SHADOW OF THE
DARK ANGEL

Book 2 in the series,
THE CRIME FILES OF KATY GREEN

Also by Gene O'Neill

SHADOW OF THE DARK ANGEL

Book 2 in the series,
THE CRIME FILES OF KATY GREEN

by **Gene O'Neill**

with illustrations
by Greg Chapman

DARK MOON BOOKS
Los Angeles, California

SHADOW OF THE DARK ANGEL
Copyright © Gene O'Neill 2009

Interior layout by Eric J. Guignard
Cover design by Eric J. Guignard
www.ericjguignard.com

Front cover illustration by Jelena Mišljenović
www.instagram.com/jelena.misljenovic

Interior illustrations by Greg Chapman
https://darkartiste.wordpress.com

First Dark Moon Books edition published in June, 2018
Library of Congress Control Number: 2018940993
ISBN-13: 978-0-9988275-8-2 (paperback)
ISBN-13: 978-0-9989383-6-3 (e-book)

DARK MOON BOOKS
Los Angeles, California
www.DarkMoonBooks.com

Made in the United States of America

This book is dedicated to:
Mu Chuisle

CHAPTERS

God spared not the angels that sinned,
but cast them down to hell, and delivered them
into chains of darkness.

—2 Peter 2:4

PROLOGUE

The boy lay at the foot of his bed, almost dropping off to sleep, but determined to stay awake. Every few minutes he roused himself and peeked at the door adjoining the bedrooms, making sure it was ajar just a crack. He'd been fighting sleep for two hours, waiting for the girl to return from work. He still could not believe what he had seen last night, when he accidentally awakened after she'd come home from her part-time job at Burger King.

So, early this evening after the three other boys were asleep, he had tiptoed to the adjoining door to the bedroom of his two foster sisters and quietly cracked it open, just a quarter of an inch. Then he returned to his lower bunk bed, turned around with his head at the foot of the bed, so he could easily peer through the crack into the dresser mirror across the girls' bedroom.

But his enthusiasm was beginning to wane as the hour grew late, his eyelids drooping, and he had actually dozed off soundly for a few minutes, awakening with a start as he dreamed he was falling off a cliff—

A footstep in the hall.

It was her!

A nightlight blinked on in the room. In the mirror the boy saw his older foster sister move into view, glance around, then smile at her apparently still sleeping roommate, just out of the boy's sight. He froze, holding his breath when she looked directly at him, hoping she would not see the cracked door.

His pulse raced.

No, please don't close it...

Then, after an eternity, she moved out of view, obviously not noticing the opened door.

The boy sighed deeply.

The girl returned to view, wearing only her underwear. Standing squarely in front of the mirror, she reached up and brushed her shoulder-length reddish-blonde hair, her lips mouthing the number of strokes. But the boy was not watching her hand; he was staring wide-eyed at her underarm, the little tuft of golden-red hair in her armpit.

Staring transfixed.

After completing the prescribed number of strokes, she finished and dropped the comb onto the dresser.

Then, the girl unhooked her bra and placed it beside the comb, exposing her smallish breasts, and the boy shifted carefully on the foot of his bed, pulling himself a few inches closer, anticipating what he had seen last night.

Hoping, hoping.

She bent over and stepped out of her panties, placing them on the dresser beside the abandoned bra; at that moment she was squared-up perfectly in front of the mirror.

The boy saw it, again!

The tiny patch of hair at her crotch. Tonight she touched herself there, her fingers covering the patch for just a moment. Then the hand was gone.

He clutched his mouth, stifling a moan of delight. Beautiful reddish-golden hair.

Who would've thought? None of the boys had hair down there. Only a naked dangle. Even though the girl had no dangle, she possessed a marvelous hidden treasure.

Secret golden-red hair.

Suddenly the light was out, the show over.

The boy reluctantly slipped back to the other end of his bed, frowning, one of the Voices echoing in his head: *Bad boy, bad boy!*

SAMSON

t is still unusually muggy outside, especially for 11:00 at night, almost as oppressive as the laundry room back at the hospital, your T-shirt stuck to your sweaty underarms, your shorts bunching uncomfortably, and your crotch feeling gritty. Despite the heat, you keep your blue stocking cap on, rolled down to your ears, and you don't even consider pulling up the sleeves on your khaki work shirt.

No indeed.

You pause outside *The Red Impala Diner* on your way home, peer in the front window, scanning the bright emptiness; as you first suspected, there appears to be no one in there to hassle you. An iced tea would be good, help cool off.

You take a seat at the counter, and the cook, a clean white apron around his waist, steps out of the kitchen. "What'll it be, pal?"

Sucking in a deep breath to stave off the funnytalk, you ask almost perfectly,

"G-got ice' tea?"

He nods, turns, and draws a big glass full from an urn near the order window into the kitchen. "Lemon?" he asks, a bored, tired expression on his face.

You shake your head. The iced tea is good. You stare at the tall glass, remembering...

It had been your favorite drink at Chula Vista. You didn't like milk or coffee, and the Kool-Aid was always too weak, watered down. You'd spent six years at the California Youth Authority facility south of San Diego, long, difficult years. Those first years often violent, spent defending yourself.

But you'd met Father Nathan there, and he'd been more than just a priest, kind of like a mentor, helping you learn to cope with many things, including the teasing and ridicule of the other boys because of your funnytalk and the hair thing. Eventually he'd even managed to help you with your speech—taught you how to breathe deeply, relax, focus, and speak slowly. He stimulated the desire to read books, suggested titles, helped you begin your self-education. And even though you'd never directly mentioned the Voices to Father Nathan, under his positive tutelage, They'd gone away. You hadn't heard either of the Angels whisper in over three years.

The bell jingles at the door, interrupting your reverie.

Someone slides onto the stool next to you.

For a moment you consider gulping down your drink and leaving. You've avoided most human contact, including even the most casual, since being released from CYA three months ago, especially eliminating any contact with the females at your job at the hospital. But you sneak a quick glance right and freeze.

She's wearing a bright yellow blouse with cutoff sleeves, exposing her shoulders, her underarms, and *reddish-blonde kinky hair.*

You can't tear your gaze away.

"What can I get you, lady?" the cook is asking her.

You glance up at him, then quickly back to the woman.

She points at your glass. "Is that iced tea he's drinking?" she asks, smiling at you.

You look at her more closely.

The bright clothes and hairdo—reddish-tinted brown and spiked real short—seem appropriate for a younger person, and are at odds with her facial features, her heavy makeup not quite hiding the crow's feet at the corners of her eyes or the faint lines radiating from the sides of her mouth when she smiles. But it is her eyes that really give her away. Even with the green shading and careful black lining, her brown eyes are dull and flat, as if they've seen too much.

She's really old, you finally decide, maybe even forty or so.

The cook nods, still wearing the same bored expression.

"Then, I'll have some, too," she says, looking more closely at you. Her voice seems genuinely warm and friendly, making you feel better about her ancient eyes.

She takes a sip of her drink. "Hmmm, pretty good." Still facing you, she asks, "Hot, ain't it?"

You nod, looking away shyly. You should leave. Just get up and go, now. But you can't resist sneaking another glimpse at her exposed armpit and the untamed curly reddish hair that contrasts so dramatically with the manicured lighter spikes.

"I just got off at the Golden Pheasant Club, up the street," the woman continues in her friendly tone, adding, "a beverage server." She takes another sip of tea, before saying, "Nick, the bartender who works there, too, he says that earlier it was almost a hunnerd outside in the shade, and he notices stuff like that. Course it was cool at work, air-conditioning and all. But we weren't too busy. God, must still be ninety outside, though. Weird this hot late at night. Doan' you think?"

You nod your head again, saying nothing, just staring at your glass of tea, wondering about a cocktail waitress *not* shaving her underarms. Some kind of feminist thing, maybe. There's lots of stuff like that in the magazines.

Then, she is actually making contact with your arm. "My name's Mary Ann," she says in a lower, almost confidential tone.

You feel a sense of panic, staring at her outstretched hand. But her position gives you a clear view of the hair in her armpit. You suck in a breath.

"I-I-I'm Sam," you say hoarsely, silently thanking Father Nathan that you aren't completely paralyzed by the funnytalk. "W-work at the h-hospital laundry," you add, pointing back in the general direction of L Street. It comes out pretty well, everything considered.

Mary Ann shakes your right hand, grinning. And you even think you see a faint glimmer of life in her old, flat, dark eyes.

After the introduction, she leans real close, so close your nostrils are flared by the overpowering smell of her perfume, and she whispers, "I've got some sun tea at the apartment. Beats this stuff all to hell. Got a nice little fan, too. We could be more comfortable, you know what I mean?" She sits back straight on her stool, holding her glass of tea in her left hand, with her eyebrows lifted questioningly.

No, no, Sam Boy, one of the old Voices suddenly whispers in your head. Of course you recognize the Light Angel, even after all this time. *You have not forgotten that other young girl and all the trouble?*

But you ignore the Voice, unable to keep yourself from staring at the few strands of kinky hair barely exposed now; and you can't keep your mind from wondering about her secret hair.

What does it look like?

Is it reddish-blonde, too?

Thick or thin?

Soft or coarse?

Maybe even wiry, like her underarm?

The panic turns quickly to excitement.

So, again you breathe deeply, and, finally, you nod your acceptance.

She reaches in her purse and leaves money for the teas. Then, boldly, she possessively grasps your arm. "C'mon, Sammy."

You stand up, following her lead.

"Oh, my, you are a big one," she says, smiling and winking suggestively. And though you've never heard the word spoken in your entire life, her bold stare makes you shiver, as if her *lascivious* gaze were X-ray vision, rendering you completely naked.

Mary Ann's third-story apartment, just over a few streets from *The Red Impala*, is hardly more than a bedroom, with adjoining bathroom and tiny kitchen. But she turns on the fan, and it complements a slight breeze blowing in the open window. She pours you a glass of tea, as promised, turns out the light, "so it's cooler," and excuses herself to go to the bathroom.

You actually begin to relax slightly, thinking it might be all right. Maybe the Light Angel is wrong. Mary Ann's just lonely, not a bad person, not like that other one so long ago, interested in doing bad things. And you tell yourself convincingly that you are a good person too, with only right thoughts in your head, *except* for the erotic image of her underarm hair that lingers in your mind, like a festering sore.

Then, she is standing in place in the opened bathroom door, her back to the light, stark naked. You're unable to keep your gaze from sliding down to her crotch—

You stifle a moan.

Her secret hair is dark red, luxurious, and bushy... and not just a tiny patch that can be covered with a hand, but thick and spreading out, growing along her inner thighs, and even a thin dark line up to her belly button.

You groan as if punched in the stomach.

She moves across the room, reaches up and takes your face in her hands, kissing your lips wetly, forcing her tongue between your teeth and into your mouth.

You're stiff with fear now because bad things are indeed happening, just like the Angel suggested.

"I'll bet you're *big* all over," Mary Ann says, her voice changed to a hard, husky whisper; and her eyes, her dark, dead eyes, are shiny bright and alive now.

She tries to touch your stocking cap, but you manage to brush her hand away. So, she lets her hands slide down to your work shirt. She unbuttons it and strips it off. Then your pants. You're like a statue, now, unable to even feebly resist. She kneels and pulls down your shorts—

"Ohhh, my God!"

Her expression is a mix of surprise, disbelief, and shock, as she abruptly stands back up.

"No," she gasps loudly, still staring down at your hairless crotch, your limp member. "What, wha—" Mary Ann just shakes her head, staring at you for some explanation.

You are silent, paralyzed with fear and shame.

After a few moments of strained silence she reaches up and peels off your stocking cap, exposing your bald head. Then, in her regular voice, she says, "Who shaved all your hair, Samson?" She cackles loudly at her own cleverness, nodding.

You want to tell her that your head hasn't been shaved, that the hairless condition is something you were born with, a rare state called alopecia by the doctors. But you are completely tongue-tied now, unable to speak. Silent, naked, hairless, vulnerable—almost like the other time; and you hope the Dark Angel will *not* speak again this time.

Her hand reaches out and touches you down there, and you flinch, chilled by her cool fingers and embarrassed by your nakedness.

At that moment, Mary Ann begins to really laugh.

She laughs and points at your shriveled, limp member. "You are truly weak, aren't you, Samson?" And she roars at her own cruel joke until tears stream down her cheeks.

By this time you've partially recovered from your paralyzed state and are struggling back into your clothes, even managing to pull your stocking cap into place, covering your baldness. And you try to shout over her laughter, *Not Samson, that is not my name.* "N-N-N—" But it's no use. Even stamping your foot down solidly doesn't break the stammer. "N-N-N… "

Your exaggerated funnytalk and obvious anguish only make the woman laugh harder, until she's actually howling, like some kind of crazed animal. Finally, unable to stand the mocking sound, you head for the door with your hands covering your ears, pausing and glancing back over your shoulder. Even the sight of her remarkably thick, red bush can't hold you in the tiny apartment, and you jerk open the door and run down the stairs, fleeing from her insane howling.

Bad woman, bad woman.

Two blocks from the apartment, you slow to a walk, the woman's taunts left behind, lost in the street noise; but your heart thumps rapidly against your ribs, and you choke off a sob of frustration, your eyes moist with the tears of shame. At the same time you are thankful that the Dark Angel had not spoken.

2

The humiliating aspect of the encounter with Mary Ann is gradually pushed to the back of your mind with all the other affronts—almost, but not quite forgotten. You tell yourself that you're grateful you were fortunate enough to escape before she could do something real bad. You try to lose yourself in your reading. But you cannot forget her marvelously luxuriant secret hair. You see it in your mind's eye several times a day, at your work on the big extractor at the laundry; you dream about it at night; and every time you pass a female on the street, you are unable to keep your gaze from dropping to her crotch, wondering curiously about her secret hair: its texture, color, and thickness. Just knowing what is there underneath the flimsy dress or blue jeans or shorts makes your blood rush with excitement. You develop a permanent ache, an unfulfilled longing.

So as time goes by, what had been a fascination all these years turns to more of an obsession; every night after work you roam the streets, searching for open windows, hoping to spot a woman unclothed, revealing her hidden treasure. A small chance of success, as there are few ground floor apartments in your section of the city, even fewer with windows at the street level; and your efforts go unrewarded. In the end you're even picked up by a squad car, the questioning policemen eventually letting you go, but threatening to arrest you for prowling if they catch you again around any of the apartment buildings. Fortunately they don't check and discover that you're on probation from CYA.

You give up the random wandering around at night; but you decide to try something you've heard the men at work joking about. *T & A.* A burlesque club downtown, showing mostly X-rated film, but each weekend night featuring one live exotic dancer.

3

You sit up front, right next to a ramp running perpendicular to the stage, splitting the theater exactly in half. You are next to an older man, who gropes himself noisily whenever the couples on the screen engage in sex. You feel cramped, disgusted by the sleazy film and the man's behavior, but there are no nearby vacant seats. And you cannot just get up and go, not until the live performance. You are trapped. The films leave you unfulfilled, showing mostly bare breasts and behinds, and focusing on a variety of sex acts. Dirty, filthy films. And only fleeting glimpses of secret hair.

Bad, bad, bad.

Very bad, indeed.

Between movies, the old man wants to engage you in conversation, as if nothing has happened, as if he's just an everyday film buff.

"Hey, man, howja like that last one, huh?" he asks, elbowing you in the arm. "Didja see the lungs on that blonde? Man, could she give head?" He doesn't really care about an answer; he seems to be in a kind of trance-like state of perverted, sexual excitement, his gaze still locked on the gray screen.

Suddenly, the man in the worn tuxedo is back on stage with his microphone in hand. "And now, ladies and gents, the featured attraction of the evening," he is saying, as the drummer in the band pit in front of the stage does an exaggerated drum roll. "Here now, all the way from Hong Kong, the exotic Dragon Lady!"

The lights go out, then one big spot centers on a woman in a red gown, matching gloves, and high-heeled shoes, with stunning Asian features and beautiful shoulder-length shiny black hair.

She turns around slowly, her backless gown revealing a huge iridescent tattoo covering her entire back—the main body of a dragon, its lower half curling down across her bared buttocks then out of sight.

She begins to dance, her motion indeed serpent-like, graceful except for the occasional sudden gross bump made with her hips and pelvic area…

Your pulse picks up as she begins to take off clothing: her gloves, her earrings, her necklace, and then her shoes; finally she steps out of the red gown, but clutches the garment in her arms, covering her breasts. Slowly she lets the gown slip from her grasp to the floor.

She is completely undressed except for two tiny red dots covering the nipples of her breasts and a string that holds a larger red dot over her crotch. For tantalizing minutes she dances around the stage in this attire, making a number of exaggerated pelvic bumps. Then, after discarding the breast dots to cheers and whistles from the audience, she turns her back, the light shrinking to a small spotlight; and she steps from the stringed circle covering her crotch, the fully exposed dragon shimmering luminescently on her backside in the dimmed light.

The spotlight blinks out abruptly, and she turns around; in the darkness you can still see she's covering her pelvic area with her hands. In the dim light she moves along the ramp, coming closer and closer to where you sit, stopping at each row or so, squatting, raising her hands, and briefly exposing her complete nakedness. Because of the angle you can't really see anything, but the suggested revelation has the crowd in a noisy uproar of anticipation.

She is directly above you, squatting, and—

You now have a direct view of her crotch, only a couple of feet away, but there is nothing to see.

Only her wrinkled dark lips.

No secret hair.

As she stands and moves down the ramp, you remain in place, staring ahead, at the empty stage, feeling numb.

No hair.

None at all.

Shaven.

Finally, the theater is emptying out—all the noisy, bad people—the spectacle is over. Drained, you stand up and leave, feeling extremely disappointed and cheated.

4

Getting off work an hour early on Tuesday night, with the oral directions and lewd encouragement given you by Wilbur at the hospital laundry (he works close to you on the big washers) you take the downtown municipal bus to Seventh and L Streets near the huge Greyhound Bus Depot.

As you dismount the bus into the crowd of pedestrians, your senses are bombarded: *loud noise*—cars braking, horns blaring, people shouting, western music thundering from an open entry to a bar; *bright light*—colorful neon glowing, headlights glaring from cars, stoplights blinking red, yellow, green; *varied smells*—gasoline and diesel, spicy barbequed meat, sweet perfume; and an *electric tingling* of excitement in the muggy air, just like before a thunderstorm.

You gasp, senses overloaded, stumble out of the moving crowd, and lean up against a window front, wiping the sweat from your face with a handkerchief.

A hoarse voice whispers behind you, "Yo, big fella."

You turn and stare.

The tall black woman is dressed in a low-cut, leopard skin blouse, black vinyl mini-skirt, dark high heels, her short kinky hair dyed a blondish-red color. She tries to smile through gaudy facial make-up, managing only a kind of leer.

You almost shudder, but restrain yourself. "Y-Yo b-back."

She chuckles, moving in closer, massaging her large breasts against your arm. You can smell the heavy perfume, but it doesn't quite mask a stronger, very unpleasant odor, something vaguely familiar… like a locker room full of many men, sweating heavily: dirty socks, dirty jocks. You close your eyes, but are unable to keep your arms from goose-pimpling.

"Hey, man, y'all lookin' to party or what?" asks the painted woman.

You nod, stammer, and stamp your foot, finally able to ask, "H-H-H… How much?"

The woman stares back, then shrugs slyly, "Depends, what y'all got in mind, big fella?"

This time you have to stamp down hard, "J-J-J… Just want to l-l-l—" but it's no good; you're unable to get out the last word. "L-L-L-L—"

But the black woman helps. "Say, *look*?"

You blink and nod, gratefully.

"Y'all want to watch me do another guy?"

You shake your head vigorously.

"Ah, another chick?"

"No," you manage to say forcefully.

"Well, what do you wanna see?" she asks impatiently now, a puzzled look marring the painted mask.

"J-J-Just you." You point at her and smile encouragingly.

"Jes' me, nekkid?"

You nod.

She nods back. "Okay, how 'bout, ah… " she pauses, gazing into your eyes as if searching for the right number. "Oh, twenny bucks? Twenny bucks to look at me nekkid for a coupla minutes."

You nod, reaching in your pocket for the money.

You are in a dingy hotel room, and the painted woman is facing you, completely stripped of clothes.

You just stare at her naked crotch, speechless.

Her secret hair is very kinky down there but dyed an unusual tone, the color of a flamingo. You can't believe it. You edge a step closer, point with your finger, and shake your head.

The woman giggles. "Hey, I know, cute, ain't it?"

Cute?

You can't resist reaching out and touching her down there with your fingertips, the tight pink curls drawing your hand like a magnet. Then you grab her tightly around the waist in one arm, while you stroke her secret hair gently, amazed by its stiffness and almost metallic texture. Pink steel wool—

"Hey, big fella," the woman hollers angrily into your face, "Y'all paid to look, not cop a feel."

She struggles to get loose, but you are gripping her even more tightly now with your free arm, pulling her to you roughly.

She screams loudly, "Hey, back off, mister. Charlie, hey, Charlie—?"

The door of the room bangs open, and a huge black man rushes in, swinging something from his hand.

A blinding thunder rumbles through your head, and you sink down into dark nothingness.

You awaken in an alley behind the hotel, your head bursting with pain. You have to get home, but your wallet is gone and all your change. Despite the throbbing and huge bump on your forehead, you must walk, each step sending a sliver of steel jarring into the sinuses behind your eyes.

On and on, back up L Street you go, block after block, a mile or more...

Eventually you make it back to your apartment on 26th near the hospital, and to bed. Before you drop off to sleep, you hear a Voice in your head—but it's just a far-off weak echo, *Sam Boy, it is time to call Father Nathan. You need his help, again.*

Yes, it is the Light Angel's voice, but so distant and weak.

You are too hurt to respond and so very drowsy.

5

You awaken again after dozing briefly, your head pounding, your mouth dry, your tongue thick, dim light shining into your room from the streetlamp outside your window. Even after a shower and two Excedrin, you still feel funny. Kind of like you are watching something happen, not really involved, your movements directed by someone else.

You lie back down on the bed and remember the business with the bad woman, her amazing pink-colored, kinky hair, and the black man bursting into the room, hitting you over the head with something very hard—it all seems unreal, not something that actually happened to you, but more like remembering a scene from a movie you've just watched.

The Voice that shouts loudly in your head is real: *The time is at hand for vengeance.*

You gasp with recognition.

It is Him, the other one, the Dark Angel…

Then, the glare from the streetlight outside the open window is partially blocked out by the silhouette of a winged figure who casts His shadow halfway across your room, the humid air stirred into a swirling gale by His beating wings; and for the first time in your life you actually see *Him*.

The Dark Angel hovers before you in the dimness of your room.

You squint, attempting to get a clearer view, but it's like trying to make out a figure on a photographic negative held at arm's length.

"Yes, it is really me," He admits, as if reading your thoughts, his throaty-hoarse voice growling loudly in the tiny room.

You are too stunned to even answer, but you manage to rise again from the bed, forgetting your aches and pains.

"It is time to cut down your enemies with impunity, one at a time," he says, still hovering, wing beats continuing to churn the heavy air. You move a step or two into His shadow and stop, the temperature appearing to drop at least thirty degrees. You briskly rub your arms, trying to warm yourself.

"Here is your instrument of vengeance," the Dark Angel announces.

A glint catches your eye, and you reach out, forgetting your chilled state, accepting the instrument, an ebony-handled, straight razor.

"My shadow will hide you from your enemies, protect you," He says, moving back toward the window.

You follow Him across the room, able to pause only momentarily, trying to catch a fleeting glimpse of yourself in the mirror over the dresser, before stumbling along in his wake. The mirror reflects *nothing* except a faint shimmering distortion in the middle of the shadow, where you should appear even in the dimness.

Amazing!

But before you can speak, the voice of the Dark Angel again thunders in your ears, ordering, "Come. The woman with the thick red hair made fun of your name, your manhood, and mocked you."

In the icy darkness, you nod to yourself, slowly growing angry. It is time now, time for vindication. You follow Him out the window.

6

The Dark Angel hovers overhead, as you wait in His shadow at the far end of *The Red Impala Diner*, blending into the darkness, an unseen part of the night. You wait patiently, feeling confident and strong, smiling wryly to yourself.

Footsteps.

Here she comes—Mary Ann—walking carefree, obviously happy to be off work at the *Golden Pheasant Club*. She passes within inches of you, her shoulder almost brushing against your chest; but you shrink back into the wall, deeper into the shadows, letting her pass by untouched.

Then you follow.

At the entrance to her apartment building, Mary Ann pauses, turns, looks back directly at you, a frown of suspicion on her face, as if she senses something awry. After a moment she shrugs and takes out her key to the building's main door.

You hurry to her side, always in His shadow, slipping in behind her when she opens the door, unseen; then quietly you follow her upstairs, into her apartment.

Finally, you are inside her tiny room again. You glance around, vividly remembering the last time: Her mocking jokes, her howling laughter.

She goes into the tiny kitchen, opens the refrigerator for a drink or something.

She re-enters the bedroom, flipping on a bright light. Then, Mary Ann gasps with surprise, not more than a croak really, her throat paralyzed with fear—

For you have left His shadow as the Dark Angel hovers in the night just outside the opened bedroom window; you face the terrified woman, clutching the instrument of vengeance in your right hand. Slowly you flip open the straight razor, the glint of its steel matching the glint of fear lighting up her ancient, dead eyes, and making your pulse race wildly.

You edge closer, doubling your left fist.

And this time it is Mary Ann who remains frozen in place like a statue...

7

You stare into the mirror over the dresser at yourself, reaching up, wiping the trickle of red from your forehead, and adjusting the tuft of spiked reddish-brown hair, then you look down at the patch of coarse darker red hair, and you smile, glancing at your partially-thickened manhood.

Looking back over your shoulder at the woman lying still on the bed, you chuckle and announce flawlessly, "That's right, Mary Ann, I am indeed Samson, and I have recovered my strength."

You dress, then begin to move across the tiny room toward the window, but you pause, hearing something. A distant whisper. Someone calling your name, *Sam Boy?*

You strain to hear more, cocking your head and listening intently for a few moments.

There is nothing more.

It is indeed too late now, there is nothing to hear except the whirring sound of the Dark Angel's impatient wing beats, beckoning you and you step to the open window, back into the chill of His shadow, shivering violently.

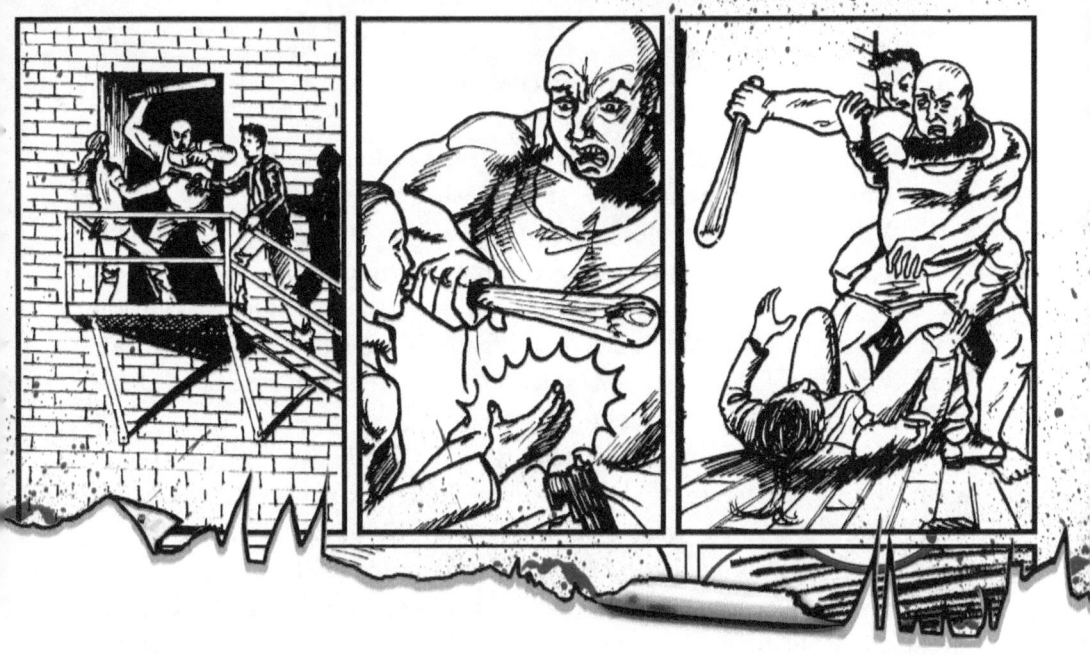

THE GREEN HORNET AND CATO

L ate Tuesday evening Katy Green is standing before her desk and Mac computer, stretching her athletic frame; at 6-foot, with lean build, healthy complexion, strawberry-blonde hair pulled into a short pony-tail, and the slight frown of concentration, all suggest an athlete-in-training, resting and thinking after a workout, rather than a writer taking a break over her word processing program. But Katy Green *is* a professional writer, although part-time, with over fifty short story credits in the science fiction, fantasy, and mystery magazines and anthologies, under a male pseudonym.

She sits back down, still frowning at the screen, then she glances at the digital clock on the left side of the desk: 11:30 p.m.

"Whoa," Katy says aloud, surprised by the lateness of the hour. I guess time does fly when you're having a good time, she thinks, enjoying the triteness of the old cliché. She grins to herself, realizing she has not eaten a thing since breakfast. *At this rate, I'll certainly have a good rough draft of the novel completed to show the agent at BayCon in three and a half weeks, if I don't starve to death before then.*

Katy is genuinely pleased with herself. *The Indigo Man* is coming along nicely, better than she had even hoped for when she'd taken three months unpaid leave of absence from the crazy intensity of her regular job as a homicide detective with Sacramento PD.

She gets up and heads for the kitchen, wondering if there is anything at all to eat, because she has not shopped in over a week. Rummaging through the cupboard she finds a can of tuna fish, opens it, and begins making a sandwich. But she pauses before taking a bite, the frown returning, as the reality of the situation hits her.

She is thirty-three, still single, a well-paid detective career on hold—actually the *only* female homicide detective in the entire Sacramento Police Department—living off her savings, hoping to sell a first novel, and a science fiction novel at that. Not really a high-probability success venture, and for sure not really a well-paid undertaking. But she has a slight edge on most first novelists. For the last eight years, since her senior year at Sac State majoring in Police Science, she has been writing and selling the occasional story, actually none of them primarily science fiction, fantasy, or mystery. She considers herself a writer exploring the darker side of life, continuing her college fascination with abnormal psychology, her main characters usually odd, offbeat, often sociopathic or psychotic. And, in fact, the theme of *The Indigo Man* revolves around psychological issues. She is expanding a short story she first published in *The Twilight Zone Magazine*, "The Burden of Indigo," a time in the future, when criminals are color-coded based on their crimes, dyed permanently and banned to roam the devastated wastelands. The indigo man is a sex criminal, an old man who has wandered for thirty-plus years since his color judgment, who believes his color is suddenly starting to fade. The short story examined the last four days of his life and his eventual redemption. Katy is extending the story into a novel with flashbacks, exploring the old man's early years of wandering the wastelands and his youth growing up in a domed coastal city: A longitudinal psychological probe of a convicted sex criminal.

Munching on the sandwich, Katy chuckles to herself, enjoying a kind of ironic parallel.

Her writing life is not that far removed from her everyday detective life. In the last four years, since being assigned to homicide, she's built a reputation within the local law enforcement community, a knack for being able to track down sociopaths and psychos, the most recent being the infamous Double Jack.

The image of the fat rapist-murderer makes her drop the sandwich and rub the aching scar just below her right elbow. She presses along the bone, imagining she can feel the pin, her thoughts shifting back to four months ago...

2

The *Bee* had dubbed him, *The Good Samaritan Rapist*, then later at his trial, Channel 10, after putting the image of the huge man on local TV, tagged him *Double Jack*. Whatever his nickname, he preyed on female motorists who had broken down or had a flat tire along the freeways during the late evening commute, offering to help them fix the flat or whatever, gaining their confidence, test driving them to a more secluded spot, then raping and strangling them in the back seat of their own cars—at least once in broad daylight. Fortunately, the last of his five victims had gotten loose and survived his attack, able to accurately describe the 400 pound Jack Malenko.

Katy and her homicide detective partner, Johnny Cato, had floundered with few leads other than the description, until Katy finally had a sudden insight and suggested they begin showing Jack Malenko's composite drawing likeness at health clubs/fitness studios around the greater Sacramento area.

Eureka!

They obtained his name and address from the fifteenth place they visited, *Fun & Fit*, a club on Arden Way out near the state fairgrounds. Jack Malenko lived in a nearby run-down apartment complex off of El Camino Avenue.

Early the next morning after visiting the fitness club, they checked to make sure that Jack's 1979 gray Courier pickup was in the parking lot of his apartment complex. It was parked between a pair of beat-up wrecks with flat tires. In fact the lot resembled a junkyard, most of the run-down apartments occupied by welfare recipients, many single mothers, who owned or were making payments on the assorted collection of broken down junkers. Katy had been in here a half-dozen times four years ago, when she still worked child/spousal abuse before her present homicide assignment. She knew her way around fairly well.

She leaned over and peered in the pickup, wondering how the devil a man Jack's size got in and out of this smallish cab. She started to comment to her partner—

But Johnny was violently shaking his walky-talky. "Damn it!" he swore, finally holstering the piece of equipment. "It's past time the department sprung for cell phones. I think the batteries or something are shot in this thing." He took a deep breath, then continued: "Not sure what's going on with our backup. They could be anywhere in here. This complex is a friggin' maze, Katy. We better wait and make sure they're in the right lot, headed for the right building, you know."

"Uh-uh," Katy said, checking her standard issue .38. "He's home, now. Let's take him, *now*."

Johnny rubbed his badly broken nose—he'd been an outstanding light heavyweight as a college freshman before Sac State gave up boxing, finally following the course of other NCAA schools—something he always did when nervous or unsure of himself. "Ah, Katy, you know the drill. Captain Silver will have our asses sucking buttermilk if anything goes wrong out here, and he finds out we broke procedure by *not* wearing vests and then, of all things, going ahead of our backup arriving."

She nodded, smiled sweetly, and said, "Long John doesn't ever have to know, pal," then beckoned him to follow with her drawn weapon.

At the edge of the parking lot, they paused, peering around cautiously, looking for residents, and staring at the stairs leading up to the second level and Jack's apartment, number 2217. They saw no one, not even kids, although there was a pair of abandoned Big Wheels, a skateboard, and an old bike lying near the stairway.

"Where in the hell is everyone?" Johnny whispered, a sharp edge of puzzlement in his tone. "This place is quieter than a graveyard after midnight."

"Too early yet," Katy whispered back, glancing at her watch. It was just 7:15 a.m. "Few mothers work in here, everyone's probably still asleep, including all the kids. And that's good for us."

They left the cover of the parking lot, hurrying to the stairway, the cemetery-quiet stillness of the big shabby complex unnerving. At the second level, Johnny signaled for Katy to wait, and he leaned out from the railing, surveying the parking-lot-disguised-as-a-junkyard. He frowned, rubbed his nose, and shrugged at her. Still, no backup.

She smiled and mouthed: *Oh well.*

After checking the first apartment door to the left, 2210, Katy signaled for them to turn right and led the way past 2211, easing by two more odd-numbered doors before she paused, pointing at the next apartment, her heart pounding in her chest, her pulse racing. *Jesus*, she thought, taking two long, deep breaths, *I never get used to this shit.*

Johnny bent over and duck-walked, so he wasn't visible in the window of 2217—even though ragged shades were drawn, blocking a view in or out—and moved to the far side of the apartment door, Katy staying in place just beyond the door to adjoining 2215.

Suddenly, the apartment door *behind* her, 2215, jerked open and there was shirtless Jack Malenko, wearing only a pair of boxer shorts and an angry scowl, his wet hair pulled back in a pony tail, reminding Katy of a sumo wrestler gone berserk, except this sumo wrestler was holding a baseball bat, waving it in a threatening manner and moving toward her. The address had been wrong, or maybe he'd been visiting a girlfriend last night, or who knew what—?

"Stop, Police!" Katy said, the command little more than a pair of indistinct croaks.

"Cops," the fat man growled fiercely, spitting the word out as if it tasted bad on his tongue. Then he grabbed the bat in both hands and swung it like Mark McGwire in the on-deck circle, but looping it forcefully in the direction of Katy's head.

She frantically jerked off a round from the .38, hitting the big man high in the chest; but, even though he shuddered noticeably, he still managed to follow through strongly and whack her with the bat, the blow glancing off her right arm, which she had instinctively raised to shield her face. Katy was driven back by the terrific force of the blow, almost flipping over the railing behind her, sharp pain exploding just below the elbow and shooting up her arm. Only by quick reflex she caught her balance in time, but dropped her revolver, clutching her right elbow with her left hand, overcome with pain, knowing the bones in her lower arm must be shattered into a million sharp pieces, each sliver stabbing a nerve.

"*Oooh, Jeee-sus,*" she moaned, her vision tunneling, sour juices flooding her throat and making her wretch with nausea.

Then, through the red veil of pain she saw Johnny solidly punch the wounded man in the face, snatch the bat away, and toss it over the railing—he'd jumped between Malenko and Katy with his weapon still holstered, apparently afraid of shooting her.

Snorting angrily now through his bloody nose like a wounded elephant, the enraged Jack Malenko was more than a match for the much smaller detective. He clutched Johnny before the detective could get his .38 free from his shoulder holster, jerked him off his feet, and shook him as if he were little more than a rag doll; then the huge man pulled the detective close, locked an arm around his head in a strangle hold, and squeezed.

Helplessly, Johnny gasped for air, his face turning dark red as he tried to struggle free, his arms pinned against his sides.

Katy fought back her nausea, blinking and searching the deck for her gun, the pain in her arm momentarily forgotten. This fat-ass nut is strangling my partner!

My gun, where's my gun?

Aha.

She picked up the .38, in her left hand, trying to hold it steady and draw a bead on the fat man. But her aim was shaky with her off hand. Instead of jerking off a round at a shifting target, she reached out with the revolver and slammed the barrel down hard on the big man's bare foot.

He roared with pain, tumbled over near the railing, but managed to maintain his grip on Johnny, pulling the semi-conscious detective down to the deck alongside him.

Time slowed, Katy's vision again blurring, as she tried to aim the unsteady barrel of the .38 for a clear shot at the giant.

Oh, shit—!

Just as she began to squeeze off a shot, Johnny was jerked around, partially shielding Malenko.

She was forced to ease off on the trigger.

Finally at the last moment, their backup arrived—Harlan Bundy and Patrick McHugh, two other homicide detectives—thundering up the stairwell; Katy later swore, that moments just before they arrived she heard a cavalry charge bugling in her head, just like an old western movie. The two clubbed the huge Malenko with their drawn revolvers, until the wounded man finally released the unconscious Johnny, who crumpled up on the deck beside Katy like a discarded rag doll.

The collar had been a fucked-up fiasco, a close call for both of them.

Katy was hospitalized for three days after the arrest, her badly broken ulna requiring surgery and insertion of a pin. In fact, she testified before the grand jury with her casted arm in a sling, her partner with yellowing bruises on his throat. But she had come out of the courtroom a media heroine, getting credit for figuring out that anyone the size of Jack Malenko would probably be trying to control his weight, then searching until she found *his* fitness club.

While on worker's comp she ignored her celebrity status, refusing invitations to several talk shows including Channel 10's persistent Serra Melendez of *Saints or Sinners?*. Instead she went to the range as soon as her arm was sufficiently healed, getting Range Master Andy Montin to recommend a new sidearm and the appropriate ammo—something with sufficient stopping power to take down a huge, fired-up, sociopath like Double Jack with *one* hit. Andy had suggested a Sig Sauer P-220, a .45 semi-automatic, not really much heavier than Katy's standard issue .38, but with three times the stopping power. They had practiced every day with 180 grain JHP rounds until she felt comfortable firing the new sidearm; in less than a week she was an expert with the more efficient weapon.

3

Even now while working on the novel during her leave of absence, Katy never goes out anywhere without wearing the Sig Sauer in her back holster hid by a windbreaker or some other garment, because she occasionally suffers a recurring nightmare about being at a 7-Eleven and suddenly a sumo wrestler comes lumbering out of the video game toward her with a huge sword, his face a fierce grimace, and after the sword slashes her, she awakens in a cold sweat, sitting up and rubbing an aching arm.

Katy drops her hand from the scar below her elbow, sucks in a deep breath, centers, then, with an effort of will, she forces the memory of Double Jack and the pain he caused to the back of her mind, shifting her attention back to her writing.

As she eats absently, washing down the tuna sandwich with a glass of milk, she hopes she can do the story correctly. Not just filling in words like a lot of fixed-up novels based on previously published stories. No, she really wants to do the premise and story justice. Make it psychologically honest. She frowns again, because she feels a kind of tense pressure conflicting with her better intentions—she's used up over two months of her leave of absence. She can almost hear the clock ticking.

The phone jars her from her thoughts.

"Hello," Katy says tentatively, feeling a little apprehensive about receiving an unexpected call almost at midnight.

There is only a male voice making a weird, loud sound: "Buzzzz…"

"What's up, Johnny?" she asks, annoyed now, knowing it's her detective partner trying to be funny. Since the Double Jack case, the *Bee* and both local TV Channels have been calling her and Johnny: *The Green Hornet and Cato.*

"You off your recovery wagon or what?" she asks, not hiding the biting sarcasm.

"No, no, Katy," he answers in a mock hurt tone, "I'm still on the bus, going to an AA and a NA meeting every week, staying off *all* mind altering substances. Actually this isn't really a middle of the night maudlin call like the old days. It's strictly business."

Oh, oh.

"I'm at an apartment on H Street, back of Sutter's Fort," he explains. "Murdered woman—"

"Hey, Johnny," Katy snaps, cutting him off, "I don't want to hear it. I'm almost through a rough draft of my book, on a leave of absence, looking at a deadline of about three weeks to attend a science fiction convention and meet with this hotshot agent, who wants to see a *complete* draft of the book. You do remember, I hope?"

"I know, Katy, I know how important this is to you, but this one might be *special*," he explains apologetically.

She shakes her head with exasperation, but can't quite restrain her own curious nature. "Special?"

"Yeah," he says. "Looks like the perp might be some kind of psycho. He cut her throat, then of all things he took a swatch of her pubic hair as a trophy… " He pauses, waiting for her to react, say something.

"Jesus," Katy finally mutters, all thoughts of her writing project momentarily forgotten. She murmurs to herself, "Who in the hell would do that to someone and why?"

"I know I'm going to need your help on this one, Katy," Johnny says seriously. "Your special insight into sick perps like this guy."

"You remember I'm still not on active duty, haven't been since the broken arm and taking off on worker's comp."

Johnny snorts dismissively. "Captain Silver asked me to call. He's taking care of the paperwork, getting you back on limited duty, but full pay status." He waits a second then adds, "The forensic team has been here already, dusted the place, taken pictures, and all that, but I've got the Coroner's guys holding off moving the body. Everything is pretty much like it was when she was discovered."

A pause of almost a minute…

"Okay," Katy says and sighs heavily. "But only a week, and you do all the grunt work. Then I've got to get my book ready for the San Jose convention to give to the agent."

In an elated voice Johnny Cato gives his reactivated partner the address.

4

Katy's first impression is a claustrophobic sense of being smothered by the cramped, muggy smallness of the woman's place, only a *tiny* studio apartment. And so dreary, too, with very few personal effects. Nothing decorating the walls. Looks almost like a motel room, except there is no TV or phone, she thinks. It's obvious that this woman was a transient. But at least she had a fan, Katy tells herself, after glancing around, spotting the active window fan, and basking for a moment in its slightly cooling breeze as she wipes the tiny beads of perspiration from her forehead. Jesus, it can't still be this hot this late at night.

Johnny leads her to the bed. "The perp probably used a straight razor," he says pointing at the gaping crimson smile across the victim's throat, a pillow and the upper bed cover completely soaked the same dark color. "Her name was Mary Ann Olson, a cocktail waitress at the Golden Pheasant Club, on the other side of Sutter's Fort. Apparently walked back and forth. Neighbors say she often brought men home."

Katy looks up at him questioningly.

"Nah, she wasn't really a hooker," he says, answering his partner's silent question. "At least she's never been arrested for that."

Katy stares down at the murdered woman's features. Used too much makeup, made her look kind of sleazy. A redhead—

And what's this?

"Johnny?" She points at the bloody bald spot just above the woman's forehead.

"Yeah, I mentioned he kept some pubic hair. Well, he took a small patch from her head, too. Sliced it away with the razor. Weird. And something else funny too. Even though her dress is hiked up around her hips and panties removed, there are no traces of sex. And he didn't keep her underwear, either. Forensics bagged them."

She looks up, momentarily puzzled. "No sex at all, even post-mortem?"

"Nothing vaginal or anal, none of her orifices violated with foreign objects. Nothing, whatsoever. The forensic boys are pretty sure there was no sex, period. No semen on the bed or floor either. So he didn't masturbate unless he did it into a condom."

She nods, accepting the unusual fact in a crime of this nature, glancing again over the partially naked woman for another minute or two, looking closely at her arms and hands which bore no apparent bruises, cuts, or even abrasions; she sighs, signaling the waiting Coroner's men that it's okay to bag the body.

"I got Patrick McHugh to contact the bartender from the club," Johnny continues, as Katy now carefully looks over the small room. "He called back just before you arrived. Mary Ann usually picked up men at work. But *not* tonight. She left work alone. The bartender's cooperating, trying to make up a list of those men he knew she'd seen in the past. Wasn't really any regular guy, though, so it's kinda tough. She just seemed to need company, you know. Picked up whoever was available. And the bartender says she had few female friends from work, no one calling her at the bar either."

"Family?" Katy asks.

"No one in Sac," Johnny replies, glancing at his C.S.—*Crime Scene*—notebook. "She moved here from the Twin Cities about six months ago. Still got a mother in a rest home in Minneapolis."

"What about neighbors? What did they hear tonight?"

Johnny grins wryly. "Mrs. Crane is a widow, across the hall, very familiar with Mary Ann's coming and going, and saw a *number* of her male visitors, you know. Anyhow, Mrs. Crane doesn't think Mary Ann had a friend with her tonight. She heard her come in about 11:15 or so—alone. And she heard her unlock the door, so it apparently hadn't been left unlocked. Actually she went over to visit as was her custom when Mary Ann was alone after work. No answer to her repeated knocks, so she called the manager downstairs. They found the body about 11:25."

Katy nods, moving over near the mirror. Maybe he was already here, waiting, she thinks, glancing around, wondering how he got in. Through the window? Probably not. Too far from the ground, unless he was some kind of sheer rock climber or a circus acrobat—not too many of them around, but something to consider. Maybe he had a key, just walked in.

"Better check and see how many keys were issued to her, Johnny."

Abruptly she kneels, after spotting several drops of blood in front of the mirror. "Forensics see this?"

Johnny replies, "Yeah, they took a sample. They think it's hers, Mary Ann's."

What's it doing over here? Katy asks herself. The room is actually remarkably clean of blood, except for these three spots. He must've used something—the pillow?—somehow to prevent spraying the room. And Mary Ann never left that bed after the perp cut her throat. He must've dripped it here himself afterward. Maybe off the straight razor? But what was he doing over here? Looking at her reflection in the mirror... admiring his work, what?

Johnny shakes his head when she looks up, as if privy to her silent questioning about the location of the mysterious blood drops.

Katy sucks in a breath, filing the questions away in the back of her mind.

"Seen enough?" Johnny asks, peeling off his latex gloves.

"Too much."

"What do you think?"

She shrugs. "I'm not sure. If the guy is already here, how did he get in? Or Mary Ann brings a guy home without the neighbor noticing—at least we *think* it was a guy—but not from the bar as usual. Where did she pick him up? And they don't have sex. Instead, he cuts her throat without spraying the room with blood... then pulls off her panties and shaves off a patch of her pubic hair plus another swatch from her head. And all this in less than ten minutes or so with absolutely no signs or sounds of a struggle. Then, to top it all, he leaves without the neighbor spotting him."

She shakes her head, more than a little puzzled.

"Why would anyone do that, Johnny, take her hair like that?"

He rubs his nose. "I've asked myself the same question, several times. And, hey, it's racist, but all I can come up with is an *Indian* scalps people," he says, staring questioningly at his partner. "Then takes the scalp with him as a friggin' trophy?"

They both stare at each other, silently mulling things over.

Then Katy clears her throat and says, "Well, let's check the public places between here and her work—you know, bars, restaurants, convenience stores, anything that was open around 11:00 or so tonight? Any place she may have picked up someone. Maybe we'll be lucky, get his or her description. And be sure to check out her number of door keys—he may have let himself in and been waiting. Carefully check the outside of the building up to her window—any possibility of a climber scaling the building? Oh, and let me see the complete forensic report as soon as you get it."

"Yeah, yeah, okay."

Katy takes one more look around the dismal little apartment, then says dismissively, "Yes, I've seen more than enough."

They start to leave, Katy following Johnny out, pulling off her gloves.

She stops suddenly, grabbing the back of his shirt. "You know, the Indian thing might not be a bad angle, at least the *scalping* part. Check out the M.O. See if you come up with anything in the last year or two from the state computers including CYA. Might not be a bad idea to check out the feds at NCIC, even if it takes a while longer."

He rubs his nose, then nods, as they leave the apartment together. "It's good to be working with you again, Katy," Johnny says. "I've missed you during the last couple months. How's the arm doing now?"

She just nods and shrugs, resisting the impulse to rub the damn scar in front of her partner.

5

The phone awakens Katy the next morning.

She glances at the digital clock on the nightstand and groans: 8:09. Then she picks up the phone, answering sleepily, "Hello, Mr. Cato."

Her partner chuckles. "Good morning, Miss Green Hornet—"

"Hey, c'mon, Johnny, lay off with that phony media bullshit, okay? It's bad enough calling me in the middle of the night and again this morning so early. So just *can* the funny stuff."

He agrees in a serious tone, "Okay, Miss Sunshine." Then, with a grin in his voice, he says, "Got lucky with quick results on the computer check. Get a load of this, kiddo. You ready?"

She doesn't answer, but nods.

"Indian kid was just released a few months ago from CYA down south. Supposed to still be in L.A., but his probation officer can't locate him. His name is Little Fox, but naturally he goes by the nickname of Chief. Did three years for aggravated assault. Beat his girlfriend up with his fists, then—get this—scalped her with a straight razor!"

Katy sits up in bed, unable to keep the excitement from her voice. "Hey, that's really interesting, Johnny."

"Yeah, but it gets even better. Little Fox has an Aunt... Emma Berglund, who lives in Elk Grove, and he apparently visited often with her before he got sent to CYA. So, he kind of knows the Sacramento area."

Elk Grove? Katy repeats to herself. It's a little town about ten miles or so downriver from Sacramento.

Man, it can't be this easy, she thinks, remembering all the wheel-spinning before they finally caught Double Jack. But, who knows, maybe we deserve to be lucky this time—the gods balancing the scales of fairness. Wouldn't that be great if we could wrap this up now, and I could get right back to my book?

"I hope you have an address for the aunt, Johnny?"

"Hey, c'mon, what do you think?" the grin gone from his voice.

She smiles to herself, knowing she unintentionally got to him. She lets a few moments pass, then says, "Just kidding, partner. Sorry."

"Well, funny girl, shall we go down and visit Auntie Em?" he asks, still a little tightness in his tone.

"I'm going to shower and get dressed right away."

SYMPHONY OF THE BIG MACHINES

The clock next to Mr. Clark's office door, on the other side of the laundry above the mangle, reads 4:55 p.m.

Wilbur and Danny have already gone to dinner early.

You are finally alone with the sounds of the big machines: *In your Sanctuary.*

You lean back against the bleach urn in front of the three washers that resemble huge stainless steel iron lungs and close your eyes. All the machines are humming their special music to you: The washers making their *sloshing* sounds, each slightly lower or higher depending on the content of their loads; and in addition, from the far right corner of the laundry is the high-pitched *wet whining* sound of the huge extractor bolted into its cement footing—even though you've never seen a particle accelerator, you imagine the extractor looks like a smaller version of one; next, about forty feet away to your right, centered in the back wall is the commercial dryer, with its huge bulging glass eye, a *tumbling, flopping* sound; and behind you, running half the length of the right wall, the slight *whirring* of the mangle masks the chattering of the four women, two at each end; and finally you isolate the nearby sound of the three industrial fans, high on the wall above the washers, making a faint *sucking whoosh* as they pull the muggy air from the basement of the hospital and dispel it into the night outside.

Still, the temperature of the laundry hovers around a hundred degrees.

You ignore the itchy, sweating discomfort, concentrating on the blend of sound playing in your head, resonating like a full orchestra, and the feel of the machines vibrating the cement floor, running up your legs, stirring your blood, and the muggy air thick with the fresh linen smell of the clean hot sheets coming off the far end of the mangle, out of sight behind you.

It's all so much better than the smaller laundry back at CYA, back where the machines first sang their special song, reverberating with your soul, making that special spot inside your chest vibrate warmly as if it were a tuning fork, back when you first discovered sanctuary from the Angel Voices.

You smile to yourself, in your element.

A loud human voice interrupts your almost trance-like tranquility, grating, raising the hair on the back of your neck, like the sound of fingernails scratching along a blackboard, making you blink, jarring you back into the steamy reality of the hospital laundry.

"Sammy, Sammy, please do your thing with the dryer."

It's Shelley, calling from behind you, where she's been feeding sheets with the other woman into the mangle, the two women on the far end catching, folding, and stacking the clean, pressed sheets onto a linen cart.

Shelley is pointing at the dryer, which has finished a tumbling cycle, drying another load of sheets.

You nod and move lethargically from the urn, first glancing at each of the brass plates governing the cycles of the three washers—still a few minutes until the middle load needs a bucket of bleach and the end one needs softener. You reluctantly relinquish the last of your special feeling and move across the room to the dryer against the back wall, catching the overhead control panel in your hand. Then you simultaneously flip open the glass door, tilt the dryer forward about forty-five degrees, and spin the inside drum exactly one half turn, your deft touch dumping the load of dry, warm sheets into the women's flat wooden loading tray.

"*Gracias*, Sammy," Shelley says and smiles broadly, pulling the tray stacked high with sheets to the mangle and her waiting helper.

Of course it's the women's responsibility to dump the dryer—your primary work assignment is the extractor, which requires your full attention and skill in balancing the two halves properly, so that the machine doesn't trip its circuit breaker after wobbling erratically, when one side loses water too much faster than the other half. But the women hopelessly tangle up the thinner stuff, like sheets, when dumping the dryer, making it difficult for them to pull apart almost-knotted items. Each separate piece must lie flat to feed into the mangle.

You nod back without speaking, the other older woman raising a hand, acknowledging her gratitude for the tray of untangled sheets. You do not want to even try to speak. It's been less than twenty-four hours since you walked in the shadow of the Dark Angel, but the funnytalk has already come back big time, your confidence eroded by the fear that lingers at the back of your consciousness—fear of being caught for the thing you did to Mary Ann and being sent back to a place even worse than CYA.

Bad, bad, bad.

That's why you've been so thoroughly losing yourself in the music of the machines since the two washers went to dinner. You do not want to think for even one second about Mary Ann or the Dark Angel.

The extractor is silent now—a double load of blankets needs to be emptied, and the whistle will blow any minute for you to feed bleach into the middle washer. It can be a busy time when Wilbur and Danny go to dinner or take a break at the same time. Terry, the slightly-retarded black man, who is responsible for emptying the four dirty laundry chutes in the outside hallway—linen dropping from the hospital's six stories above the basement—has all he can do, trying to keep the chutes clear and separating the mixed tubs of dirty stuff into washing bins.

He's no help.

Mr. Clark, the boss, usually doesn't let both of the washers take a break or go to dinner at the same time, but Mr. Clark left work early today for personal reasons.

When Wilbur and Danny are on their own, they do what they want regardless of Mr. Clark's instructions—go to dinner early and together, or tease Terry unmercifully, or whatever. You chuckle wryly to yourself. They decided *not* to tease you about the funnytalk or wearing a roll-down cap and long-sleeved work shirt despite the wet heat of the basement, after they saw you lift a pair of the eighty-pound plastic bleach containers, one in each hand, and easily dump them into the urn, your first day on the job.

No, indeed.

Still, they often exploit you like tonight; except sometimes when stuff is backed up at the extractor, and you need to do mixed halves— like blankets and sheets—they help you balance some of the loads. But neither one is quite as good as you on the big machine and occasionally their loads will begin wobbling when the extractor reaches high speed, eventually tripping the circuit breaker. Then you have to lift out both halves from the extractor with the overhead crane and re-balance the loads, taking out a few blankets from one side or adding several sheets to the other, using the crane as a weighing balance, gauging the proper degree of tilt of the wetter and heavier half.

The good thing is both men respect you now, even though you have not been working here long—they know you really understand the machines. Wilbur always says, "Sam, you talk to the machines, man, and I think they actually answer you back."

Simultaneous to your last thought, a high-pitched whistle *blasts* from the brass plate governing the middle washer, accompanied almost at the same time by a whistle *blast* from the machine next to the hallway, where Terry is frantically separating gowns and bedding, trying to keep up with the constantly filling laundry chutes.

You smile to yourself—another pair of shrill sounds added to the orchestra—scooping up a rubber bucket full of bleach from the urn for the middle washer, then a minute or so later you drain a bottle of softener into the far load of diapers. Fortunately both men should be back before either load is ready to dump into the metal extractor halves, which will then be rolled to you for balancing, hooked together, and finally lifted with the overhead crane into the extractor.

But you frown, glancing at the clock which already reads 5:40 p.m., remembering that two of the women also took their *half* hour lunch breaks with the men—Yolanda and Gisela, the new German girl with the flaming orange hair.

You close your eyes momentarily, trying to blot out the image of the young woman and her remarkable hair. But, in your mind's eye, you still see the brilliant color, and the sight takes your breath away.

"Wha' y'all need nex'?" Terry asks in his characteristic slur, poking his head in from the hallway where he now has three full bins of different items separated.

You blink and stammer over the sound of the washers, "I-I-I think b-blankets."

Wilbur usually makes that decision, unless Mr. Clark comes out from his office and says that you need to catch up on gowns or whatever, when the hospital floors above call down to him with their immediate needs. But that rarely happens because Wilbur has a pretty good feel for anticipating the entire hospital's needs. He's worked at the laundry ever since he graduated from high school—twelve years now. He's married, got two kids, but that doesn't stop him from flirting with the women on the mangle, even the older ones like Theresa, who must be in her fifties. All the women are married, too

Your frown deepens.

Bad, bad, bad.

Then beyond Terry and down the hallway, you hear the men and the two women turn the corner, returning from the cafeteria… Wilbur has said something, and they're all laughing and giggling like school children, even Danny who is usually pretty reserved around the women—he recently got married just before you came to work at Sutter General Hospital.

Bad, bad, bad.

Your mood has changed, the euphoria from communing with the music of the machines gone now, replaced by a darker feeling, a sense of lonely isolation—the secret of Mary Ann and the Dark Angel locked away deep inside you, but festering like a sliver lodged in your soul.

"Hey, Sam, my man," Wilbur shouts as he comes out of the hallway with Danny. He beckons you with a lascivious expression on his face, looking like he wants to tell you a dirty joke

You cautiously move away from the bleach urn to meet him.

Wilbur slaps your shoulder as you stop near the middle washer. He laughs, glancing once in the direction of the mangle, the view of the back end blocked by a partition that extends from the hallway entry and ends near the bleach urn. Then he leans close and whispers in a confidential tone, "Man, that Gisela is something, you know, really hot to squat."

Danny is just standing there, grinning.

You want to turn and go to your extractor, but Wilbur reaches out and clings to your shirtsleeve.

"Hey, I'm not kidding, Sam. Her old man has been sent TAD back to Germany from McClellan Air Force Base for several months. She's here all by herself. Hardly knows anyone at her apartment complex. Me and Danny been talking you up. She likes big strong guys and is interested, right, man?" He punches Danny playfully in the shoulder.

Danny nods at you. "That's right, *esé*."

"Yeah, man, if I were you, I'd be all over her like a strawberry rash," Wilbur adds, gesturing with his thumb toward the out-of-view far end of the mangle where Gisela must be folding sheets now. "Won't take much, Sam, to get her to give it up." Then he shrugs. "But I don't know, Danny, maybe our man here can't handle that red-headed German tiger. What do you think?"

Danny shrugs, then both men laugh as they turn toward the washers.

"Hey, Terry, you got a bin of blankets out there?" Wilbur shouts over the sounds of the machines into the hallway.

You turn and move back to the extractor with mixed feelings—embarrassed by Wilbur's lewd suggestion, but unable to restrain a rising sense of excitement. You can still picture the fiery hair even though Gisela is out of sight and you cannot help wondering about her secret hair.

Is it the same color?

And the texture—heavy and dense or soft and fine like her head?

Or maybe a total surprise, like Mary Ann's much darker, bushy thicket?

The projected possibilities of Gisela's mysterious secret hair make your blood rush, and you gasp aloud as if hurt.

You swallow hard and look back at the other men sheepishly, hoping neither heard you. Fortunately they are both busy, unloading the middle washer into the extractor halves. You breathe a sigh of relief. But your hands are wet and slippery as you grab the control box for the overhead crane, your dry throat remaining tight and constricted.

2

Much later, after dinner, you take your break at 9:00. Usually by now the three basement fans have cooled off the laundry; but not tonight, the early summer heat wave outside lingering, and it's stifling inside, your shirt soaked with sweat. Your mouth is dry and you are thirsty. So, you head down the hallway, past Terry, who is emptying the first laundry chute, but you stop abruptly when you hear your name called out.

"Sam?"

You turn.

It's her, taking a break now, too.

The orange-headed girl, Gisela.

She hurries to catch up, smiling, and asks, "Are you going to the cafeteria?" Her English is actually quite good, with only the slightest trace of accent. The other women on the mangle, all Hispanics, mostly Mexican-Americans, have much thicker accents, several of them not bothering to speak English at all.

You've never spoken to her before, never been this close; even though she has beads of sweat dotting her upper lip and on her forehead, you can smell her strong sweet essence—a spicy lavender scent, which flares your nostrils. Her eyes, the color of blue-tinted ice, contrast sharply with the oppressing temperature of the hallway. You restrain a shiver and nod, afraid to risk the funnytalk right now.

"Good, I am going now, too, for something cold to drink," she explains. She touches her hand lightly against the back of your arm as she begins walking down the corridor toward the cafeteria, an almost intimate leading gesture. "It is too hot," she adds, wiping her upper lip with a forefinger. "Is it always this bad at night during the summer here in Sacramento?"

"N-no," you respond, as you both enter the almost deserted cafeteria. The line is closed now, but there is a bank of vending machines. You lead her to the cold drink machine.

She reaches in the pocket of her white uniform for a pair of quarters and slips them into the machine, making a selection—a Mountain Dew. Then she frowns kind of quizzically. "Are you not thirsty?"

You nod, blushing. You've been staring dumbfounded since she reached out to deposit the coins, her uniform's short sleeve stretched tight, crimped up and revealing her *unshaven* underarm—beautiful silky hair, perfectly matching the orange of her head. The sight makes your heart pound in your chest.

Fumbling clumsily in your pocket you find a handful of small coins, and manage to insert the proper amount, selecting a can of root beer.

"Shall we sit down?" Gisela asks, leading the way to a table in the far corner.

You follow, thinking: This is a mistake, a big mistake. I should just walk off.

Since beginning work, you have never taken dinner or a break with *any* of the women. Usually you avoid even Terry. But this orange-headed woman, especially the sight of her unshaven underarms, is an overwhelming attraction. Unable to resist, you sit down, determined to stare only at your drink; but your will is weak, and you sneak another peak at her underarms.

So beautiful!

Of course your attention drifts to thoughts about her secret hair, although you manage to resist looking in the direction of her crotch, which is hidden now by the table as she pulls her chair closer. Still you cannot help speculating about the characteristics of her hidden hair. It *has* to be orange and silky like her underarms. You squirm on the hard plastic chair, resisting the almost overwhelming urge to drop something, glance under the cafeteria table, and up her dress. For a second you close your eyes, trying to visualize something else—the laundry, the big machines—and imagine the sound of the extractor.

She has been saying something to you.

You blink, and with an effort, you focus, concentrate on her words.

Gisela is talking about the climate in the little town of Germany where she was raised. She talks about her mother, who came from England—which explains Gisela's good command of English. She chats on about her homeland, her family, and finally mentions her husband, who she met when he was stationed in Germany in the Air Force. They've been married only six months. And now suddenly he has to go back for several months, leaving her all by herself in a strange place.

"I am very lonely, Sam," she admits, her icy eyes staring at you directly. "I have no relatives here, and do not even know my neighbors yet." She manages to force a weak smile at you, gazing deeply into your eyes, as if expecting you to answer some unspoken question.

You dare not speak. No, indeed. Instead you point to the clock on the wall: 9:15.

She looks up and makes an exaggerated sad face.

You begin to rise, but Gisela clutches the sleeve of your work shirt. "This was fun, Sam. I like your company even if you do not say much. You are a very good listener. Maybe we can eat together, even tomorrow. I know, I will fix a, oh, what do you say… ah, *picnic* dinner. We can go to the park where it will be much cooler." She gestures southwesterly in the direction of the park just beyond Sutter's Fort. "Mr. Clark will be gone again, so we can run over a few minutes if need be." She has it all smoothly worked out, as if she'd carefully planned it beforehand.

You do not answer, rising stiffly like a robot.

She leads you out of the cafeteria, glancing back and asking, "Do you like homemade potato salad?"

You nod, not really sure you have ever eaten homemade.

"It is settled then," she says with finality. "We will meet in the park at 5:00 tomorrow. No one else needs to go or even know. It will be our private picnic. Okay?"

No, you think; but, as if your head and brain are not connected, you nod your acceptance.

You are in the hallway now almost back to the laundry.

Gisela stops you, glances around. Only Terry is in view, but he has his back turned, sorting laundry into bins. She smiles mischievously, stands on her tiptoes, pulls your head down, and gives you a quick, moist kiss on the cheek. Then she hurries back to work, chuckling to herself.

Stunned, you stand there a moment in the hallway, then you touch the wet spot on the cheek where she kissed you. It is a bad thing, you know, the kiss provocative, a flirtatious act. Gisela is a married woman, you a single man. But your fingers linger at the spot and, after another moment, you decide it does not really feel all that bad. No indeed. You decide it's just an innocent thing, a kiss between friends, more like a parting hug. Gisela is actually a very sweet person. Wilbur is wrong, very wrong, when he suggests she is interested in men like you in that other vulgar way.

You enter the laundry, smiling to yourself; for the first time when returning to work you pay little attention to the music of the big machines, other thoughts swirling in your head.

At the extractor you reach up to grab the control box on the crane, your hands trembling noticeably as if you're a palsied old man.

3

Later that night in your room, you lie on your bed in the darkness, unable to sleep, thinking about Gisela and her remarkable hair, and the fact that she actually likes you. You can almost visualize her bright orange triangle, soft and fine, and the image makes you toss and turn, the bedding feeling sticky and hot.

Hours seem to slip by...

Then, despite the lingering heat, you eventually drift off to sleep, retaining an image of the young, orange-headed woman, accompanied by the symphony of the big machines humming sweetly in your head.

WORLD CLASS
COOKIES

On Wednesday afternoon, Katy and her partner drive down to Elk Grove in Johnny's sky-blue Mustang, both excited by the prospect of an early arrest, ignoring the heat waves already shimmering off the sweltering asphalt of the narrow levee road winding along the Sacramento River.

In Elk Grove, they eventually find Emma Berglund's address on a cul-de-sac south of the town proper. It's a wood-frame stucco house, in a neighborhood of recently-constructed, two-story houses well-landscaped with newly-planted trees, shrubs, and lawns. Everything upscale, expensive.

"Wow, I didn't expect this," Katy says aloud, "a new grand house." As she speaks, Katy realizes she has no right to expect anything more modest just because the woman is a Native American and has a nephew recently released from the California Youth Authority.

Johnny shrugs. "She's a widow. Guess the old man had some insurance. Actually this is a recent move for her. She lived closer to town three years ago, before Little Fox went down."

Katy nods, getting out of the car.

At the door, despite the upper-class surroundings, they both slide a little to each side, Katy cautiously touching the Sig Sauer .45 holstered on her hip out of view. No more surprises like when Double Jack suddenly jumped them from behind, she thinks, unable to suppress her anxiety as the door opens.

Aunt Em is a slight, gray-haired woman, with only a hint of Native American features—dark eyes and high, rosy cheekbones. She smiles kindly, wiping her hands on a red-checked gingham apron. "Yes?"

"Emma Berglund?" asks Johnny, showing his gold detective shield.

The older woman nods, just a pinch of a frown deepening the lined forehead. "Yes, I am, officer."

"This is Detective Green and I'm Detective Cato," Johnny says. "We are wondering if we might talk to you for a few minutes about your nephew, Mr. Little Fox?"

Still frowning slightly, Aunt Em steps back and beckons them in. "Certainly, but we'll have to talk in the kitchen. I'm in the middle of baking for the church social, coming up this Sunday." She leads them through the immaculately neat house into the kitchen—all white and chrome—to the oven. Taking a potholder from the nearby rack, she opens the oven door and the room is flooded with the sweet, rich aroma of freshly baked cookies. The frown is gone now, as Aunt Em explains proudly, "My special recipe for raisin oatmeal," and begins pulling out two trays of thick, golden-brown cookies, placing them on the sink counter behind her. Then, from the counter next to the oven, she inserts two more trays into the oven. "Peanut butter, chocolate chip." Done for now, she hangs the potholder back up and wipes her hands again on her apron. She points at the little table, "Sit down, please. Can I offer you both some coffee?"

Katy replies, "Please."

Johnny nods.

Aunt Em pours the coffee, then prepares a little dish of the hot oatmeal cookies, setting coffee cups, spoons, a container of cream, sugar bowl, and cookies out on the table.

"Now, what's all this about my nephew, who I haven't seen in, oh, about three years, since your folks down south put him in reform school," she says, just a hint of sharpness in her voice indicating her disapproval. Her forehead remains heavily creased.

"That's what we want to talk about, Mrs. Berglund," Johnny explains. "Exactly when was the last time you did see him or talk to him, even on the phone?"

The old lady's mahogany eyes are sad as she explains, "Haven't seen him since just before he got in all that trouble down south. He came for a visit, oh, it's better than three and a half years ago. I know he's out now, though. He wrote me just before he got released, hmmm, three months ago, I think. Haven't heard from him since then…" She pauses, then, looking directly at Johnny, adds, "He hasn't phoned either, officer."

"In his letter he didn't say anything about maybe coming up for a visit when he got out?" Katy asks.

Aunt Em shakes her head. "In the letter he said he missed me, but when he got out he'd be on probation. Probably have to stay around there for a while… "

She pauses again, pushes the plate of cookies to Katy first, then Johnny.

"Oh, these are terrific," Johnny mumbles, mouth full, after biting into his thick cookie and stuffing in all the remainder in a second huge bite.

Katy nods and smiles. "They *are* good."

Aunt Em grins back.

"So, you haven't heard anything recently, then?" Johnny asks, wiping his mouth with a napkin. "Have no reason to believe he might be here or maybe up in Sacramento?"

"No," the old lady replies, shakes her head, then takes a sip of coffee.

"Would he call or come see you, if he did come north to Sacramento, Mrs. Berglund?" asks Katy, declining the offer of a second cookie. "I mean if he had some other business bringing him up here."

Aunt Em shifts her gaze evasively from Katy to the dish of cookies. "I don't think so, officer. Anyhow, he has no other business up here."

Katy nods, glances at Johnny, and stands. "Well, we thank you for your cooperation and the wonderful cookies, Mrs. Berglund. Your church congregation is very fortunate, indeed."

The old lady smiles at the compliment, then asks, "What has he done this time—my nephew?"

Johnny responds with the party line, "We don't know that he has done anything, Mrs. Berglund. Just a routine investigation. Thank you for everything. Have a good day."

They leave.

2

Outside, back in the Mustang, Johnny says, "Well, what do you think?"

"I think she is pretty much what you see," Katy replies, "a nice old lady, who cares a lot and worries about her nephew."

Johnny starts the car.

"Except she's obviously being evasive with that last response."

"About him not coming to see her?" Johnny says, easing away from the curb.

"That's a lie," Katy says. "She knows damn well he'll come, if he's in Sacramento, probably anywhere in Northern California. She thinks she's protecting him if he is in the area. But I don't think she has heard from him yet."

"So, what do you want to do?"

She grimaces at Johnny. "I don't see any way out of a stakeout, here, do you? At least for a little while. We can get Patrick and Harlan to help if it drags on."

Johnny rubs his nose.

"Okay?"

He sighs, finally nods reluctant agreement, then swears in a forlorn whisper, "Jesus H. Christ, another friggin' stakeout."

Katy shrugs sympathetically. Despite the public's romantic perception, so much of detective work involves long periods of doing nothing but repetitive or boring tasks, and stakeouts are the most monotonous of all. Both her and Johnny despise them with a passion.

3

That evening, with the Mustang parked across from the cul-de-sac, but Aunt Em's house in full view, Johnny says, "Man, what a day. Hot and sweaty. I must look like a wrinkled wino after a three-day binge."

"No, not really," Katy says sweetly, glancing at him with a straight face, before adding, "more like *five* days." Then she can't restrain a chuckle.

He looks over at her, frowning, and says, "Well, you ain't exactly ready for Atlantic City, either, Miss California."

She combs her hands through her hair, which does feel kind of oily and gritty, her blouse sticking to her underarms and ribs, the material feeling wrinkled and damp. She nods, realizing she has to look pretty wilted, too.

Staring at each other they both burst out laughing, relieving some of the muggy tedium of the evening.

"You been out to see the Monarchs yet this year?" Johnny asks, after he's wiped his eyes, knowing how keen Katy is on basketball, especially Sacramento's entry in the WNBA.

She shakes her head. "Been too busy with the book and all." But she has been following carefully the Monarch's progress in their first few games on TV news clips and in the sports section of the *Bee*, especially after their star Ruthie Bolton-Holifield went down with ligament damage to a knee. She really likes the play of Adia Barnes, who resembles Katy in size and build. "Got to get out soon."

In addition to working out regularly now, Katy played college basketball for Sac State, and even before that she'd played in high school and a tough PAL league down south.

Thinking about basketball reminds Katy of Geri Robinson, the black woman who is like an older sister to her. She stares absently out the car window, momentarily forgetting the hot, sultry evening, her thoughts drifting back to the night fourteen years ago when she first met Geri...

4

Between her junior and senior years in high school in San Diego, Katy's school basketball coach, Gavin McCloud, suggested she try out for a PAL girls summer league team, and gave her the name of his friend, a cop-coach, Geri Robinson. Coach McCloud knew Katy had been having problems in school at the end of the year, struggling with her studies, after experiencing an abrupt transfer from one foster home to another because the previous foster father had been making sexual advances. It had even affected her appearance. She slumped now, trying to hide her breasts, her appearance almost slovenly.

Coach McCloud had called her on Sunday afternoon with the address and location of the PAL team.

Monday, after work as a waitress at her daytime summer job at Bob's Big Boy Burgers in the Mission area, Katy took the bus to the edge of the central projects, growing apprehensive as she got closer, finally getting off and walking to the Metro Rec Center just before dusk, pausing to glance at the graffiti spray-painted around the entry to the dismal gray building. It looked more like an institution of some kind rather than a recreational/educational facility—a battered fort in the heart of the surrounding slums. She was indeed sorry that she had promised Coach McCloud that she'd keep the appointment.

But I'm here now, Katy thought with forced resignation, stepping inside, walking down the hall to the gym. Might as well check it out.

The place was noisy with bouncing balls and shouting spectators standing about on the sidelines, the two side baskets cranked down, and all four hoop areas busy with games of three-on-three. A tall, black woman with a whistle in her mouth roamed around center court, apparently watching all four games closely, often stopping the action of one game or another, shouting over the noise to point out something—usually a defensive error, like reaching instead of moving the feet when guarding a driving opponent.

These girls all look pretty good, Katy decided after only a couple of minutes of observation, the four games very physical, no one going to the hoop uncontested. And all the participants were black or Hispanic, most probably coming from the surrounding housing areas.

She felt nervous now, really out of place.

Then a pair of big, heavyset black girls, spectators, shuffled over to Katy, and for a moment just stared at her in a kind of hostile appraising manner.

"Whatcha doin' down here, girl... slummin'?" the biggest of the pair asked sarcastically, her expression reinforcing the aggressive nature of the question.

"Yeah, *whitey*," the other one added, "what ya lookin' at?"

Katy didn't say anything, her pulse racing; she shrugged and smiled good-naturedly, thinking: *This is just what I need.*

The biggest girl moved closer and bumped her. "Whatcha grinnin' at, fool? Y'all think I'm funny lookin' or somepin'?"

She was right in Katy's face now, so close Katy could smell the Doublemint gum the girl chewed.

The shrill sound of a whistle diverted their attention, as the black woman ordered the four groups of six players: "Take ten laps, then shoot free throws, two at a time." Then, the woman came over and announced, "Yo, Gertie, Twilla, this is *my* new ballplayer. You girls find someone else to hassle. Scoot!"

As the two big girls shuffled off, both glancing back with soured expressions on their faces, the woman leaned forward and asked in a low voice, "You *are* Katy Green, right?"

Katy nodded, still feeling slightly intimidated by the confrontation with the two husky bullies, thankful for her rescue.

"Okay, let's have a brief talk in my office," the black woman said, leading Katy to a tiny office beyond the far end of the gym.

"I'm Geri Robinson," the woman said, sitting at her desk. "Gavin told me all about you, losing your parents when you were ten, the foster home hassle last year, your problems at school, and even suggested that he thought you might make a pretty good basketball player, someday. So, we don't need to deal with any of that ancient history tonight, right?"

Katy nodded. The woman gave off an air of gruff, authoritative competence.

"Let me tell you what I'm about," Geri said. "I'm the coach of the Panthers in this little eight-team summer recreational league. All my girls play on high school teams just like you, except most are seniors. But for them this is much more than recreational or therapeutic. For them it's a way out of the projects. We'll have as many as a half dozen scouts from southern California colleges watching some of our games. In the last five years, since the league began, I've had *five* players get full scholarships and go on to play college ball. Another six continued at local community colleges, three of them eventually going on to four-year schools. Eight girls college educated, with a chance for a better life. So, where does that leave you?"

Katy shrugged, not knowing how to respond. "I hadn't thought about going on to college. I just, I don't know, needed *something* now."

Geri nodded. "Well, I'm doing Gavin a favor even letting you try out this late. I'm going to keep only ten players on the Panthers. First cut is next Monday. Last cut the following week before our first game. If you are a player, we'll soon find out. If not, I can't risk taking a spot from another girl to provide therapy for you. Is all this perfectly clear?"

Katy nodded, not really sure what to think about this woman and her kind of blunt, aggressive, straight forward way of talking. Finally she responded, but a little too loudly, "Hey, it's all real clear."

"So, you still want to try out, knowing how it is?" Geri asked, her tone slightly softer now.

Katy thought a minute, staring back at the black woman, her earlier apprehension replaced now with a sense of stubborn resolve, and she blurted, "Yes, I think I really do want to try out, see if I can make it."

"Well, I'll say this, Katy Green, you got guts even coming down here at all, much less trying out," the woman said, her stern expression slowly dissolving into a wide, toothy, sweet smile.

They stood, and Geri surprised Katy, coming around the desk and giving her a big, warm hug. "Welcome to the Panthers." Katy couldn't help but like this plain-talking, tough woman.

She just barely made the team, the tenth and last spot, by hustling during the week of tryouts, diving for balls, playing hard-nosed, physical basketball.

Surprising even herself, Katy soon worked her way into a starting forward spot, focusing her physical and mental abilities on rebounding and playing defense—much like Dennis Rodman of the Chicago Bulls—realizing the Panthers already had several great shooters. With this philosophy she quickly found her niche on the team; by the third game she walked straight and tall, respected by everyone she knew at Metro Rec, even Twilla and Gertie, the two heavyset spectators who'd hassled her that first night at practice.

After the season, Geri had all her girls over to her house for a barbeque, her husband, Herb, doing his "world class baby back ribs." At the end of the evening Geri had separated Katy from the rest of the team for a special chat, leading her into the study.

They sat down side-by-side on a leather couch.

"Well, you know me by now, Katy. No preambles. I'm going to say exactly what's on my mind." She paused a moment, apparently collecting her thoughts. "Even though you weren't the star of the team by any stretch of the imagination, I'm more proud of you than either Lulu or Lisha," Geri continued, referring to the Panther's two best all-around players, who had both recently received offers of full rides to Pepperdine. "You made a major contribution to our championship season even with your modest shooting ability. So, you helped the team get serious attention from all the college scouts. I wanted to say thank you. And I hope you got something out of it, too. More than just a little basketball and a championship trophy."

Embarrassed by the older woman's complimentary frankness, Katy managed to reply softly, "Thank you, Geri. I did learn a lot from you and the team." She had indeed learned about real teamwork, struggling against adversity, and many of the other almost trite-sounding, character-building benefits attributed to playing team sports; but perhaps most importantly she had learned that heart and perseverance could be as important to success as pure talent. It had been an invaluable experience, a pleasure to play for Geri.

"You're coming back next summer?"

"Try and stop me," Katy responded, laughing. "Maybe I can go on to college, too, like Lulu and Lisha, you know"

Geri smiled. "Maybe you will. But in the mean time, we need to do something about your appearance. You're a beautiful, tall woman, and don't need to be ashamed of it." She held out an envelope. "This is a little thank you present from me to you."

Katy opened it.

It was a paid appointment at one of San Diego's most prestigious beauty salons. She looked up at Geri with moist eyes.

"We'll start there," the older woman said gently, standing and giving Katy a big hug.

At the end of her senior year of high school, after summer PAL basketball, Katy was *not* offered a basketball scholarship—she had continued to concentrate on rebounding and defense, never shooting much, and didn't personally catch the attention of any of the college scouts. Then, a few days after the end of the season, Katy had decided she really wanted to be a cop like her coach. Since Geri couldn't discourage her career choice, she arranged for Katy to go on to Sacramento State College, which had a good police science training program and a pretty good Division II women's basketball program, even though they gave no scholarships. Everyone was a walk-on at that time.

Katy blossomed at Sac State, doing well in her studies, playing power forward for the Hornets. Good grades. And in her English classes, she soon discovered she had real writing talent—receiving As and glowing praise from instructors, especially on her stories in Creative Writing. During her college career she kept in close contact with her good friend, Geri Robinson, who flew up special from San Diego to Sacramento the day Katy graduated *magna cum laude*.

5

Returning to the present, Katy is flooded with a sense of guilt. She hasn't written or even called Geri for several weeks. Maybe after this book thing in San Jose I can get down and see her, she thinks, the thought not really making her feel much better. Or maybe I can get her to come up for a short visit *now*, take her out to Arco Arena for a Monarch's game. After all she is footloose, retired from the SDPD last month. Yeah, that sounds a lot better, Katy decides, the decision easing her conscience. I'll call Geri tomorrow morning first thing—

At that moment she spots a shadow slide between the Berglund house and the neighbors. "C'mon, Johnny," she says, the pitch rising in her voice as she slips out the door, reaching back for her .45 automatic.

"I see him," Johnny whispers.

They separate as they leave the cover of the car, quickly moving across the street and into the shadows of the adjoining homes. Katy stops at the front of the neighboring house and peers around the corner into the darkness, as Johnny takes up a spot at the corner of the

Berglund place. She sees nothing now, even after blinking and squinting.

But she hears *him*, dragging something toward her.

Katy glances over at Johnny, just barely visible in the shadowed overhang of the adjacent home. He nods, indicating he too hears the sound.

What the hell is he dragging? Katy asks herself, trying to control her racing pulse by taking several deep breaths.

The sound gets closer.

Then Katy jumps out, assuming a Weaver stance and shouts, "Hold it! Police. Hands up!"

She hears a gasp from the shadowy figure, as he releases whatever he's holding.

Johnny closes in from her left. "Easy, pal," he says, in a voice just slightly tighter than normal, "keep them hands where we can see them."

They both edge closer, the figure clearer now.

He's frozen with his hands over his head, standing in front of a garbage can.

"What are you doing?" Katy asks, keeping her eyes on the man's hands.

"I'm, I'm just taking out the garbage," he says in a voice little more than a hoarse whisper. "Tomorrow is pickup day."

"At this time of night?" Johnny asks.

"I just got off work," the man replies.

"Where's your car? How did you get here?" Katy says

"My friend was driving, left me off the next street over." The man turns and points back into the darkness. "I came through a gate in the backyard, like always when I ride with him."

"You live here?" Johnny indicates the house to their right.

"Yes, I do, officer. What's wrong? I, I didn't do anything."

"Okay, turn around, reach back with your left thumb and forefinger and take out your wallet. I want to see some I.D." Johnny moves in close.

Katy maintains her shooter's stance, a sense of disappointment beginning to erode her tense alertness, as it becomes obvious to her that this older guy can't possibly be Little Fox.

The man is a very frightened Mr. Michael Hruska and does really live next door. He's a systems programmer for the State, usually working odd hours, often coming home late like tonight.

After apologizing for frightening Mr. Hruska half to death, Katy and Johnny slip back into the Mustang, both feeling a little sheepish.

"Well, that kinda takes care of our stakeout," Johnny says, the exasperation evident in his tone. He starts the car. "Might as well head home. Right?"

"Yeah," Katy replies, realizing she's exhausted. The long, monotonous stakeout, then the adrenaline rush after seeing Hruska creeping around suspiciously, followed by the disappointing let-down. "Man, I'm tired."

6

The next day, about noontime, Katy answers the phone. It's her partner.

"Got some good news, and some bad news," he says with a kind of forced jolliness in his voice.

"Okay, hit me with the good news."

"The forensic report is done, but I don't see much in it, except their revelation that Mary Ann was probably unconscious when her throat was cut by a straight razor. He apparently knocked her out, laid her on the bed, then used the pillow to block spraying blood after cutting her throat. Anyhow, I'll bring it over."

"And the bad news."

"Well, first, there is only one key to Mary Ann's apartment, accounted for in inventory of her stuff, and I don't think anyone scaled her building last night—no evidence of anything like that.

"Secondly, Little Fox's P.O. called a few minutes ago. Our man has surfaced in L.A. In fact he was never gone. Apparently had the flu or something, running a low profile. So, that lead is a big, fat, raggedy-ass zero."

After a few moments thought, Katy asks, "No other scalpings in the computer or from NCIC?"

"No, not even a crew cut."

Despite her disappointment, she laughs. "Man, nothing really gets you down anymore. You are one cheery soul."

"Hey, kiddo," he replies, "did you forget my recent past. I used to have to drink Jack Daniels and snort blow to stay on an even keel. But you're right. Life goes on, even if Little Fox isn't our perp and yesterday was definitely a wild goose chase. Hey, you had a world class oatmeal raisin cookie at Aunt Em's, you know?"

She just chuckles wryly, only partially buoyed by her partner's good cheer, regretting the lost time taken from working on her novel. "Okay, what now?"

"I'm going to talk to Mrs. Crane again, make absolutely certain she remembers Mary Ann bringing *no* one home with her Tuesday night. See what else she remembers about Mary Ann's past boyfriends. Then I'm going to check around the neighborhood again with Bundy and McHugh, making sure Mary Ann didn't pick up someone. And, later, I'll drop off the forensic report. Maybe you can get some writing done in the meantime, okay?"

She nods to herself, recognizing the hint of guilt in his question. Then, after a moment, she suggests, "Hey, Johnny, maybe I'll fix us something to eat tonight. Or better yet we can have a barbeque outside in back by the complex swimming pool. You can stay for dinner, can't you?"

He doesn't say anything for almost a half a minute. And Katy can guess what he's probably thinking.

When they first became partners four years ago, he was going through a nasty divorce, drinking and doping heavily and jumping from one-night-stand to one-night-stand. Of course he suggested the everyone-sleeps-with-his-partner routine, and he suggested it seriously after he began to sober up, regularly going to AA and NA meetings, and trying to rejoin the human race, often calling her late at night.

But Katy had kept Johnny at arm's length with, "Hey, man, I'm not interested in being a rebound item. You get some time under your belt being a human being again, and we'll see what develops." She knew it was still at the back of his mind as they became more comfortable as partners—in fact it was at the back of *her* mind, occasionally catching herself looking at him in that appraising kind of way. She admits to herself that he is an attractive guy despite his broken nose and a little scar tissue over his eyebrows, even taller than her, which is really a bonus. But to date, they've just been partners and close friends.

Waiting for his answer about dinner, she asks herself: How do you feel about that, you and Johnny just being friends? She doesn't really have an answer.

"Sure, Katy," he says, kind of guardedly. "I'd really like that. Can I bring *you* some wine to drink or some dessert for both of us?"

She laughs, easing a slight sense of tension. "No, partner, just bring your appetite. We'll have my special fresh peach smoothies to drink, cook something on the grill. Maybe take a swim if it's still steamy outside, so you can bring your suit—no skinny dipping in the complex swimming pool."

"You got a date, partner," he answers enthusiastically, and she can detect the grin back in his voice. "What time you want me there?"

She thinks a moment, remembering tomorrow will be Thursday. "Make it just after 8:00, okay? It's my workout night over at ARC."

Tuesdays and Thursdays at 6:00 p.m., despite anything else pressing including the deadline with the book, Katy has recently resumed her workout schedule at American River College gym, where her friend and ex-Sac State team mate, Artis Johnson, is a P.E. teacher and coach of the ARC women's basketball team. They play for an hour and a half each night, Artis usually digging up four of her ARC players for three-on-three, half court games. Katy is just getting back in playing shape, after recovering from the broken arm, not really shooting well yet; and in the previous two sessions a sister of one of Artis's junior college girls has really been drubbing her. CeCe Reyes is almost Katy's height but broader, quite a bit heavier, an all-city basketball player at Natomas High School, headed for ARC in the Fall.

Katy is looking forward to tomorrow's workout, because she's ready to bring her A-game.

PINK STEEL WOOL

You are nervous, on edge all day, anticipating the picnic with Gisela, unable to read, watch TV, or listen to the radio, constantly checking the time for going to work: 12:00, 1:30, 2:00. Finally, you go over for a walk in the park next to Sutter's Fort, enjoying the shade and a slight breeze. Still you are unable to relax. You know it's a mistake, seeing this young woman alone in a private place, just like that time long ago, when the other one surprised you, and the Dark Angel growled in anger...

2

You were fifteen, just transferred to a new foster home over in El Cajon. It was Sunday and all the other foster kids had been taken to the movies, except you, in trouble for *stealing* a cookie from the kitchen that afternoon. At least you thought everyone had gone to the movies. You wandered back into the kitchen, thinking about taking another one of the chocolate chip cookies, but then you decided that your new foster mother had probably counted them. Seemed like the type.

You turned to leave and jumped with a start.

She laughed, Susan, the oldest foster sister. "Scared you, huh?"

She was a couple of years older than you—seventeen or so—her face slightly pock-marked and too angular to being even close to being called pretty. But her brown hair had a reddish tint when it reflected the light, which you liked, and she had caught you staring at her several times since moving in the day before. You flushed when caught the last time, because you had been speculating in your mind about the color of her secret hair.

"Y-Y-You didn't get to g-go to the m-m-movies, S-Susan?" you asked, wondering what terrible offense she had committed.

"I didn't want to go," she answered. "It's a stupid picture for kids." Then she moved closer. "Besides, I wanted to get to know you better." She smiled crookedly, the facial expression reminding you a little of the movie star, Ellen Barkin.

Be careful, Sam Boy, the Light Angel spoke in your head.

The older girl reached out and took your hand. "C'mon, I want to show you something in my bedroom."

No, Sam.

But you disobeyed the Light Angel's command, for some reason compelled to follow Susan.

In the foster sisters' bedroom, a cabin back of the main house, she turned and faced you boldly, still gripping your hand. "I've seen you looking at me," she said, her voice almost accusatory in tone.

You began to squirm.

"And I know why," she said, dropping your hand, then leaning close.

You react by moving a step backward.

"Hey, I'm not going to bite."

Then she kissed you on the mouth, before taking a few steps back herself.

That was when you first noticed that she was wearing a San Diego Padre's T-shirt and realized there was nothing underneath. You could see the nipples of her small breasts straining against the navy blue material.

She slowly pulled off the T-shirt.

Leave right now, Sam Boy.

But it was too late.

She had reached down and started to unbutton her jeans.

You were too fascinated to move.

"Yes, I know exactly what you're interested in," she said, her voice a low, raspy whisper now.

You swallowed as she stepped out of the jeans, barely stifling a moan, for she was wearing nothing underneath the jeans either.

For a moment she just stood there in the middle of the room, stark naked except for a pair of dangling earrings, hands on hips, smiling crookedly.

And you, you just stared in awe at the slight patch of reddish-brown pubic hair. "Ohhh," you moaned aloud with delight, marveling at the glorious sight, the girl's unattractive facial features all but forgotten now. You shook your head, unable to speak at all.

She nodded and moved close, reaching up and taking your head in her hands. She kissed you roughly on the mouth, then laughed, and said huskily, "Was I right about that, Sam?"

Still you could not speak, and you wanted to shake your head, but you were frozen in place now. You knew bad things were going to happen, but it was all out of your control. You should have listened to the Light Angel.

Too late for second thoughts.

Susan began unbuttoning your long-sleeved shirt, then massaged your smooth chest and said, "Actually there is something I want you to show me, too." She reached for your zipper, then hesitated.

"Okay?" It wasn't really a question.

Oh, no, you thought, pulse racing, feeling a sinking sensation in your stomach. No one in the last year or so, not even the two other teenage foster brothers at the last home had seen you down there. You were too embarrassed by the complete lack of all hair; they'd both been so proud of showing off their sparse crotch patches, often walking around naked in your communal bedroom.

You twisted away, and shouted at the girl, "N-no!"

"No?" she repeated, as if not understanding the word, an incredulous look on her face.

Aggressively she reached out and pulled you close.

"What do you mean, *no?*"

Then she reached down and almost tore your zipper off, exposing the white of your jockey shorts. You were too shocked to resist, to even move. And encouraged by your lack of resistance, she eased her hand slowly into your shorts and fondled your penis.

"Why, you're completely soft," she said, dismayed, looking into your face with a questioning look.

After holding your limp member a moment longer, she jerked out her hand and pulled down your pants and shorts, exposing you completely.

She stared, her mouth hanging open, then whispered her discovery, "No hair." She looked up into your eyes with a confused expression, as if searching for an answer, then repeated, "No hair?"

Slowly an angry look crept over her dumbfounded features, her face flushing, making her even uglier. Finally she found her voice and shouted, "You're just a big *queer,* you know. No hard-on, no hair. A big, big… sissy!" She pushed you hard in the chest, making you step back to recover your balance, then she added, "Asshole! Why didn't you tell me this in the first place?"

No, the voice shouted angrily in your head. It was the other one now, the Dark Angel.

She is wrong, inconsiderate, making fun of you. She is a bad person, a stupid person, an ugly person, an evil person.

Slowly, moved by His emphatic prodding, you grow angry, your nakedness forgotten, your embarrassment turning to a shaking rage.

Make her pay, He commanded. *Now.*

You reached out and clutched her right hand in a steely grip, pulling her closer, squeezing, squeezing, crunching the bones, until you saw the pain and tears in her eyes.

Harder.

She slapped out with her free hand, hitting you weakly in the face.

Strike back.

And the red rage welled up, blurring your vision, as you struck out blindly with your left fist, feeling it smash solidly into soft flesh. You blinked and watched the girl crumple to the floor, completely defenseless now.

Like an animal leaping on its wounded prey, you were on her, pinning her down with your knees, pummeling her with both fists in the face.

Hit, hit, hit.

Sam Boy, Sam Boy, the other Angel cried out, breaking into your rage, finally gaining your attention. *Stop, look what you have done.*

You gasped, blinked, finally able to focus.

The naked girl was lying on the floor, groaning, her face badly bruised, her nose and mouth bleeding.

Oh, no, you thought, standing up, but not really knowing what to do, remaining rooted to the spot, absently pulling up and zipping your pants, as the girl sobbed with humiliation and pain…

But soon they all returned from the movie. Then it was a confusing bedlam and, before you knew it, you were whisked away and questioned by frowning strangers. You said nothing about the Dark Angel's instructions and direct involvement, and could really offer the strangers no explanation for your suddenly explosive behavior. It… just happened, like to somebody else in a movie.

A little later in juvenile court:

Sexual assault.

Battery.

Then, six long years at CYA.

3

You blink and gasp, returning to the present, looking about the nearly empty park, feeling slightly disoriented. It must be close to 3:00 p.m. now, time to walk over to Sutter General Hospital and punch in to work at the laundry.

See Gisela.

You shudder at the thought, the other young woman's battered face still fresh in your memory.

4

You find it difficult to attend to the extractor, to keep your eyes from wandering in the direction of the mangle and the orange-headed girl. It's very hot, but the sweat on your body is clammy, making you shiver; you feel an almost irresistible urge to flee from the situation. But you manage to hold on, even balance most of the loads properly, trying to concentrate on the soothing rhythms of the surrounding big machines.

Sloshing—Whinning—Flopping—Whistling—Whooshing—Whirring: the special symphony eventually eases the knot in the pit of your stomach.

Then you glance up at the clock near Mr. Clark's empty office—he left just after the shift started, calling both Wilbur and Shelley into the office for instructions before he departed.

4:55.

Wilbur knows you want to go to dinner early, believing you have an errand to run and may even be back late a few minutes.

"No problem, man."

So, as the big hand hits 12 on the clock, you hustle along the hall past Terry working in chute four, along to the outside door, and out into the bright sunshine, your legs feeling like you've run five miles, your chest tight, your heart thumping rapidly, your pulse racing.

You walk down the street a block and glance around, at first not spotting Gisela, thinking maybe she forgot or changed her mind; and you experience conflicted feelings—disappointment/elation.

At that moment, from across the street, at the edge of the trees encircling the park, you see her waving at you, holding a large brown shopping bag in her other hand.

Stiffly, you wave back and cross the street.

"Hi, Sam."

You force a smile and reply, "H-Hi," trying to control your racing pulse. Deep breath, deep breath.

She takes your hand, leading you into the heart of the park. "Here is a private table where no one from work can see us," she says, putting the shopping bag on the picnic table. She begins taking out paper plates and other stuff. Then she glances up and tells you, "Sit down, silly. We will eat first, talk later."

It's almost cool here deep in the park, the thick cover of trees a barrier against the heat and bright sunshine, even screening the normal city noise of the late afternoon. Peaceful. You just sit idly and watch her prepare two plates of food, after pouring you a large glass of iced tea.

"There," she says, sitting down.

Feeling relaxed now, you bite into the sandwich—ham and cheese—and nod your head at Gisela's questioning glance for approval. Then you scoop up a plastic spoonful of the potato salad and taste it. "Oh, this is really g-good!" you say almost perfectly. It has a different, sharp vinegary taste, not at all like sweeter deli stuff you know.

Gisela smiles knowingly. "It's the German kind. I don't think you quite have anything like it here."

As you eat slowly, you notice that she is wearing heavy makeup and dark red lipstick. This makes you frown slightly, because it brings to mind both Mary Ann and the black woman downtown. You look down at your plate, feeling annoyed. You like Gisela better when her face is plain, her natural orange hair and ice-blue eyes her only adornments. But you say nothing.

Bad, bad, bad.

After you finish the delicious salad and sandwich, washing the last bite down with a big gulp of tea, you try to say, *very good*: "V-V-V-V—"

But you're locked in a stammer.

Gisela reaches across the table and touches your hand. "You enjoyed it, right?"

You nod, gratefully. "Y-yes."

She says, "Good," packing everything back in her brown shopping bag.

Then after looking at her wristwatch she says, "I wanted to ask you something, Sam, before we have to go back inside to work."

"G-Go ahead," you say, encouraging her to continue.

"My two next door neighbors, young women attending Sacramento City College, are going to have a party for me. Very small, several of the other neighbors I do not know yet, and maybe a few friends from here at the laundry. I wanted to invite you. It's tomorrow, late Friday night after work. Say you will come." She pauses, taking a card from the bag. "My address, with instructions how to get there."

You take the card and put it in your pocket, but you don't say anything for a moment, knowing it will be a probation violation because they'll probably have beer or something else alcoholic to drink. And you don't usually do too well in crowds, even small ones make you extremely edgy. So, you suck in a breath and shake your head. "I-I don't g-go to p-p-p—"

"Oh, Sam, why?"

You flinch at the hurt look on her face, in her icy blue eyes. And you do try to explain without mentioning CYA and probation. "I j-just c-can't stand c-crowds. T-Too l-late. I-I-I—"

"For me? You cannot come for me?" Her gaze is more than icy now.

You just shrug, then shake your head emphatically.

Her painted face flushes darkly, and she stands abruptly, obviously very angry now.

You almost decide to tell her the real reason you can't go; but before you can explain, she turns to leave.

"It is 5:40," she says, her tone almost as cold as her gaze. "We better get back."

You nod and follow her out of the park.

At the door back into the basement of Sutter General Hospital, Gisela stops and faces you for a brief moment. "Sam, I really want you to come to that party tomorrow night. I think we can be very *special* friends."

"I c-c-can't c-c-c—"

You close your eyes and stomp, trying to forcefully break the stammer.

You blink.

But she has gone back inside.

Quickly, you follow her inside with a sinking heart, suspecting it is too late. You are right. Gisela has already disappeared into the women's locker room. You won't have the opportunity to explain, not tonight, anyhow.

Reluctantly, you return to work, feeling confused, even slightly angry yourself.

"Hey, man, did you get it done?" Wilbur asks as you pass him and Danny, heading for your spot by the extractor.

"Y-Yes, I did," you respond wryly, grabbing hold of the overhead crane's control box, almost ripping it away from its thick, insulated cable. Yes, you really did do it this time, hurting your new friend's feelings; now she's really upset with you.

Yes, indeed.

5

Later, after work, despite your attempt to catch her attention, Gisela completely ignores you, heading straight out to the parking lot, talking only with the other women.

You watch them all disappear into the night toward the freeway just north of the hospital, Gisela slipping into an older model Dodge and driving off.

You walk several blocks downtown in the opposite direction toward your apartment on 26th with a heavy heart, feeling discouraged and sad. You think about her orange hair, the potentially brilliant triangle, but even that exciting image does little to make you feel better.

You unlock your apartment, the gloomy, stuffy interior a sweatbox.

It is much too hot to sleep.

You turn on the tiny TV—a recent purchase at K-Mart last payday—but you can't concentrate. Then, you switch to the radio, some background music, standing before the window shirtless, trying to catch a whiff of air. But the muggy night closes in around you, like a steamy blanket, and you just stand there, sweat rolling down your ribcage, gasping for breath.

6

You must have pulled a chair near the window and dozed off, because you awaken suddenly with a start, feeling chilled, sitting up straight. And you hear something—

It's Him!

The Dark Angel is hovering outside the window, blocking the street light, His Shadow darkening most of your room, his wing beats stirring the air around you, chilling your sweaty, partially naked body.

"It is time for more vindication," he commands in his hoarse throaty voice. "Another of your enemies has forgotten her insults and goes about her business with impunity. Pick up your instrument of vengeance."

In almost a trance, you shuffle across the room to your bed, still in His shadow, which extends up the far wall and you reach under the mattress feeling for the hidden straight razor.

Clutching the ebony-handled instrument in your hand, you move back to the opened window and the dim light.

"I have i-it," you say softly.

"Good," He says, drawing away. "Come."

Without hesitation, you follow the Dark Angel outside, feeling like a spectator watching a dark film at the movie theater.

Nothing real, everything an illusion.

But in His shadow you feel calm, protected, safe, confident, strong, though chilled to the bone.

You both move southward, downtown.

And soon you recognize the area, His shadow screening away the loud sounds of the night, even the bright lights somewhat dulled now. Nothing as overpowering to your senses as the last time you were down here by yourself.

The Dark Angel slows along the K Street walking mall near 7th Street, searching, searching; you follow inconspicuously among the crowd, always remaining in His chilling shadow, still moving like a puppet jerked about in a dream.

He stops suddenly.

"There."

You spot the woman across and down the street half a block, standing and talking to the black giant, the man she called, Charlie. She's wearing her same working uniform, the low-cut leopard skin blouse, the black vinyl mini-skirt, and the dark high-heeled shoes. Even at this distance you can see the heavy, gaudy make-up; but her short, kinky hair is different from last time, not dyed reddish blonde, but darker, almost an indigo color.

Still, there is no question that it's her, the painted woman.

You shiver, remembering that other night not so long ago, when you saw and touched her remarkable secret hair, your rapture abruptly destroyed by the huge black man bursting into the room and smashing you over the head. You reach up and gingerly rub the back of your head, which is still slightly tender, growing disturbed with the painful memory.

The woman beckons to a young man dressed in jeans and a cowboy shirt, who has been staring at her from a few feet away, leaning against a storefront.

Charlie quickly slips away up the street.

The young cowboy and the painted woman negotiate for a few moments.

Then, as you watch, the woman says something to the cowboy, who shakes his head vigorously and gestures down the street to the entrance of an alley, almost directly across from your location.

She laughs, clutches his arm against her ample breast, and moves him down the mall, hesitating for just a moment at the narrow mouth of the alley, looking about nervously, before both suddenly disappear into the darkness.

"Come," the Dark Angel commands, his deep tone almost gleeful now. "She has made a fatal mistake."

And you follow in His shadow, quickly crossing the street before halting at the mouth of the alley, peering into the darkness, squinting, unable to make out much of anything in the blackness.

Then you can hear the painted woman speaking softly, and she isn't very far away.

"Oh, c'mon honey, five more ain't gonna kill you."

A few moments silence, then a sigh, and a petulant male response, "Okay then, *here*."

You can make out their two figures now that your vision is adapting to the lack of light. You move carefully, the Dark Angel above you, hovering in the night, his wing beats silently stirring the humid air around you in the narrow alley.

You see them both more clearly now.

Two figures, one kneeling in front of the other, and you hear the standing figure making odd sounds… like moans.

Closer, closer.

You're so near now, that you can almost touch the engaged figures.

It is the fully-clothed woman kneeling, plying her trade, the cowboy, pants and shorts bunched around his knees, leaning back at the waist against the brick building, making the faint, almost childish, moaning sounds of pleasure.

Bad, bad, bad.

Abruptly it is over.

The cowboy disengages from the woman, pulls up and buttons his jeans; then, without another word or even a glance back, he hustles away, the sounds of his boot steps echoing slightly in the dark alley. The woman rises very slowly from her knees, watching as the cowboy disappears into the lighted street, her shoulders slumping slightly, as if she is very old and wearing a heavy but invisible backpack.

Then, suddenly sensing a foreign presence, she straightens up, her gaze jerking around, settling in your direction, her lined eyes squinting into the darkness, peering. "Who's that? That you, Charlie? C'mon, man, doan' play with me. I'm tire'."

You step from the Angel's shadow and move in closer.

The painted woman shudders, and exclaims, "Hey, you ain't my Charlie."

"No, I'm n-not," you say almost perfectly, deftly flipping the straight razor open in your hand as you slide even closer. "But you do know me don't y-you? Remember?"

"No, I—"

Her voice cuts off as she notices the glint of the metal in your hand.

You edge closer still.

"Whatcha gonna to do with that, big fella?" she asks, pointing at the razor, voice trembling with fear, her heavily painted face reminding you of a sad clown.

You remain quiet.

Her gaze suddenly darts left toward the lighted mouth of the alley, her thinking transparent.

She looks back at you, gauging the distance, her chance to run, then she glances down at the high-heels, her faint hope evaporating like morning mist under a burning sun, and her shoulders slump a little more. She knows she is completely at your mercy; there's no chance of escape.

You nod your head, then order, "Take off your skirt."

Her tense expression softens slightly, and you realize she is again feeling a glimmer of hope—maybe sensing another way out if she cooperates.

"No problem, big fella," she says, her confidence growing.

Quickly she wiggles out of the tight skirt.

"The panties, t-too."

She obeys, stepping easily out of her shiny, red underwear.

You suck in a long, deep breath.

Even in the dim light you can see her triangle is still dyed the bright flamingo color. You swallow with difficulty, your throat tight, your pulse racing out of control now.

"Oh, baby, how 'bout puttin' away that nasty ole thing," she says, stepping in close, her voice a sexy, husky coo. So close you can smell her heavy cheap perfume, which still does not quite mask the scent of all the unwashed male bodies lingering on her skin.

You shiver slightly, attempting to breathe only through your mouth.

"Momma gonna treat you right, y'all see," she adds, maintaining her soft coo, trying to look seductive, despite her gaudy, smudged mask, which is much the worse for wear now, the close, claustrophobic nature of the narrow alley compounding the sticky mugginess of the sultry night.

She moves within arm's length of you, reaching out with her long fingers toward your belt buckle—

You strike without warning, a swift, short left hook, twisting from the hip, setting down for leverage like a boxer, your pronated fist catching her squarely on the right side of her jaw.

Her head snaps back, her lined eyes widen and roll up, as her wobbly legs sag beneath her, and the painted woman collapses into a heap at your feet.

A few minutes later, you hear a heavy step crunch at the mouth of the alley and you look up, only partially finished with your work using the ebony-handled instrument of vengeance. Oh, no.

It's the huge black man, Charlie.

You leave the woman where she lies up against the brick wall, and after withdrawing a few steps backward under the Dark Angel's protective shadow again, you press yourself flat against the darkness of the far wall and freeze.

After a few moments, you silently creep by Charlie, looking back for a minute over your shoulder.

"Is tha' you, baby?" he asks in a worried, concerned tone, spotting the unmoving figure crumpled up in the debris against the far wall in the dark.

He edges closer, his body language stiffening with the awareness of exactly what he's stumbled onto.

"Oh, baby," he groans, bending down, reaching out gently with one hand. "Oh, no, whatcha gone done now?"

At the mouth of the alley, almost in the light, you ignore the sounds of the grieving giant and look down at the small bloody patch of pink steel wool held in your hand.

Beautiful.

Then, the Dark Angel's rapid wing beats are swirling a large pile of debris against the side of the building, whipping it around the mouth of the alley with almost gale-like force. You fold the straight razor, put it in your pocket, and catch a discarded McDonald's napkin to wrap your prize in. You will have to try it on later. Remembering that the black man interrupted you before you could shave a patch from the painted woman's head, you sigh with regret.

Too bad, too bad.

"It is time to go," the Dark Angel whispers forcefully in his deep throaty voice.

After again glancing briefly back into the alley at the man bent over the prostrate woman, you follow the Dark Angel into the night, over a block on 7th, before turning north on L Street.

Vindication is sweet, you think, unable to suppress a smile of deep satisfaction.

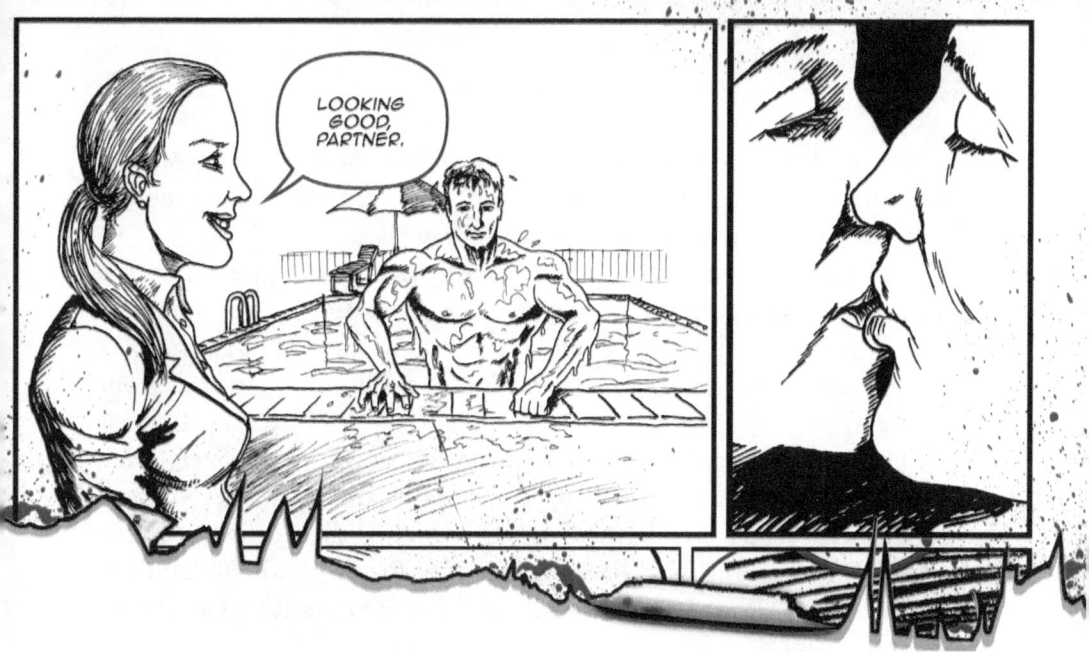

THE FAST EDDIE FELSON EFFECT

oming out of Artis's P.E. office at the American River
College gym, where she has changed and locked up her gun
in her friend's desk, Katy bumps into CeCe Reyes and her
older sister, Tanya, hurrying into the building.

"Hello, ladies," Katy greets them. "Really glad you could make it,
CeCe."

The big girl smiles back, kind of a cocky expression on her face.
"Yo, Katy. Wouldn't miss it for anything, you know what I'm saying."

Tanya adds a simple, "Hi," as the two sisters continue up the
hallway, headed for the women's locker room to change from their
street clothes.

CeCe obviously remembers drubbing her the last two workouts and is probably expecting to do it again, Katy thinks, smiling kind of ironically to herself. Well, we'll just see about that.

She watches the two young women quickly disappear into the locker room, noticing the sound of basketballs noisily thumping the floor from the open double doors to the gym at the end of the hallway, and she turns back to ask her friend, Artis, "Who else is working out, tonight?"

The smaller black woman locks her office door then answers, "The Adams twins, played for me a couple of years ago. They've been coming semi-regular for awhile now. You missed them when you were off for three months with your broken arm. Pretty good ball handlers. Dana's a good shooter, too, started small forward her last year at ARC in... ninety-six."

They move into the gym, Artis introducing Katy to the Adams twins, Dana and Donna, before the four players all begin to warm up and shoot around, waiting for Tanya and CeCe, Katy first doing a set of stretching exercises, limbering her tall frame.

Loose now, Katy takes her first shot, a jumper from the free throw line, and she thinks she feels it finally coming back, the *touch*. All good shooters have it when they're at the top of their game, an almost magical sense in their fingertips when they shoot. She hits a couple of more shots, really feeling it now. It's almost inexplicable, she thinks, the feeling difficult to put into words. You just know when you have it.

Dribbling the ball in place for a minute, Katy recalls a favorite scene from the movie, *The Hustler*. Paul Newman, playing Fast Eddy Felson, is trying to explain to Piper Laurie what it feels like when a good pool hustler is at the top of his game, when he is on, when he has *it*. With a glow of almost reverence lighting his faded-denim eyes, Fast Eddy explains that the cue ball, the cue stick, and the shooter's arm are kind of magically linked, an extension of the shooter's central nervous system, all in perfect sync. Down go the numbered balls, *thunk, thunk, thunk*. And, amazingly, the shooter knows they are going down even before the balls drop into the pockets, because he senses he has *it*, a special feeling in his shooting arm.

Great movie.

Katy thinks this touch in basketball is something like that, too; when a shooter is in the zone, she feels the same way as the hustler in that movie, super-confident, playing at a different level, knowing the basketball is going to swish, even at the point of release: The Fast Eddie Felson Effect.

She hadn't always had *touch*, being more of a defensive player and rebounder in college, similar to when she played for the Panthers in the PAL. But in her senior year at Sac State, Katy had been forced by an early season-ending injury to the Hornet's star shooter into taking more shots, suddenly developing her touch and becoming the team's leading scorer, averaging a solid 14.5 points per game for the year.

Katy swishes a couple of more practice shots, glowing inwardly now. It's going to be an interesting night.

Tanya and CeCe join them, warming up and shooting around for a few more minutes.

Usually they play three games to twenty which makes for a good hour and a half workout, Artis dividing the teams as fairly as possible by ability and size, insuring the games are close, contested workouts. As the most experienced players, she and Katy always play on opposite sides.

Tonight, Katy and the Adams twins will take on Artis and the Reyes girls. Katy and CeCe, the tallest players, will guard each other.

During the first possession, Artis misses on a drive, a little off balance, and Katy rebounds and tosses the ball out past the free throw line—as is customary in their half court games—to one of the twins. Dana bounces the ball immediately back to Katy, who has drifted out toward the left corner; then Donna screens CeCe, and Katy gets off an uncontested, clean, 12-foot jumper, the ball leaving her fingertips softly, spinning in a perfect spiral to the top of its arc, and dropping down through the basket, rippling nothing but net. A thing of beauty, a thing of *touch*.

Two!

Winners out at the top of the key—as is also customary in their workouts.

This time Katy fakes a jumper from the free throw line, drawing CeCe in close, over-guarding, and Katy drives left around the huskier girl, dishing off at the last minute, when Tanya slides over to pick her up, leaving Dana open, who hits a slick 5-foot bank off the glass.

"Way to go, Dana," Katy says, slapping her teammate's hand.

Four, zip.

Katy swishes another jumper from the left side of the key, then a lay-up, followed by a 15-foot set off another screen by Donna. She's really feeling it now, the F.E.F. Effect, absolutely certain that each of her shots is going in at the moment of release.

Ten, zip.

"Hey, Katy *Jordan*, do we get to ever touch the ball again?" Artis jokes, retaining the game ball in both hands after the last shot, her team with hands on knees, catching their breath.

"No," Katy snaps back with a ruthless grin, slapping the basketball from her friend's hands, "it's *winners'* out, remember?"

She's right. The first game ends 20-2. A blowout.

They break for a drink of water, a brief rest, everyone sprawling out on the gym floor except Katy, who remains standing, not the least tired, anxious to keep going.

They get back up and finish another game, Katy still hot, knocking down every shot she takes, really feeling the special shooter's touch.

20-4.

Another brief rest.

The Fast Eddie Felson Effect continues through the last game: 20-2.

Three blowouts in a row are really unusual in their workouts at ARC.

"Hey, we'll get you next Tuesday, Katy," CeCe says, hands on knees, gasping for breath, trying to maintain her cockiness in the face of three severe booty whippings. "You were unconscious tonight, you know what I'm saying."

Katy smiles, then agrees, "Yeah, you're probably right, CeCe. Who knows, maybe it will be your turn to be unconscious *again* next Tuesday, like the last two workouts before tonight. You know what I'm saying?"

A good sport in the end, CeCe laughs and admits, "You were really awesome tonight, Katy. But isn't your shooting arm just a little tired and sore?"

Katy returns her high-five.

In the office shower, Katy wonders why she even cares about shooting well, winning, showing CeCe and the others what she can do when she is fully recovered from her arm injury—after all these are just workouts to stay in shape, right?

Wrong.

She knows they're more important than that to her.

Why?

Is it just competitive spirit?

Maybe. Katy realizes she is competitive all right, but that's probably too simple an answer. She suspects the explanation is much deeper, more complex than just competitive spirit.

The games at ARC actually remind her of the workouts down in San Diego at Metro Rec long ago, when she was proving herself in front of Geri and the other Panthers, a white girl competing against blacks and Hispanics for respect on their home turf.

Those workouts and the games had actually been a kind of rite of passage for her.

Perhaps down deep that's still part of it—a need to prove herself? And maybe the racial angle does have something to do with it, too. Artis's ARC teams are mostly blacks, with maybe a Mexican-American, and only occasionally a white player; in retrospect, Katy realizes she'd been the only white person on the court tonight. Funny, she doesn't normally think along racial lines. Artis has always been just her friend, not a *black* friend. But Katy knows most athletes pay close attention to the racial mix on basketball teams, even blacks, often joking about it being a black person's game—anyone who cannot jump or move quickly has WMD: *White Man's Disease.* Once in a game at Sac State in her senior year, after Katy had scored 20 points and pulled down 10 rebounds against the University of Pacific, a Division I team, their star—a six-three, black woman—had grudgingly complimented Katy by saying, "You aren't too bad, girl, considering you're skinny, slow, and white."

Walking out of the ARC gym, Katy waves goodbye to Artis, then chastises herself: *Girl, get a grip, for chrissake.* She laughs aloud, thinking that all the writing is making her too fucking introspective. These are just workouts, and it's simply more fun to win than lose, period.

2

Katy reaches her townhouse on Watt Avenue out close to Sac State just about the same time as Johnny, who has a big grin on his face, a wrapped towel under one arm, and a folder in the other hand.

"Hello, kiddo. How'd the workout go?"

"Not bad," she replies, unlocking her door. "Not bad at all. The old wing is starting to loosen up. It was a lot of fun."

Johnny follows her into the kitchen, where she takes a pitcher out of the fridge. "If you aren't starving to death yet, pour us a smoothie and we'll talk about the Mary Ann Olson case," Katy says, spotting the blinking message-waiting light on her phone. "Okay?"

Johnny nods, digging out some glasses from the cupboard, while Katy punches the message button.

It's Geri in San Diego, replying to Katy's earlier call: "Hey, me coming up for a visit and checking out the Monarchs is a *great* idea. Cheryl Miller's Phoenix Mercury will be playing there Saturday night. I've been wanting to catch their act anyhow. So, I'll see you at the airport. My plane gets in at 10:00, Saturday morning. But I can't stay Sunday like you suggested. I have to fly back Saturday night at 11:30, because Herb and I have something special planned for his younger sister on Sunday morning—it's her fiftieth birthday… " There's a brief pause, then Geri adds, "It will be really great to see you again, Katy. It's been too long between visits. I'm excited."

Still staring at the phone, Katy silently agrees.

And Geri flying home after the game won't be much of a strain— Arco Arena is almost right next door to Sacramento International Airport.

"Here's the forensic report on Mary Ann," Johnny says, sitting down at the kitchen counter, opening the manila folder he'd been carrying and sliding it across the counter toward her. "Check it out, then I'll tell you something pretty interesting that we dug up today."

She takes the peach smoothie and sits down next to Johnny, reading over the material, studying the dozen or so black-and-white photos.

There isn't anything new in the report that they don't already know, except it confirms what Katy had suspected at the scene.

The drops of blood by the mirror do indeed belong to Mary Ann—no explanation, of course, why they're in that location.

No defensive marks, bruises, abrasions on Mary Ann's hands or arms.

No skin, hair, anything under her finger nails.

She apparently offered no resistance to her attacker at all.

No pubic hair or semen from the perp, no other evidence of sex that night.

The guy just moved in close enough to knock her out, drop her on the bed, cut her throat, then take a swatch of pubic hair and a small patch from her head. Seemed almost too easy. Of course she might've been too terrified by the sight of the straight razor to resist or make a fuss. Or maybe the guy really surprised her, and she didn't have a chance to resist. Or, who knows what—?

Lots of latent prints around in addition to Mary Ann's, but nothing really good enough for a computer match. He didn't leave any of himself behind—just lucky or actually smart?

The report isn't really much help at all, Katy decides, and the graphic black-and-white photographs do little more than depress her.

She takes a sip of her smoothie, the icy drink tasting especially good after her workout at ARC. A neighbor brought her the fragrant white peaches yesterday, picked fresh from an orchard up in nearby Yuba City. She ruffles through the pages of the report again, thinking, then she looks up at Johnny, who has almost finished his smoothie. "I wonder if she actually knew this guy, maybe from a past visit?"

He shrugs thoughtfully, rubs his nose. "Maybe. That would fit with two bits of information we turned up today, if they are indeed related, like I think they are."

"What do you have?"

"Well, I went back to see Mrs. Crane, the neighbor across the hall, and talked to her for quite awhile. She's a pretty observant old gal. Keeps up on what's going on around her, you know. Anyhow, she remembers about a week or so ago—we can't pin down the exact day—that Mary Ann had a friend visit. But something went wrong, an argument or something. Then suddenly Mary Ann was making a lot of loud noise—laughing and shouting, and finally she actually chased this dude out of the apartment into the hallway—"

"Did Mrs. Crane get a good look at this guy's face?"

Johnny frowns and shakes his head. "No such luck. Of course she was curious about the hubbub, but all she got was a glimpse from her cracked door at his back as he ran down the stairs."

"Just his back?" Katy repeated, disappointed.

"Yeah, but she noticed several specific things," Johnny says, pouring himself and Katy some more smoothie. "The guy was big, huge, maybe six-five and real husky. And—get this, kiddo—he was kind of bundled up, even though the muggy heat was still stifling that time of night."

"Bundled up?"

"Yeah, a rolled-down, stocking cap—dark brown, blue, or maybe black—and a long-sleeved, tan work shirt. Dressed kinda like a friggin' cat burglar, you know."

"But she never saw his face?"

"No," Johnny answers. "But Mrs. Crane's description is a fairly good match to another eye witness, if I have the right night, right guy." He takes a long sip of his smoothie, obviously enjoying the fresh peach drink, and stringing Katy along at the same time.

She just stares at him coolly, finally blurting out an impatient, "What other witness, Johnny, for chrissake?"

"McHugh first dug up this guy. A cook on the evening shift—four to twelve—at a 50's diner on K behind Sutter's Fort—*The Red Impala*. Patrick showed him a blow-up of Mary Ann's driver's license photo. The cook definitely recognized her. He thought she'd been in the diner once in the recent past when she'd picked up this young dude—"

"This isn't just last Tuesday night?"

"Nah, this is over a week ago, I think the same night as Mrs. Crane saw this big guy's back. Cook's description is similar. Huge guy, all bundled up in a long-sleeved shirt and some kind of hat rolled down over his ears. The cook doesn't remember much about his features except he was much younger than Mary Ann, maybe only twenty-five, somewhere in there. Two specific things that he did recall was the young dude's height when he got up, at *least* six-four, and the guy stuttered badly when he talked."

A twenty-five-year-old giant stutterer?

After thinking for a moment, Katy says, "You're probably right, Johnny. It could've been the same night, same person Mrs. Crane spotted."

The grin returns to Johnny's voice. "Yeah. And maybe, just maybe, he's the same dude showed up last Tuesday night and did a number on Mary Ann. Guy that size could easily knock someone out with one punch. Apparently he had a reason to be pissed at her, getting run off last week."

"You may be on to something," Katy admits.

Then, as if playing the devil's advocate, she asks in a thoughtful whisper, "But why didn't he kill her the night they first fought, instead of running away? Why come back a week or so later and cut her throat? Does that make any kind of sense at all? Not to me."

Johnny shrugs.

Looking around, he asks, "We still cooking outside tonight or what?"

"You bet," Katy replies, getting up and taking a plate out of the fridge. "My secret recipe, marinated ground chuck burgers, pal." She hands him a tray and the plate of four meat patties. Then she takes out a bowl of tossed salad and a package of hamburger buns from atop the fridge, stacking them all on the tray that Johnny is carrying now. "I'll take the drinks. Is that your swimming suit?" she asks, pointing at the wrapped towel on the counter.

"Yeah, you sure I'm going to need it?"

"I got it, *flash*," she says, rolling her eyes in mock disgust, slipping a well-worn Sac State green and gold gym bag over her shoulder, then picking up the pitcher of drinks. "C'mon, I got us a grill already loaded with charcoal and a table out by the pool. Everything else is out there already, under a tablecloth—condiments, plates, glasses, eating utensils."

"Sounds great, partner," Johnny says, following Katy out of the townhouse, down the stairs, and around back to the pool area.

3

Even though it's still hot and humid outside at 9:00, the pool area is empty of people, except for three teenage boys clowning on the diving board, doing cannonballs, yucking it up, making lots of noise—everyone else apparently worn out by the heat wave, too exhausted to even swim, hanging out in their air-conditioned townhouses.

Katy starts the pyramid of charcoal in the grill next to their picnic table, then they change in the nearby dressing rooms and meet in a few minutes back at poolside.

Surprised, Katy sees that Johnny is lean, tan, and in really good shape for a guy almost forty and once a heavy-duty boozer and drug user not that long ago. "Hey, you been working out on the sly, pal, or what?" she asks, wiggling her eyebrows up and down in an imitation of a Groucho Marx ogling look.

"Actually, I've been volunteering three days a week the last couple of months in a boxer's training program for cons up at Folsom," he replies, kneeling down and splashing himself with water from the pool. "So, I've been spending quite a bit of time on the big bag, the speed bag, jumping rope with the boxers, and sparring a few rounds each visit... And I'm running a couple of miles now early every morning. After Double Jack handled me so easily, I figured I better get my ass back in shape, you know. Hey, you don't look so bad either in that two-piece swimming suit, partner. How come you never told me *before* that you were a girl, for crying out loud?"

She laughs.

The teenagers finish diving, leaving the pool empty of people, the whole area quiet and still now, except for a faint breeze coming off the nearby American River and stirring the leaves in the crepe myrtle trees lining the picnic area.

Johnny abruptly dives in the water, leaving Katy standing there beside the pool. She watches him swim a half lap, then shouts out, "Hey, wait for me, *Tarzan*."

They both are good swimmers and easily finish twenty or so laps of the pool, before resting, Katy hooking her arm in the ladder at the deep end of the pool, wiping her eyes and face.

"Feels good," Johnny says, slowly dog-paddling closer to her.

"Yeah, just the thing for this kind of weird weather. You recall it ever being this muggy this late at night in Sacramento?"

"Nope," he says, grinning mischievously, cupping his hands and splashing her dry face. Then he turns over, dives down, and disappears deep under the water.

Katy spots him coming back up under her, where she is hooked onto the ladder. He grabs her ankles in a steely grip, jerks her under a foot or two, moves real close, then blows a stream of air bubbles against her chest between her breasts… tickling.

She giggles, swallowing water, choking.

They both explode up out of the water, gasping for air, Katy coughing but managing to pull herself up the ladder and out of the pool.

"Where you go, Jane?" Johnny says, looking around with a dumbfounded expression. "Come back to Tarzan."

Catching her breath by the side of the pool, out of his reach, Katy dries her hair with the towel, and says, "Okay, ape-man, I'm going to put on the burgers. I'm really famished."

"Me, too," he says, pulling up out of the pool. When he's out, he shakes himself like a dog, spraying both Katy and the barbeque.

"Hey, pal, cool it," she says, snapping her towel at him playfully.

Johnny grins and picks up his towel. "About time you lightened up a little, partner, had some fun," he says, drying himself off. "Rehabbing the arm, writing the book, this bizarre murder, and all, you've been pretty uptight, lately, you know."

She just shrugs, then puts the hamburgers on the grill, thinking Johnny may be right. She's glad they have had this chance to relax, enjoy each other's off-duty company. Time for a break from everything… And now that she thinks about taking a break, she's really stoked about Geri coming up Saturday morning, even though she will only be staying the day.

"Hey, it's time you met my friend, Geri," Katy says to Johnny, who's stacking the buns with thick slices of pickles, onions, lettuce, and tomatoes.

"I'd like that, Katy," he replies, licking his fingers. "You make her sound like almost family, you know. An aunt or something."

Katy nods, flipping the meat. "She is family."

They eat, enjoying the food, ignoring the still sultry night, each wolfing down two burgers and a big plate of salad. Finished eating, Katy goes back in the dressing room and peels off her clinging-wet suit, checking herself out in the mirror. Well, the breasts are a tad small, but, hey, for a skinny, white girl, I guess I don't look too bad.

Cleaning up, stacking everything back on the tray, Johnny asks kind of shyly, "You, ah, ever see Tolbert anymore, Katy?"

She stares at him a moment before answering. "No, Johnny, I haven't seen him since the Double Jack case."

He's referring to Shane Tolbert, a lawyer in the public defender's office. When Katy first teamed with Johnny as a homicide detective four years ago, Shane and her were still an item, at the end of a semi-serious long romance. For a number of reasons, over recent years they had slowly drifted apart, until they were still friends but not really very close.

She frowns, reminded that she hasn't had a serious relationship with anyone since Shane.

"Hey, good," Johnny says and laughs, carrying the piled high tray back toward the apartment.

"What do you mean, *good?*" she snaps back—annoyed more by her last thought than anything Johnny has said—following and eventually opening the door for him. "Shane's a neat guy, attractive... and single. Doing well in his career. I probably messed up letting him get away."

Johnny shrugs apologetically, blushes slightly, and rubs his broken nose. "I don't know, just... well, shoot, Katy. You know what I mean."

She looks steadily at him for almost a minute, then smiling, she leans close and gives him a quick peck on the lips. "Yeah, I know exactly what you mean."

"Thanks for the forgiving kiss, *grandma*," he says, clearing his throat. "I feel like I'm a clumsy seventeen-year-old on a first date, with my foot in my mouth."

For a few seconds they stare into each other's eyes, Katy sensing that they're about to cross some kind of undefined line in their relationship; but Johnny's pager suddenly goes off and shatters the moment.

He reads the number aloud and mutters in an annoyed voice, "Oh, shit, I think that's Bundy's cell phone number."

Katy knows Johnny and the other detective aren't tight buddies, hanging out after work, so it must be homicide business.

Johnny returns the call from her phone, a deep frown creasing his features as he listens for a minute or so. "Okay, Harlan, *okay*, we'll be down right away," he says, then hangs up.

"Well? What is it?" Katy asks.

"Our boy has hit again, left a hooker dead in an alley near the Greyhound Bus Station downtown. Cut her throat. Same M.O."

4

The alley is blocked by two patrol cars, four others, with colored light strips flashing, blocking off the walking mall along K Street, the uniformed cops keeping a camera crew from Channel 3 and a small group of onlookers back from the cordoned-off crime scene.

Patrick McHugh and Harlan Bundy meet Johnny's Mustang just beyond the blocked-off area and guide them into a reserved spot closer to the noisy scene. Katy and Johnny get out and follow the other two detective partners to the mouth of the alley.

"Okay, Harlan, what have you got?" Johnny asks. "You were first here and interviewed the guy who found the victim and an initial suspect, too?"

Bundy nods toward the two patrol cars blocking the alley. "They're sitting in the back seats if you want to talk to them. Big black guy with the shaved head is her pimp, Charles White. The young cowboy, Edgar Ray Jennings, in the other car, was her last customer, right up here in the alley. Naturally White fingered the cowboy, but after talking to him, I don't think he killed her. He just got off a Greyhound from Texas. Did a three spot in Huntsville for burglary, released late Tuesday afternoon, supposed to meet an uncle here tonight, who lives in Roseville, but was delayed and is coming later. The cowboy gets restless waiting, has a couple of drinks in the bar over next to the bus station on 7th and L, then wanders over here on the K Street mall looking for some action—female type. Finishes his business with the victim, Pearl LeDoux, in the alley and heads back over to the bar. From down the street, White sees him leave, goes back in the alley to pick up Pearl, and finds her dead, throat cut. Of course he suspects Jennings. Anyhow, the cowboy says he was still in Texas when our boy hit Mary Ann last Tuesday night. And that's going to be real easy to check."

"Let's look over the scene," Katy says to Johnny and Patrick McHugh. "Keep those two locked in the cars for awhile, Harlan, okay? We'll talk to them in a minute."

Bundy nods and shuffles over to the occupied patrol cars.

Katy, Johnny, and Patrick slide past the two cars and into the narrow, littered alley, the immediate area lit up brightly by the headlights from the police cars, the beams focused on the naked body, halfway up the alley and only partially hidden by the surrounding debris.

"Forensics been in and out already, Patrick?" Johnny asks, as they move toward the victim.

"Yeah, you just missed them," the detective answers, leading them nearer the body. "They think it's the same guy hit Mary Ann, but the M.O. is a little different from last Tuesday night, as you'll see."

They stop at the foot of the prostrate woman, the gaping crimson-crusted slash across her throat adding to the bizarre appearance of her death mask—the colors of her thick makeup melted and run together into a ghastly harlequin pattern.

"Jesus," Katy murmurs under her breath.

"Apparently her boyfriend moved her slightly," McHugh explains. "When he found her, her head and upper back were propped there high against the wall, that piece of cardboard laid across her chest. White tossed the cardboard aside, pulled her flat, and straightened her out. He also covered her crotch with her vinyl skirt. She was nude from the waist down when he found her."

Katy kneels, her gaze moving from the woman's slashed throat, across her blood-soaked leopard skin blouse, and resting for a moment on the nearby blood-splattered piece of cardboard. "I assume forensics dusted the cardboard for prints?" she asks.

"Yeah, but they don't think they got anything much except White's," McHugh replies, in a matter of fact voice.

Then, Katy's gaze moves down the body to the woman's naked crotch. A small swatch of pink-dyed pubic hair is missing. She glances back up at the woman's scalp.

"That's the M.O. deviation—he didn't take a patch of hair from her head?" she asks, rising back to a standing position.

"Yep," McHugh answers. "He might not have had time. From the moment the cowboy left the alley, passed her boyfriend headed for the bar over near 7th and L, and the exact moment the boyfriend found her, it couldn't have been more than four or five minutes—boyfriend's estimate."

Katy and Johnny both prowl around the body for a few minutes, moving debris about with their shoes.

Katy asks, "Forensics pick up her panties?"

"Yeah," replies Patrick. "They were already off, so you know they won't find any hair, semen, or anything from the perp—"

"But he didn't have sex with her anyhow, did he?" Johnny asks.

"The forensic boys don't think so, but this time it's a little harder to rule out. In addition to the cowboy, the boyfriend says Pearl had four other customers earlier tonight. But the perp probably wouldn't have had enough time, even if he were so inclined."

Katy looks the body over again, then lets out a long, loud, sad sigh. "Hell of a way to end your life. She must only be in her late-twenties."

"Actually only twenty-three," McHugh corrects.

Johnny doesn't say anything, but makes a sad face and throws up his raised palms—*What're you gonna do?*

"Let's get out of here," Katy snaps, signaling the waiting Coroner's crew to bag the body.

At the patrol car, she pulls Bundy aside, out of earshot of the two seated in the cars.

"Harlan, keep the cowboy down at jail, until you actually verify his alibi. Ask if he maybe *sensed* someone else in the alley, right after he was with Pearl. Or if he saw anyone going in as he was leaving. Our perp must've been there, or went in immediately after, if White is correct about the short window of time for him to kill her. Anyhow, get a full statement."

Bundy takes the cowboy out of the patrol car and heads off to his own vehicle.

Katy introduces herself and Johnny to Charles White, the big man with the shaved head. "Charles, you're sure about the time elapsed after you saw the cowboy leave Pearl in the alley and when you actually found her? Four or five minutes doesn't seem very long to me."

The huge black man frowns deeply, wrinkling even his bare scalp, and says in a half-pissed voice, "Like I tol' the other *po*-lice officer, five minutes tops... " He pauses a moment, anger welling up in his dark face. "'Sides y'all got the muthahfucka done it, right there—that lil' dude *cut* my Pearl!" He pokes his finger in the air in the direction of the departing Bundy and cowboy.

Katy holds up her hands. "We're checking him out, Charles, but we have to cover all the bases. We know what we're doing. Let us do our job, okay?"

The big man sighs, the anger turning to sad resignation. After a minute or so he shrugs and says in a listless voice, "Yeah, you the man, all right."

Katy says, "I truly feel bad about Pearl, Charles. She was way too young to, to... I-I... I'm just sorry." She touches him lightly on the shoulder.

The bald, black man stares hard at her for a moment, then his expression softens slightly, and he drops his gaze.

She clears her throat, before asking, "When you walked into the alley, did you see anyone else come out after the cowboy departed?"

"No."

"Is it possible that when you found Pearl, someone else was still in the alley? You know, like hiding?"

"Doan know 'bout that," he answers, still looking down at his feet. "Kinda upset when I spots her. Doan know if she dead or what. So... " He pauses and shrugs again. "Wasn't payin' much 'tention to anythin' else, yah unnerstan'?"

Johnny asks, "Did you actually see this cowboy take Pearl into the alley?"

"Yeah, I's up the mall, but I sees 'em turn in. Usually Pearl take her bidness to a hotel 'nother block over on 6th. And I follow, make sure no rough stuff, or they pay. So I's watchin' close. But I guess this lil' dude inna real hurry, willin' to settle for his ashes haul inna alley."

Mention of the hotel over a street surprises Katy. She knows most downtown hookers take their customers to motels over in West Sacramento—just across the line in Yolo County, because it's another legal jurisdiction.

"How long he take?" Johnny asks.

"Not long, five, maybe six minutes."

"Can you think of anyone who would do this to Pearl?" Katy asks. "A disgruntled customer, someone like that."

"Nah, she always do her job. We never pull a murphy or any of tha' chickenshit stuff... Course who knows?" he adds, wearing his normal cynical expression now. "Being in bidness you run into some off-the-wall dudes and some pretty weird chicks, too."

"Okay, Charles," Katy says, "the detective here is going to take you to the station for a full written statement, okay?"

"I's free to go after that?"

"Yeah, you'll be back on the street in an hour," McHugh promises, patting him on the back, then guiding the big man by the arm to lead him off.

"Well, what do you make of this one?" Johnny asks Katy as they stroll back to the car.

"Looks like the same guy, except he didn't take a head patch. Everything else seems the same. Must have knocked her unconscious, too—notice the blue bruise on her chin?—and used that piece of cardboard to prevent spraying all over when he killed her… " She pauses as they get in the Mustang. "But one thing is really starting to bug me, Johnny, about this guy."

"What's that?" he asks, glancing at her before starting the car.

"Nobody ever actually *sees* him just before or after the murders. If he's some huge guy like Mrs. Crane and the diner cook described, all bundled up funny-like in this muggy weather, how come nobody notices him coming or going at the murder scenes?"

"I don't know, kiddo," Johnny answers, and then chuckles derisively, "unless he's maybe invisible."

"Well, let's check his description on the computer, see if there are any recently released cons with a violent background against women— big, husky stutterers, twenty-five or so. Might be a good idea to check the State Hospitals and NCIC, too."

Johnny nods.

5

Before Katy gets to bed that night, Johnny phones her back.

"Partner, a little bad news. We have to be at a meeting with Captain Silver tomorrow morning at 8:00 a.m. sharp. He wants you, me, McHugh, and Bundy there. Apparently the Chief is anticipating some static from the media. Channel 3 ran a late news blurb last night about a *serial murderer* running loose in the city. So, Long John wants to coordinate, get on top of this one. You know the drill."

"This isn't a press conference, I hope?"

"No. But I think the Chief and Captain Silver will be doing one sometime later in the afternoon. This will be private, just the five of us, I think. I'm not sure exactly what else is involved, but Long John knows about your limited duty status, the book, the convention, and the upcoming meeting with your agent."

"Okay, I'll be there, partner," Katy answers, feeling a twinge when Johnny mentions the book. Even when she's had time to write during the last two days, she's been blocked. She's really worried now about making the BayCon convention with even a partial rough draft to show the agent. But what the hell can I do? Katy sighs to herself, too tired to explain all this to her partner.

"Goodnight, Johnny."

"Goodnight, kiddo. Thanks for the dinner and swim. It was all great before Bundy's friggin' call interrupted everything, you know."

Katy grins wryly and hangs up.

A few minutes later, slipping into bed, she asks herself silently: *Interrupted what, Johnny?*

DADDY WIGS

K eyed up, able to only doze during the night, you get up early
Friday morning and leave your apartment, heading west on
26th Street. As you walk, you try to examine your feelings
now that you're out of the shadow of the Dark Angel, not a
spectator watching a dark movie or walking in a dream. You feel no
guilt, only an unsettling sense of apprehension that you may be hunted
down and sent to a place much worse than CYA, even though both
women were bad, bad people. But you know that will make no real
difference. It will be just like the other time when you were sent to
CYA. They will say you are the bad person, that society demands that
you be punished. They will listen to nothing you might try to say. You
will be sent away again for a much longer time, perhaps forever—

Abruptly you withdraw from the terrifying thought and shiver,
despite the increasing temperature of the early morning.

You continue along 26th Street, walking under an umbrella of shade, mature elm trees lining the sidewalk, limbs merging with neighbors' limbs into a continuous green leafy canopy that extends out over the street. At this hour the adjacent street is quiet, nearly devoid of traffic. It will be at least another forty-five minutes before all the nearby streets grow congested with cars heading for work, trucks delivering goods, and the accompanying sounds—horns honking, brakes screeching, people shouting.

After walking three or four blocks in peace and quiet, you spot your destination, which is a park resembling the one near Sutter's Fort, but furnished with more benches, more stone tables; unlike the one near Sutter's Fort, this park is filled with people already, even at this early hour.

Old people.

Mostly old men, the majority of them wearing blue, tan, or gray work clothes, which are clean but faded from years of wear. Many are seated, playing cards, dominoes, checkers, or chess at the stone tables; some are standing, chatting quietly or actively kibitzing the games; and across the park others sit alone, reading newspapers, magazines, or books, a few of them staring off in space, completely lost in thought, perhaps exploring their much happier past. Here and there are a few older women, wearing clean but almost colorless dresses, a little frayed from years of laundering. The residential area around the park includes a number of aging Victorians, broken up into tiny apartments for their elderly occupants, the weathered exteriors of the grand old houses matching the faded appearance of the residents.

On the third of every month, the park will be nearly empty in the early morning—the third is Social Security check day—and the nearby bank branches along J Street will be busy early, serving their senior customers, who will then shop or do other business, while paying close attention to their skimpy budgets, perhaps returning to the park after lunch.

Even though there's a hint of cool wistfulness lingering in the air, like traces of morning river mist, you're strongly attracted to this senior citizen's park, feeling that despite your age difference, you share a common bond—a sense of forced isolation—with these mostly forgotten older people. You often come down here to rest on the benches or watch the card games or just walk around, occasionally peeking curiously into the heavily-lined, lonely faces, looking for some hint of recognition of a kindred soul—a smile, a lifting of an eyebrow, a slight nod; but the reaction is always the same, the immediate avoidance of any eye contact, active non-involvement—probably a judicious survival strategy for the frail elderly in a city of cold, uncaring strangers.

Today you are jumpy and restless after last night's vindication, hoping a visit to the park will settle your nerves before having to report to work back at Sutter General Hospital. But as you wander around the small park, you feel yourself growing more edgy, unable even to concentrate on the games. Finally, you force yourself to sit down on a bench in the heart of the park, trying to relax like Father Nathan taught you at CYA, by taking deep breaths and willing your body to relax limb by limb. Eventually you do settle down a bit, able to watch with some interest as an old man, sitting on the bench directly opposite from you, slowly unrolls a newspaper, removes a thick, long stick—almost the size of a child's play baseball bat—drops the newspaper back to the ground, then takes out a pocket knife, and begins to methodically whittle away—the thin, even, long shavings dropping neatly into the middle of the paper at his feet.

At that moment, beyond the whittler, across a wide but shallow pond, near 26th Street, a movement catches your attention.

A tall, thin, black man, dressed in navy blue slacks and a short-sleeved white shirt seems to be preaching to a small group of the older park inhabitants. He is too far away for you to hear anything he's saying, but his mannerisms, as he talks, have caught your eye and seem to be vaguely familiar. After watching the man's arm and hand movements for a few more moments, you frown to yourself, remembering exactly where you have seen similar gestures.

You were seven years old the day you first saw the dancing hands of Daddy Wigs...

2

"Daddy Wigs, Daddy Wigs," one of the older boys was hollering, pointing at you as you slipped from between the sheets of your lower bunk bed and dropped to the floor, the crotch of your pajama bottoms dark and soaking wet.

"Look at Sam, he done peed his bed."

The boy from the top bunk over you dropped down beside you, and in a sad whisper, announced, "Oh, you done it now, boy. You gonna get a whuppin' from Daddy Wigs."

The tall, thin black man that stood in the doorway of the Boy's Dorm, as it was called, was actually named Ishmael Wiggins, Jr. You'd met him last night just after your arrival, but all the boys in the transient foster home called him Daddy Wigs, as did even his wife, Mrs. Eudora May Wiggins.

He just stood in that doorway, staring at you for a full minute without saying anything, his stern gaze taking on a distasteful expression, as it slowly shifted from your face to the damaging evidence of your pajama bottoms then to your bedding. Finally he nodded, apparently understanding everything; as he began to talk, his arms and hands gestured in the air, as if he were conducting an orchestra or, perhaps, preaching a sermon to a church congregation.

"Ah, Samuel, my boy," he began, his tone heavy with disappointment, "your first night, and you are not doing too well." The conducting movements of his hands were actually punctuating his speech. "I guess Samuel must have been nervous," he added, in a not unkindly tone, looking around at the eleven other boys, who were all in various states of dress, frozen beside their bunk beds.

He turned back to stare at you with his penetrating dark eyes. "Did you know that you have a famous Biblical name, Samuel?"

You shook your head, unable to respond.

"Yes, Samuel was a great man, a man of God, a prophet in the Old Testament."

He nodded his head knowingly. "A great man, so we expect good things from you, his namesake. But this—" He pointed at your incriminating pajama bottoms, slowly shaking his head sadly. "This is not a good thing, Samuel, no indeed."

By now you were visibly shaking, as the tall, intimidating man moved closer.

He beckoned for the other boys to move nearer, packing them in around you. Then his hands really began to conduct vigorously, as he lectured sternly. "Now, Samuel, boys, there is good and there is evil in the world. Mostly good, but still a lot of evil. And the Light Angel reigns over all that is good, helping us stay vigilant against that evil, yes indeed… "

He paused for a moment, raising his gaze directly above the group, staring heavenward as if he actually saw that Light Angel, and then he smiled in a reverent manner.

After a few more moments of respectful silence, Daddy Wigs continued, his wrinkled brow deepening into a scary frown, his voice dropping to a just audible whisper, but his hands still dancing in the air. "And of course, *evil* is the work of the Dark Angel. Now, we all know in our hearts that Samuel is a good boy, but last night he must've been touched—just the tiniest brush—by the shadow of the Dark Angel. But I don't think this will happen again, because Samuel is going to be vigilant, always on guard, right Samuel?"

You nod vigorously.

"I did not hear you, Samuel," Daddy Wigs said in a louder voice, one hand cupping his ear, the other gesturing for you to speak up.

"Y-Y-Y-Y-Y—"

You stomped the floor repeatedly with your bare foot, unable to break the stammer; and as frightened as you were, you knew that you would be unable to escape the clutches of the funnytalk for hours, perhaps even all day.

But Daddy Wigs, smiling kindly again, just held up both hands in the stop gesture. "That's quite all right, Samuel, I know you understand. And to help you avoid the shadow of the Dark Angel while you are sleeping tonight, this evening at dinner time you will *not* drink anything. Nor will you drink any water or anything else after dinner. Nothing before you go to bed. Do you understand me?"

You nod.

"And you other boys will help Samuel, am I right?" He swept his hand and gaze across the group, indicating he meant each and every one of the eleven other current residents of the Boy's Dorm.

"Yes, Daddy Wigs," the group responded loudly in nearly perfect unison.

The tall man smiled broadly, revealing a gold front tooth that glinted in the light. "Very good. I knew you would all support Samuel's effort, watching him closely, ensuring that he is not tempted to drink even the smallest sip of water tonight after dinner, right?"

"Yes, Daddy Wigs," the boys answered again, as a few of the braver, older ones sneaked peeks in your direction.

His arms rested now, his hands folded neatly together in front of his chest, apparently indicating that the lecture was over.

Abruptly Daddy Wigs turned and left.

There was almost a visible sigh of group relief.

"You lucky, boy," your bunkmate said, lifting his eyebrows in an exaggerated expression of surprise at the apparently mild rebuke. "Really lucky. Doan be peeing in that bed again, you hear? 'Cause if you do, the shit gonna hit the fan 'roun' here for everbuddy."

That night, and the succeeding evenings were nightmares of parched thirst. From dinner on, you could not keep your mind off images of tall, cold drinks—lemonade, Coke, root beer, iced tea, iced water. You even dreamed of swimming in a pool of refreshingly cool water.

But, with the constant surveillance of your roommates, you managed to avoid the tiniest sip of any liquid after dinner. You didn't even use any water when brushing your teeth. You did not want to have anyone tell Daddy Wigs that you had disobeyed his instructions in even the slightest way.

Miraculously, you did not wet the bed all that week; though, in retrospect, bedwetting had been an almost nightly occurrence as far back as you could remember. At first you thought fear, the lack of liquids, and the group pressure from your roommates accounted for the dramatic loss of a bad habit. But as the days passed, you began to believe in your heart that it was some kind of *special* power that Daddy Wigs exercised, his arm and hand movements weaving an invisible web of black magic that snared you and determined your destiny.

Your roommates constantly changed, all eventually going on to placements in permanent foster homes within a week or so after arriving in the Boy's Dorm. But you remained for a week, then two, then three at Daddy Wigs'.

As a reward for overcoming your bedwetting problem, Daddy Wigs made you the *head gardener*, everyone having daily chores; but only a select few boys, usually the ones longest in residence, were even allowed out into the garden, much less assigned to work there. The garden was Daddy Wigs' special project, and apparently during the summer it produced nearly all of the vegetable and fruit needs of the group home.

It was out back of the dorm, a cyclone-fenced half an acre, furrows of dark, neatly-tilled soil laid out geometrically, the arrow-straight rows of beans, onions, carrots, potatoes, lettuce, cabbage, and corn, guarded over by a perimeter of fruit trees—apples, pears, apricots, peaches, and plums. But in all of this fruitful abundance, there was nothing more lush, more manicured, than the carefully staked, 3-foot high, dark-green tomato plants, the arms drooping heavily with unripened lime-green tomatoes.

In the whole garden there was not one weed robbing the vegetables of valuable moisture and nutrients. No, indeed. It was one of your main jobs, as head gardener, to supervise the careful pulling of each and every invader, seeing that the black earth around each plant was constantly turned and broken with little claw-like tools. But the tomato vines required especially cautious weeding, your helpers taking care to push the limbs aside, as the weeds, which seemed to sprout right next to the vine trunks, were carefully tugged from the ground.

These plants were indeed special. In the evening after dinner Daddy Wigs often strolled about the garden on an inspection tour with you at his side and he always ended his tour at the tomato vines, the sight of the heavily fruited plants never failing to bring a broad, tooth-sparkling smile of joy and pride to the man's dark features.

One afternoon not long after your promotion, the shaded green tunnels between the rows of green tomato plants beckoned irresistibly to you and your two weeding subordinates for a game of hide-and-tag. Oh, what fun, escaping the hot Southern California sun and the eyes of the boy who was it, crawling into and hiding in the moist green tunnels, scampering on hands and knees up and down the rows. Even at seven you were big for your age, heavy of foot, and you brushed clumsily against the sticky green vines.

Up and down, in and out, all afternoon.

Your exuberant play in the tomato vines eventually made the three of you even more wild and reckless; and, not even trying to hide, you all darted clumsily in and out of the rows, chasing each other, forcefully brushing aside the sticky vines that clung to your heads, bodies, legs and arms.

Finally, about 5:00 the three of you rested, flopping down on the ground at the beginning of the rows of vines, gasping for breath, laughing, making fun of the green-stained arms, hands, and faces of the others. So silly looking.

Then, you suddenly stopped laughing, looking over the field of play, actually seeing the sacred tomato vines.

Oh, no!

Many were completely uprooted, some were crushed entirely to the ground, and all of the remaining standing plants were missing most of their limbs, which were randomly strewn about the nearby garden area.

The tomato vines, Daddy Wigs' pride and joy, were an absolute mess, ruined, completely destroyed.

And *you* had been in charge.

You swallowed with some difficulty, surveying the damage, wide-eyed now. Maybe you could replant, straighten up, hide the torn limbs, you thought hopefully—

But a second careful inventory of the plants made you realize rehabilitation was completely out of the question. The destruction was complete and not repairable. Your shoulders sagged under the burden of guilt.

At that moment the three of you were engulfed in a shadow, and you turned slowly to face the towering Daddy Wigs.

His face was an ugly scowl of extreme pain.

For what seemed like an eternity, he said nothing, just stared incredulously at the devastation...

Finally, after he seemed to partially gain control of his emotions, he pointed at the two other boys. "Go to my office, right now!"

The two scurried from the garden, off in the direction of the main building.

"You, you Samuel, you go to the dorm, wait by your bunk," Daddy Wigs sputtered in a choked voice, not even trying to hide the anger in his tone. "I'll deal with you later, after those two are punished." He spun on his heel, following your youthful crime partners inside, leaving you to contend with the terror of facing the unknown.

What was he going to do to you?

When?

The waiting was the horrible part. You wished you were with the others, getting your punishment right now.

At that moment, from the direction of the office, you heard a series of muffled shouts of pain, each blow of the belt making you flinch.

… Five, six, seven, eight, nine, ten.

Silence.

Then, the other boy cried out, each individual landed blow punctuated with an accompanying loud bellow of pain.

Ten whacks, too.

You shuffled into the boy's bunkroom, waiting your fate, trembling, knowing it was going to be much worse than ten whacks with a belt. Yes, indeed, much worse.

And it was.

After dinner, which you missed, Daddy Wigs gathered all the boys in the dorm for another of his hand-conducted sermons.

"Now, boys, we've talked about the Light Angel and the Dark Angel," he began, his arms making flying motions in the air above him. "The Light Angel cruising over us constantly, protecting us from evil, circling and watching. But sometimes the Dark Angel swoops down, momentarily undetected—"

Suddenly his right hand was a hawk hurtling down on a field mouse—his scurrying left hand. "—And attacks the Light Angel."

He clasped his hands, squeezing and wriggling them this way and that way in a terrific struggle. "Momentarily stunning Him, diverting Him from His duty. Then that Dark Angel is able to drop down lower and His shadow sweeps across one of us… *chilling* us to the bone, compelling us to commit a bad act, an act of evil. But it is only a passing thing, a momentary aberration in the normal course of events, for the Light Angel quickly recovers, follows, engages, and this time defeats the Dark Angel, casting Him far away from us, just like God originally cast those sinning Angels down into chains of darkness. Yes, indeed."

Daddy Wigs dropped his hands to his sides, as if exhausted emotionally, speaking now in a slow, hoarse, throaty monotone.

"But occasionally, ever so rarely, the Light Angel is stunned and too slow to recover, and that Dark Angel has time to completely engulf someone in His shadow, hoping to claim that person's soul, recruit him to a life of eternal evil… "

At this point Daddy Wigs paused, garnering his moral outrage, staring directly at you with his penetrating dark gaze. "Yes!" he said, pointing a finger of condemnation; and oh, how his hands now danced as he continued, emphasizing almost every other word. "That has happened this very afternoon. Samuel was caught in the shadow of the Dark Angel, engulfed in evil, and he has been bad, very bad, destroying every tomato vine in the garden. Every *one*!"

Someone gasped, realizing the heinous nature of this high crime.

For a few minutes, Daddy Wigs's face darkened in tone, and he seemed to be too choked up with emotion to even continue.

Your pulse raced, your heart thumped out of control, and you thought about running away from this horrible judgment you faced; but your weakened legs trembled, out of control, and despite your desire to flee, you remained rooted to the spot, as if chained to the leg of your bunk bed. But you found yourself unable to continue looking into the eyes of the choked-up, black man, who seemed at the point of exploding, so you dropped your gaze to the floor.

Humbled.

Ashamed.

For another full minute it was quiet, as Daddy Wigs struggled with his feelings, attempting to regain control of himself. At last, he closed his eyes and sucked in a long, deep breath, the tenseness slowly easing from his neck muscles.

He blinked.

Then, peering at you again, he managed to continue in a subdued voice weighted with pain, his arms eventually freeing up to gesture expressively again as he talked.

"But we must try to rescue Samuel from His clutches, claim Samuel's soul back from the Dark Angel. We are this boy's only hope of salvation."

Daddy Wigs abruptly stopped again, and the dorm was absolutely silent, not one boy shifting from one foot to another, most not even daring to breathe.

Dead silence.

"Come," he finally barked out, beckoning you and all the other boys to follow him.

He led the group into the main house, into the hallway leading to the kitchen, pausing in front of a mysterious, padlocked half-door under the stairwell.

In a confidential whisper, Daddy Wigs said to the group, "We are going to hide Samuel from the Dark Angel." He unlocked the padlock and opened the half-door, a cool, musty smell of spices spreading into the hallway.

You bent slightly and peered into the area under the stairs, but it was too dark to see anything and you shuddered fearfully.

Daddy Wigs grabbed your goose-pimpled arm and pulled you close to him.

"We are going to hide him in the old pantry," he whispered, "where there is no light." He shoved you to the half-door into the pantry. "The Dark Angel will not be able to see you, because when I lock this door it will be pitch black in there."

Then Daddy Wigs pushed you down into the musty, spicy darkness, and immediately shut away the light.

Next, you heard the padlock snapped into place.

Then feet quickly shuffled away, and you were all alone, left in the fragrant dark.

You squatted, clutching your knees, trying to peer around and see something... anything. But it was no use. It was indeed pitch black, and you shivered from the icy terror. You hated close darkness, not even wanting to go to sleep with the light out—a fact Daddy Wigs had obviously noticed your first night in the Boy's Dorm.

Panic welling up suddenly, you pounded at the locked half-door, trying to shout out for help, gain release from this nightmare.

"H-H-H-H—"

No use.

You beat the door in vain, until your hands were sticky and numb, and you were completely exhausted. Then you just sat down, squeezed your eyes shut, gripped your knees, and rocked gently.

You eventually lost track of time...

Sleeping.

Murmuring to yourself.

Rocking.

Sleeping.

Murmuring to yourself.

At some point in your dark incarceration, you heard a voice speak in your head: *Sam Boy, I will help you if I can just find you.* And instantly you knew it was the voice of the Light Angel speaking directly to you, and your fear eased immediately. *Where are you?*

You began to try to answer, "I-I am—"

But you broke off.

Supposing the Dark Angel was hovering near enough to hear, too? You couldn't give away your location. No, indeed. So, despite your fear of being left in the dark all alone, you remained silent, hoping the Light Angel would speak to you again in his gentle, soothing voice, and comfort you.

Instead, after a few silent moments, a deeper, throaty voice growled in your head: *Yes, tell me where you are. I will come for you. I will help you.*

Of course you knew who that was speaking, so you clutched yourself tighter, not even daring to breathe, squeezed your eyelids tightly shut against the darkness, and continued rocking, rocking, rocking.

More time passed, an eternity.

Suddenly the darkness disappeared, the old pantry flooded with blinding light, and even though you couldn't see anything, you recognized Daddy Wigs' voice.

"Come out, Samuel. I think you are safe now. I think that the Dark Angel has gone to seek other souls. We have saved you. Yes, indeed."

On shaky legs you walked out into the light of the hallway, unable to talk at all, but thankful for your release, eventually discovering that you had only been locked away in the horrible pantry darkness overnight, less than twelve hours.

But it was long enough.

Yes, indeed.

Long enough for you to hear and recognize each of the Angels' voices in your head for the first time.

3

You blink.

You're staring at a stranger, an old man sitting on a bench, folding up his pocketknife, a nearly foot-high pile of long, thin wood shavings at his feet in the middle of a spread out newspaper.

A whittler——?

Then, glancing about, you recognize your present surroundings——the senior's park.

What time is it, you ask yourself, looking up through the trees, trying in vain to spot the sun's location. You decide it's at least afternoon, because a large number of the old people have disappeared from the park, probably gone home for lunch as most of them usually do.

You rise, but remain standing in the spot by the bench for several moments, thinking about what Daddy Wigs had said that day so long ago when he locked you in the pantry.

Could he have been right about the Dark Angel claiming peoples' souls for evil?

Could He do that?

After all these years of both voices struggling for your attention, had He finally dominated and claimed your soul from the Light Angel?

Is that why you took such extreme vengeance on Mary Ann and the painted woman?

Did you belong to Him, now?

Were you condemned to eternal evil?

You shiver despite the mugginess.

"N-no!" you deny forcefully, turning your back on the whittler. "I-I'm *not* e-evil."

You begin to walk back slowly, out of the park, back toward Sutter General Hospital, barely noticing the increase in the sultry temperature, the traffic, and the noise, your heart heavy, your tread slow, for despite your vigorous outburst of protestation, you are not really certain that the Dark Angel has not captured your soul, condemning you to eternal damnation.

No, indeed.

<u>4</u>

Eventually, you reach the laundry in plenty of time for your shift. Thankfully, the symphony of the big machines partially blots out all the nagging, terrifying questions. You are able to momentarily forget yourself in your work on the extractor.

SAINTS OR SINNERS?

aptain Kevin Silver looks nothing like a tall, one-legged pirate, nor does he really resemble a homicide detective captain, either—at least the movie or TV versions of one. He is a short, balding, pear-shaped, middle-aged, black man, with a thick, but graying mustache, his voice surprisingly high-pitched and slightly nasal. But he is always immaculately groomed, usually wearing a well-pressed dark gray or charcoal suit, a white shirt, and an appropriately tasteful tie, the conservative attire of a banker or perhaps a CEO of a moderate-sized, successful, publicly-held corporation. Therefore, the swashbuckling nickname, *Long John*, is doubly ironic, Katy thinks, taking a seat in front of his desk with the other three detectives. She manages to avoid even the hint of a smile.

"Everyone got coffee, something to eat?" Long John Silver asks in his high nasal twang, indicating the coffee pot and a plate of rolls and donuts to his far right on a counter.

The three men nod, holding up their steaming Styrofoam cups, Patrick McHugh munching on a nut-covered, chocolate donut.

Katy, empty-handed, mutters, "I'm fine, Captain."

He says, "All right," glancing quickly over the men, as his gaze settles on her. "Glad you fellows could all make it this early. You too, Katy. How's the arm, by the way?"

"It's fine, now," she replies, knowing he asks the question sincerely. If anything he is overly solicitous of the welfare of his troops. He actually came to see her every day at the hospital after the Double Jack dust-up.

Long John nods and smiles.

"Let's see, now," he continues in his high-pitched voice, after clearing his throat and shuffling some papers on his desk, as if searching for an agenda for the meeting.

Apparently not finding a script, he looks up and wings it. "Well, as you've probably guessed, I've called you all in for a meeting over these two related homicides—Mary Ann Olson and Pearl LeDoux. Channel Three apparently has put some of the facts together, linking the two as victims of the same killer and telecasting this information last night and again early this morning. Fortunately, they don't know about the perp's hairy souvenir collection, at least yet. But you can bet whatever they do learn will be on national TV tonight. The Chief is anticipating increasing pressure on the department and wants the investigation speeded up. We need to catch this sick puppy, *soon*. Before the politicians get on this over at the Capitol, and the crapola really begins to splatter, making the investigation even more difficult. The Chief's considering calling the FBI Behavioral Sciences in D.C., getting the assistance of their Profiling Unit—"

"Oh, Jesus, Captain," McHugh blurts out punctuated with an emphatic groan. "Not the feds. They always come up with the same old shit—a white male between twenty and thirty, menial job if employed, a social loser, tortured animals as a kid, wet the bed until ten, maybe started fires—"

Silver interrupts, holding up his hand. "That's not quite fair, Patrick. They've come a long way in the last few years. I think they were very helpful down in Atlanta aiding the locals in catching and convicting Wayne D. Williams. As I recall Williams was *black*, right?

Hey, I'm not too crazy about calling them in either. But, in any event, it's really a political decision, isn't it? And that's the Chief's game. Whether he does or not will depend on us, how fast we catch this guy."

McHugh slumps down a little in his chair, still looking irritated, but devoting his attention to his half-eaten donut.

It's obvious that Patrick has an axe to grind with the feds, Katy thinks, trying to remember something she'd heard about the FBI taking over a case from him and screwing it all up, before she came to Homicide. But she can't quite recall details. *I'll ask Johnny later, if I think of it,* she tells herself, shifting her attention back to Long John.

Captain Silver gestures toward all four of them. "As of now all of you are working on this case exclusively. And I don't need to remind you about leaking anything to the press, right? Patrick, you and Harlan, dump whatever else you were working on into Peterson and Kransky's in-baskets, okay?"

Bundy, looking surprised, asks, "That includes the little Martin girl's case, too?"

The captain nods with a reluctant expression. "Yeah, for now. You can pick that back up after we get this guy. Johnny you're the senior detective on this. You and I'll meet every day at 9:00 a.m. for a progress report. In addition, today at 1:00 p.m., the Chief, you, and I have a press conference. You can update us on everything current about 12:30 right here in my office—"

Johnny groans, after hearing about the press conference, then asks, "You say the four of us are full-time on this, but what about Katy? She's still officially on limited duty, you know."

Long John looks at Katy. "I know all about the book. And for now you guys can do all the grunt work. But if we don't make some significant progress real soon, I may need you on the bus full time, Katy." He shrugs an apology in her direction.

"Okay, Patrick and Harlan, you guys clear your desks of other work, bring Peterson and Kransky up to speed, meet back with Katy and Johnny in half an hour. Where at, Johnny?"

"My desk will be fine for now," he replies. "Maybe I'll set up a command center later today in one of the conference rooms after we finish this press thing."

McHugh and Bundy stand up and leave the office.

"Okay, I have a little something personal for you two, now," the captain says to Katy and Johnny, after the door to his office closes.

Oh, oh, Katy thinks, the alarms all going off at once in her head. What kind of crap now?

Long John digs through the mess on his desk until he locates a memo. "This is from the Chief to me about both of you, signed yesterday, but not really related to the current Olson-LeDoux case. Apparently this young woman from Channel Ten, Serra Melendez, has some political drag and is putting the pressure on. The Chief wants you two—The Green Hornet and Cato, is it?—to meet with her this afternoon for a taping. You're going to be the next pair of guests on her show *Saints or Sinners?*"

He pauses for a sip of coffee, making a face as if it is too hot. "I know it's a royal pain in the butt, and everyone in the division is going to rag your tails about it. But I'm afraid that's just tough… " He pauses momentarily again, an apologetic expression on his face, before adding, "She did one on the Mexican Mafia up at Folsom, last week. Did either of you see it?"

"No," Katy replies. She has never seen the program, not really watching much nightly TV.

Johnny shakes his head and rubs his nose, a deeply annoyed look on his face.

"Well, it was actually pretty good," Long John says, smiling. "She didn't romanticize those guys. She asked them some tough questions in that interview, kind of out of the blue as she went along. Really probing questions. She's a sharp interrogator and does her homework. So, you two can expect something probably will be slipped in about the current case, which you will *not* discuss. But, as I understand it, the bulk of this half-hour-program is supposed to be a character profile on you two super heroes."

"Ah, c'mon, Captain, this is all bullshit and you know it," Johnny complains, rubbing his broken nose. "It has nothing to do with our real jobs. In fact, it makes everything tougher once you get to be a half-ass TV celebrity. Appearing on the news in a press conference is bad enough, you know."

Captain Silver shrugs again. "That may be so, but the Chief says for you to do it. He thinks it's good for department public relations. I happen to personally think he's right on this one." He hands the paper to Katy. "Miss Melendez wants to see you both at Channel Ten at 7:00 tonight for taping. All the information you need is in this memo from the Chief."

2

Thirty minutes later, the four homicide detectives gather around John Cato's desk and semi-private office shared with Katy.

Johnny takes a few minutes and carefully summarizes the current status of the investigation of the two murders, then he opens up the discussion.

Katy asks Harlan, "How did the cowboy, Edgar Ray Jennings, check out?"

"His alibi is tight," Bundy replies. "Dude didn't get out of Huntsville Tuesday afternoon until about *5:00* p.m. He didn't come in on the Greyhound until last night at 11:15 just like he said. Then he had two drinks at the *Traveler's Lounge*. Each piece of his story checks out. So, no way he hit Mary Ann last Tuesday night here in Sacramento. And, I don't think he was interested in harming Pearl when he wandered over to the K Street mall. Guy raises after three years down, shagging some pussy is about *all* he has on his immediate mind... Ah, sorry, Katy."

She ignores the sheepish smile and half-hearted apology. "What did he say about seeing anyone else in the alley or someone going in when he was leaving?"

Bundy shakes his head. "He didn't see anyone, although he did notice quite a few people wandering around out on K Street when he came back out of the alley. I'll get you a copy of his statement, if you want it."

Katy nods, then glances over toward Patrick McHugh, who is no longer frowning. He says, "I got nothing much from Charles White. He didn't see anyone in the alley either. He's still half-ass convinced Jennings did Pearl. And he doesn't care about the cowboy's alibi concerning some other murder on Tuesday night. Do you want to look at his formal statement?"

Katy answers, "Yes, I do."

"I'll get you a copy today."

"Okay," Johnny says, "anyone else got any questions? We all on the same page here?"

No one says anything.

"The report from forensics and the medical examiner should be done this afternoon," Johnny continues. "I hope so, anyhow. I'll go over this morning and rattle their cages. And I expect to get something back on the giant stutterer description soon, but I bet that won't be available until Monday morning earliest, with the weekend on us. Probably later from the State Hospitals and NCIC. In the meantime, Harlan and Patrick, you both can dig for potential witnesses on K Street, anyone you can place near that alley at the right time last night. Get some precinct blues to help if you need to. Maybe check the clubs and restaurant bars around there, too. One of the bartenders may have heard something, regulars may have been out and about and saw something. Who knows? You both are familiar with the drill. Let's see… Anything else we should be thinking about, right now? Katy?"

"Yes, there is," she replies, rubbing her chin thoughtfully. "I'm still really puzzled about how this guy seems to be able to get in and out of the crime scene without being spotted. I didn't notice last night, but maybe one of you can check the alley again in daylight. Were there any fire escapes dropping down there… doorways… windows? Any way for him to get in and out without being seen from the mall on K Street? We need to think some more about Mary Ann's third-story apartment, too. It doesn't appear he climbed up the side of the building. So, how the hell did he get in and out without being spotted… Oh, and how about this hair thing? Why is he taking these patches? What's he doing with them? Anyone got any ideas?"

Johnny and Patrick shake their heads.

Harlan says, "Maybe I can talk to that retired Psych professor from State, ah… Dr. Wright, the guy who consults with the CHP. He had some pretty good ideas last year on the Spinelli case, about the apparent ritual nature of the victims' clothes and limbs at the crime scene, and that it was all actually staged by Spinelli, remember? Dr. Wright turned out to be right on."

"That's a good idea, Harlan," Johnny says, nodding in agreement.

Then Patrick adds, "We'll check that alley this afternoon, Katy, when we're trying to rustle up some K Street witnesses—Bundy and I."

Johnny rubs his nose absently. "Maybe we should also roust some of our snitches. You had good C.I.'s, Harlan, when you worked robbery. They may know something about this, if the perp is on the street and talking. In fact, let's lay the bundled-up, giant stutterer description on them, too, okay?"

McHugh and Bundy nod absently, apparently both already going over their mental files of current confidential informants.

"Anything else for now?" Johnny asks, looking at each of them individually.

They all shrug and shake their heads, including Katy.

"Let's get busy then. We'll meet back here tonight, say 6:00, sharp."

3

Katy is sitting at her computer in the late afternoon, trying to get some work done on her novel, *The Indigo Man*, but it's no use. Her mind keeps drifting from the story to all the questions surrounding the two murders:

Why does he take the hair swatches?

Why doesn't anyone see him coming or going at the murder sites?

Why were the blood drops near the mirror in Mary Ann's apartment?

Why those two victims—what's special about them to him?

Why, why, why?

Frustrated with her inability to concentrate on her writing, she shuts down the computer, and devotes her complete attention to the case, mentally backtracking, looking for anything she might've overlooked, something she missed.

Pearl...

Mary Ann...

She reads over the formal statements of Charles White and Edgar Ray Jennings. Nothing.

She goes back to the medical/forensic report on Mary Ann and carefully re-reads it, even reviewing the graphic photographs. Nothing new comes to mind. She'll compare the report to Pearl's when forensics finishes hers.

But for now?

She's stuck—no place to go.

So, Katy just stares idly at her dead computer screen, trying to blank out her conscious thoughts, hoping something will suddenly surface from her subconscious...

Nothing.

"Jesus," she swears under her breath after a few minutes, standing and stretching her frame. *We have to catch this guy real soon... I don't think he's quite finished yet.* "Uh-uh."

4

At 4:30, Johnny calls on the phone, a big grin back in his voice. "We've got an eye witness for last night!"

"No," Katy replies, "you're joking?"

"Not this time, kiddo," he says, unable to restrain his excitement. "McHugh has him in tow right now. We're supposed to meet them at 5:00 over at *Reds*, around the corner from *Fishes and Loaves* on North C and Ahearn. You know the place?"

"Yeah. I'll be there," she says, wondering why *Reds*. It's a low-rent dive near the homeless facilities area of town, catering to an assortment of minor hoods, crackheads, and bums, the closest bar to where the day laborers are paid in cash by the farm labor contractors and let off the buses, after returning from the fields.

5

It's noisy and dark in *Reds*, the smell of stale beer, booze, and cigarettes hanging in the gloom over the seedy crowd of mostly men but Katy, squinting, finally spots Patrick and Johnny sitting at a table way in the far corner with another man. She makes her way over, nodding at the other detectives before sitting down.

"Katy, this is Mouse," Patrick says, as she pulls up a chair across from a skinny, gray, old man, dressed in a tattered, filthy, black long coat and wearing a greasy-blue L.A. Dodgers baseball cap, despite the heat wave still lingering outside.

The old man barely acknowledges her presence, his attention directed instead to holding a glass down on the table with both hands, as if it were a balloon filled with helium instead of a glass of cheap red wine. He lets go with one hand for a few seconds to scratch his nose and suck in a deep breath, but keeps his eyes glued on the glass, his freed hand shaking noticeably.

"Take your time, Mouse," Patrick says, glancing over at Johnny and Katy and shrugging, his expression asking: *What am I gonna do?* "No hurry. We're government, got all kinds of time."

Mouse sighs, taking another deep breath, his beady eyes still locked on the glass. He clutches it tightly again with both hands, then bends over, and noisily slurps up a drink without lifting the glass from the table. He closes his eyes, smiles gratefully, and smacks his lips.

At that moment Katy realizes he is toothless, and she tries to guess his age. Fifty, fifty-five, sixty, maybe more? It's hard to tell, but he's at least fifty; and, noticing the foul, sour smell coming from beneath his long coat, she thinks it may have been at least that long since he's bathed. She pinches her nose, trying to keep a neutral expression, while swearing silently to herself: *Jesus.*

Mouse, still paying no attention to her or the other detectives, bends forward over the table again, carefully tilts the glass this time, and manages to slurp up another drink without lifting the wine. He waits a minute or so with his eyes closed, then blinks, and lets both hands slide away from the glass. They're still trembling but not quite so violently. He sucks in another deep breath, focuses, and picks up the now half-full glass in both shaky hands, managing to get it to his mouth without spilling anything, then quickly downing the remainder of the wine. He wipes his mouth with the back of his wrist, slams down the glass, and grins broadly, as if he's just completed an incredible feat of sleight-of-hand—transferring the entire contents from the glass to his mouth, without spilling even *one* drop.

"That's great," Patrick says half-seriously, then gets up, goes to the bar, and returns in a moment with another full glass of the red wine. He sits back down, but keeps the wine in front of himself. "Mouse, you get another drink after you tell *them* what you saw last night in the alley off the K Street walking mall where you were sleeping under your cardboard tent."

"Ah, man I tol' yah already," the gray-skinned, rail-thin, smelly, old guy whines, his voice as shaky as his hands, some of his words jammed together.

"Tell my friends."

Mouse first eyes the full glass of wine, then quickly makes up his mind to cooperate.

"Well I's sleepin' like he says. Somepin wakes me up. An when I stick my head out, I sees 'im, the vampire." He takes another wistful look at the full glass in front of McHugh.

"A friggin' vampire?" Johnny says incredulously.

"Let him tell it," Patrick cautions, patting the old wino gently on the back. "Go ahead, Mouse. Tell them what the vampire looked like."

"Well he's big, real big, an all shiny even inna dark—"

"Explain shiny to them," Patrick interrupts softly, edging the glass of wine a few inches in Mouse's direction.

"Mostly naked, real pale, so white, he look kinda wet n' shiny inna poor light comin' from the alley mouf… " He pauses, glancing first at Johnny and then over at Katy. "Yah unnerstan?"

"He wasn't wearing any clothes and was real pale," Katy replies

"Jus bottoms, pants," Mouse corrects her, his voice stronger now, his words more distinct. "His bare chess real white n' shiny."

"How'd you know he was a vampire, Mouse?" Patrick asks, gently coaching along the toothless wino.

"He ben' over tha woman fur a minute, blockin' her from view, then I sees blood cumin' outter neck where he bites 'er… "

"What's he do after that?" Patrick asks, inching the glass a little closer.

"Dunno," Mouse answers. "Can't see, vampire all ben' over down atter pussy. Then he jump up and back away inna shadows, n' then… jus' disappear!" He glances again at the glass of red wine.

Patrick moves it an inch closer, then stops. "What do you mean, disappear?"

"One minute there, nex' gone. Maybe he flies away, outta sight, I dunno fer sure. But they *can* fly, them vampires, yah know?"

"What happened then?" Patrick prods a little impatiently now, sliding the glass almost into the old guy's waiting, trembling grasp.

Mouse eyes the drink, swallows, and works his toothless mouth a little, before continuing in a drier, hoarser voice. "I pulls back inna tent, getting the fuckin' shakes, real bad by then, man."

Patrick pushes the drink into the old guy's hands, which are relatively steady now—just a slight tremor.

Mouse picks up the wine without spilling anything and drains it thirstily in one long drink, smacking his lips after he finishes.

Patrick holds up his hands and lifts his eyebrows questioningly at Johnny and Katy.

"Did you see his face?" asks Katy.

Mouse replies, "*Uh-uh*, I doan look inna his face. Inna vampire's eyes? No way, man."

"You've seen ah… the vampire before?" Johnny asks the wino.

Mouse shakes his head.

"You didn't actually see him leave? Or anyone else come up to the woman?" asks Katy.

"No," the old man replies. "I jus' stay inna tent and mine my own bidness."

"Do you think you would recognize the vampire if you saw him again?" asks Johnny.

"Oh, yeah," Mouse says, nodding. "Big guy, shiny white here and here—" He pats his chest and the top of his head, then coughs. "I knows 'im if I sees 'im."

Katy wonders what Mouse means by touching the *top* of his head like that. But she catches another strong whiff of sour body odor as he drops his arm, and she scoots her chair back noisily from the table, dismissing the gesture as probably insignificant.

Then it's quiet at their table for a few moments.

"Okay, Mouse," Patrick says, handing him three or four crumpled-up dollars. "Get yourself something to eat, and I mean something to *eat*, you hear?"

"Oh, I will officer," the old wino answers, shoving the money in his coat pocket, getting up, grinning, and slyly edging toward the door. "You knows I will."

Patrick shrugs at Katy and Johnny, as the old man leaves. "Hey, the old dog won't, but he'll be happy anyhow tonight."

"Great eye witness, has a real way with words," Katy says, her tone heavy with disappointment. When Johnny phoned earlier about an eye witness of their perp, she'd expected a description a bit more mundane than a fucking vampire.

"Hell, it's a little something, anyhow," Patrick insists defensively.

"You know now for sure that the perp is definitely your *giant*, even if he wasn't bundled up like in the other two descriptions."

Yeah, Patrick is right, Katy admits to herself. And all that pale vampire shit might actually be an accurate description, too, if the guy normally walks around bundled up, never getting any sun exposure. But why would he be bare-chested last night? Seems that would draw almost as much attention as wearing too much clothing... But maybe not though in this heat.

"And we know one more important thing about him, also," Patrick adds, a serious expression on his face.

"Oh, what's that?" Katy asks expectantly, standing up, hands on hips.

"Dude can fly!" he replies, unable to keep his straight face. "That's why no one ever sees him come or go, Katy. He flies in and out."

They all laugh, working their way out of *Reds*.

6

All four detectives meet again at 6:00 in the command center room that Johnny has set up. He's drawn up a wall chart on a blackboard with four columns: PERP'S DESCRIPTION; QUESTIONS; ANSWERS; and MISC. DATA.

All the information collected so far is listed under the appropriate column, the ANSWERS column mostly empty.

Other than Mouse, McHugh and Bundy have not come up with any other witnesses to the events in the alley. And their C.I.'s say no one is talking about the murders on the street, either. Not a peep.

"How about the alley?" Katy says.

"No fire escapes dropping down, no doors, no windows," Patrick replies. "Only one way in and out off the K Street Mall."

"Oh, and Dr. Wright is out of town, some kinda conference," Harlan says, "but I've left a message for him to call me when he gets back on Sunday afternoon."

"Well, I guess we're all shooting friggin' blanks," Johnny says in an exasperated tone. "No forensic report on Pearl yet. Nothing from the computers on our big, husky stutterer description, either. Katy, have you come up with any new ideas?"

She shakes her head.

"Well, you guys keep searching for potential witnesses out on K Street last night," Johnny says, checking his watch. "Katy, you about ready to head out for our 7:00 gig?"

She nods, not feeling real enthusiastic about the Channel 10 taping. They all leave the office together.

7

Katy is a little surprised at the Channel 10 studio for *Saints or Sinners?* It's actually pretty nondescript—20 feet by 20 feet maybe—a plain room, furnished with only a wooden desk and an adjoining cheap couch. Two cameras and cameramen back from the desk and couch, about ten or twelve feet away. And close behind them, the back wall has a door and a big window, two people in the room beyond. That's it.

A female assistant, Catherine, dressed casually in a blue and gold Cal Davis sweatshirt and faded jeans, has met Katy and Johnny in the lobby and brought them back here to Studio 4A, trying to relax them on the way with small talk.

"Sit down there, please," Catherine says, indicating the couch. "Now, let me hook these up... " She attaches a hair pin-like mike to Katy's blouse and one to Johnny's shirt lapel. "I see you both wore dark colors. Good." She takes a dusting brush and a bowl of flesh-colored powder off the desk. "This is just to take the shine off your noses and foreheads. Close your eyes, please." She dusts Katy's face first, then Johnny's. "Okay, that's it, you guys are ready for the big time. Serra will be out in a few moments. Any last minute questions?"

They both shake their heads.

The assistant grins wryly. "Hey, relax, you two, it doesn't hurt much, at least not any more than say... oh, a root canal!"

Katy chuckles.

At that moment, another woman enters the studio, dressed more formally than Catherine in an expensive but tasteful outfit, beige satin blouse, mahogany worsted skirt, with a pearl necklace and matching earrings.

"Hi, I'm Serra Melendez," she says, shaking hands. "Katy Green, right, and John Cato?"

She is a very poised, attractive, young woman—maybe thirty—her make-up professional and immaculate, her black hair cut short and spiked stylishly. But it is her gun barrel-blue eyes that catch Katy's attention—bright and almost child-like, with that intensely curious and interested-in-everything gaze often found in writers' expressions.

"We'll start in a moment. You'll know when the cameras are on by that little red light there. But don't worry too much about them. Just try to act naturally, talk directly to me. Hopefully, my questions will be intriguing enough to capture your full attention. In any event, this isn't live TV. We're only taping, and we have the luxury of editing all of this. So don't be overly concerned with what you say. Okay?"

Katy replies, "Fine," but thinks to herself: *Yeah, sure!*

Johnny, sitting next to her on the couch, just nods.

Serra takes her place behind her desk, glancing down at a clipboard apparently full of notes and questions.

The producer or an engineer wearing a headset steps out of the glassed-in room in the back and announces, "Taping in five seconds everyone... four, three, two, one. Action!"

Katy glances at Serra Melendez, who is looking into the camera directly in front of her—the red light on.

"Good evening," she says, peering at the unseen audience with her unusual eyes. "This is *Saints or Sinners?*, and I am Serra Melendez. Tonight I have two very special guests, who everyone in the Capitol wants to meet. Miss Katy Green and Mr. John Cato, homicide detectives with the Sacramento Police Department. You all know them better from newspapers and TV as the Green Hornet and Cato." She turns and faces the couch, smiling. "Welcome, you two super heroes. It's nice of you to take time from your busy schedule and come visit us here at Channel Ten."

"It's nice to be here," Katy replies, hoping it doesn't sound too insincere.

"Good evening," Johnny says, a thin-lipped smile on his face.

"Well," Serra begins, "you two have been together as partners for four years... and it says here that you have worked on and solved eight major homicide cases during that time, including recently catching the notorious Double Jack." She glances over at Johnny. "By the way, John, what does that mean, a *major* homicide case."

He replies, after clearing his throat, "A number of our cases don't really require much investigation. For example, we arrive at the scene. The uniformed police have the perpetrator—often a relative—in hand, and often the weapon, too. We take the perp to headquarters, read him his Miranda Rights—the uniformed police have already done this, but we repeat it for the record—take a formal statement, often a confession—and that's about it. Unless the prosecutor assigned from the D.A.'s office wants something checked out. But a case like the Double Jack thing, that can go on for several weeks or even more, requiring actually hunting down an unknown perp, more like what you see on TV shows, that's a *major* investigation—"

"I see," Serra says, looking directly at the camera in front of her, and continuing in a conversational voice like she's clarifying something to a friend over the phone. "Most investigations are fairly routine, but you two have a *very* good track record when things get complicated."

She turns, gazing at them again. "Katy, let's talk a little about some of those major cases, including the most recent one, Double Jack… "

For the next fifteen minutes or so, Serra Melendez asks them both a number of sharp questions about their past cases, then finally focuses on the Jack Malenko investigation—questions about each of the five victims, the description and composite drawing of Malenko, Katy eventually deciding to check out fitness/training centers, and details of the actual arrest, including how they both sustained injuries. Then she shifts for a few minutes to their special relationship—the Green Hornet and Cato bit—their training, and finally their backgrounds…

"Katy, you majored in Police Science right here at Sacramento State?"

"Yes," Katy answers, relaxing a little now that the half hour is almost up.

"Played power forward for the Hornets' women's basketball team, I see," Serra says, glancing at her clipboard, then smiling back up at Katy.

"That's correct."

"And have sold a number of short stories, too," Serra adds, looking impressed and nodding at the camera.

Katy says, "That's right, and I'm working on a novel right now. It'll be called *The Indigo Man*." May as well get in a little plug, she thinks, turning and smiling half-apologetically at Johnny.

"I know we will all want to read that book when you finish it," Serra says to the camera. Then, peering back at Katy with her curious, bright gaze, her voice dropping slightly in pitch, she asks, "*But* before Sac State, you actually grew up and went to high school in San Diego, an orphan, a ward of the State?"

"Yes," Katy replies, "My folks were hit head on by a drunken driver traveling in the wrong lanes on Interstate 5 and killed when I was ten—"

"And you had no relatives to take you in?" Serra asks, not smiling, an intrigued frown on her face now.

"No... Actually, my mother's sister, my only other relative was killed in the car wreck that night, too."

"So, you were raised in a series of foster homes in San Diego by *strangers?*"

"That's right," Katy replies, feeling the nature of the interview has suddenly shifted, and she's now being held accountable for a questionable background. "I lived in four different foster homes from the age of ten until I graduated from high school."

"And *that* background, *that* life style is what formed your character... made you want to study Police Science at Sac State, write stories or books about offbeat characters, go into law enforcement, and eventually be a homicide investigator, tracking down *sick* sociopaths like Double Jack?" Serra Melendez sneaks a peek at her audience, and raises her eyebrows suggestively, as if she is sharing revealing intimacies about her guest's shady background.

Katy suppresses a derisive snort, wondering what she means by *that life style.* Just exactly what does Serra Melendez think she is implying to the audience about her foster home background and subsequent career? Then, for the first time she really appreciates the question mark in the show's title, and she smiles inwardly. But she keeps her voice neutral and shifts the focus from the implied influences in her life.

"Actually, I do think you learn a *lot* of good things being raised in a group home situation—you know, how to share, cooperate, etc. But to your point, I was personally more influenced by a female police officer who was my coach in a summer PAL basketball league in my junior and senior years in high school. She was my role model. Her name is Geri Robinson, and she taught me to respect myself and strive to be all I could be. She was... and *is* still a very dear friend."

After a moment or two, Serra smiles sweetly and responds simply, "Oh, I see," checks her clipboard again and her wristwatch.

Then, she looks directly back at the camera and announces, "That's our show for tonight, folks. Hope you enjoyed our conversation with the Green Hornet and Cato. And remember, sooner or later we tell everyone's story here on Channel 10… So, someday you, too, could be a guest here on *Saints or Sinners?*"

The red light blinks out on the camera in front of the desk.

Serra stands, takes off her mike, and without smiling says almost dismissively, "That's *it.*"

The producer steps into the room. "Good job, Serra. Mr. Cato. Miss Green. I think with a little editing, we've got a really good show. Very informative. It'll be on this coming Monday night at 11:00 p.m."

Catherine is back in front of them, taking off their mikes. "Not too bad, right?"

Johnny shakes his head and agrees, "Not bad."

Katy doesn't say anything, just shakes hands with Catherine, the producer, and finally Serra.

Outside Channel 10 in the parking lot near their cars, Katy breathes a long sigh of relief. "Yeah, not too bad if you're into root canals."

Johnny laughs. "You did okay, partner. That was a very touching answer you gave at the end about Geri being the major influence in your life. You might want to mention the program to her, tomorrow."

Katy says, "I will but I don't imagine they get *Saints or Sinners?* down in San Diego. I think we will be the only lucky audience here in the Sacramento area."

"Hungry?" asks Johnny, politely opening her car door for her.

"Yes, I guess I am, now that I think about it," she says, realizing that she hasn't eaten anything since breakfast and is actually famished.

"Frank Fats?"

"Sounds good. Meet you there."

They both head south on Broadway, downtown to the landmark Chinese restaurant.

8

Later in the restaurant parking lot, Johnny opens Katy's car door again for her. "Man, it's still muggy out here," he says, leaning down, his elbows on her opened window.

"Well, thanks for the Chinese feast," Katy says, noticing that in the street light his icy-blue eyes have tiny wedges of *warmer* amber under-tint bursting from the black pupils, giving his eyes a gentler, kinder expression, which softens his hard, roughed-up, tough, boxer's features. "You know, partner," she says, "you really have very interesting eyes."

He looks kind of startled for a moment, as if she may be putting him on. Then he grins, pushes himself in closer, and kisses her softly on the lips.

She cradles the back of his head, tugging him even closer, and kisses him back more roughly, nipping at his lower lip with her teeth, then tracing the outline of his mouth with the tip of her tongue.

They break apart.

Katy grins wryly, thinking that they have definitely crossed a line now, and she whispers just audibly, "How was that, partner, just another granny kiss, right?"

Johnny laughs. "If it was," he says, "it was a young and very sexy grandmother."

PARTY FAVORS

"Hey, Sam, take a break," Wilbur shouts over the symphony of the big machines. He and Danny have pushed two metal halves loaded with blankets behind the four other halves waiting to be balanced and dropped into the extractor, the working aisle in front of the big machines resembling the morning commute backup on Interstate 80.

You nod absently, handing Wilbur the control box.

He looks kind of puzzled as you pass by. "Sam, you ain't been talking to that machine today… or you ain't been listening. Whatcha got on your mind, man? You in love or something?"

You shake your head.

He's right.

It's been your worst day at work. The basement is exceptionally stifling—at least one hundred ten degrees—and you've been distracted and unsettled not only by the recurring question of domination by the Dark Angel, but tonight is Gisela's party and you want to explain to her truthfully why you can't come. But you've been unable to catch her eye all day, and short of just walking up to the end of the mangle and grabbing her arm, which you can't do in front of all the other women, you haven't thought of any other way to catch her attention. It's almost like she's avoiding even a passing glance in your direction. She's angry at you.

You check the clock on the far wall on your way past the washers, 9:00 p.m. Maybe she'll take her break now, too, like the other day, and you will have time for a private conversation. You hurry down to the cafeteria, buy a root beer, and wait in vain, finishing your drink alone.

No question in your mind now that your friend has been intentionally avoiding you the last few days. The realization compounds your sense of isolation. Tonight, you would've even welcomed Terry's company but, as usual, he is behind in his sorting work and apparently not able to even take a break.

You go back to your station in the stifling laundry, but before you take charge of the extractor again, Wilbur says, "Mr. Clark wants to see you right now in his office."

"W-What about, W-Wilbur?"

He just shrugs—*Who knows?*—shakes his head, and moves back to join Danny in front of the washers.

Of course you know what the boss wants. He's going to chew you out for daydreaming, backing up the production of the entire laundry staff. You pause for a moment then force yourself to knock timidly on the partially-opened office door, dreading the confrontation with the normally mild-mannered laundry supervisor.

"Come in, Sam," Mr. Clark says, not unkindly, from behind his tiny desk. "Have a seat."

You sit down and wait for the axe to fall.

"Sam, I spoke to Father Nathan this afternoon on the phone. He called, wanting to talk specifically about you."

Of course he is referring to your mentor down at CYA, who four months ago had contacted and convinced Mr. Clark, an old friend, to give you this job in the laundry at Sutter General Hospital.

"H-How is he?" you ask with genuine concern. You've thought about calling Father Nathan for advice a number of times—the Light

Angel even suggested it. But too much has happened in the last few days, too quickly; it seems much too late for advice now.

"He's fine," Mr. Clark says, picking his glasses up off the desk and wiping them off with a clean handkerchief. Even in his normally closed office, the fine mist of lint that hovers constantly in the laundry air penetrates, and by this time of night covers everything on Mr. Clark's desk with a faint coating of white dust—actually every horizontal surface in the entire laundry is covered.

"He's mostly interested in how you are doing. So, I told him that you were one of my best employees. Always on time, reliable, conscientious, a gifted knack with the machines. Of course he knew all this before, from your past history with the machines in the laundry at CYA. What he was really interested in was how you were getting along with your fellow employees, and your state of mind. I told him that I thought everything was fine, but I didn't know for sure about your mental state. Shelley says you are polite and very helpful, but never initiate any contact with the girls on the mangle, always remaining kind of distant and standoffish. Wilbur has nothing but great things to say about you and your work with the machines, but he admits you don't really talk much with him or Danny. And I've noticed you never tease Terry or have much of anything to do with him. So, I guess you get along okay, although you're a bit of a loner, reserved. Is that about right?"

You nod back.

"I conveyed most of this to Father Nathan," Mr. Clark continued, "but he didn't seem particularly satisfied with my partial take on things. And I was surprised to learn that you haven't called him or written even once. Between you and me, I think maybe a letter from you would be a good idea. I know that Father Nathan would be grateful. It might ease his concerns. What do you think?"

Is this the real purpose of Mr. Clark calling you into his office, not to chew you out, but to encourage you to communicate with Father Nathan? For a moment you are taken aback, thankful that you're apparently not going to be chastised for daydreaming this afternoon, but at a temporary loss of exactly how to respond.

"I-I-I guess I really should write h-him," you finally agree, feeling sheepish and self-conscious about Mr. Clark, almost a stranger, knowing that you haven't communicated with your old friend, Father

Nathan, since leaving CYA. "I haven't done it b-because I-I don't write too w-w-well yet," you offer as a lame excuse.

"He'll understand."

"I-I'll do it *tonight*," you agree, forcing an enthusiastic response. But inwardly you shudder, for you know it will be a difficult letter, because you cannot be completely forthright with your old friend. You have never mentioned the Dark Angel. Now it's too late for that; and there is so much more to keep secret. Too much more.

Yes, indeed.

"Good," Mr. Clark says, and he looks real pleased for a moment or two. "But there is one other thing, Sam." He frowns, shifting his gaze down to the papers on his desk. "I'm going to retire soon, and who knows how my successor will relate to you, your probation officer, or whoever. If it's Shelley or Wilbur or anyone else for that matter, they'll obviously feel no obligation to Father Nathan—they don't know about him. They may see your interpersonal behavior as perhaps a little odd, even frightening considering your CYA background."

He stops suddenly, still frowning.

"I guess I'm not being perfectly clear," Mr. Clark continues, obviously struggling with what he wants to say. He sits more upright and adds, "I just wish you would be… oh, more friendly with everyone here at the laundry. Maybe make friends with some of the women. Even smile more. Look happier. Most importantly, I hope that none of the mental behavior that apparently got you in trouble and sent to CYA begins again. You do understand?" Mr. Clark looks a little funny now, apparently embarrassed by the need to discuss his concerns for your welfare, especially your mental state.

"I-I think I understand, Mr. C-Clark," you say. "Thank y-you for m-mentioning i-it."

Leaving the office, you're not really sure you *do* understand all his concerns. Why is he bringing this up now? It is almost like he senses something wrong is going on with you, suspects something. But what?

Is there any possibility that he knows you're walking in the Dark Angel's shadow?

Suspects that you are involved in taking vengeance on Mary Ann and the painted woman downtown?

But how would he know any of that?

You wipe sweat from your face and shake your head.

Uh-uh, no way he knows about that.

The police would have come by now if that were the case. Mr. Clark is just overly concerned about you because he's Father Nathan's good friend, and he feels he won't be around long to help you. That's all. He knows nothing about the Dark Angel. He suspects nothing else—he couldn't. The realization makes you feel much better, and less depressed than earlier.

You stand for a moment at the extractor, thinking about your old friend, Father Nathan. Absently you grab the overhead control box, and you recall the first time you met the Catholic Priest in the infirmary down at CYA...

2

The shower felt good that afternoon, the hot water pounding on your back, relaxing the tightness. You closed your eyes, relishing the few moments alone away from the hubbub in the dorm wing in the warm comfort, the wide-open, stream of hot water causing a steamy mist to slowly fill the tiny shower room—

A noise.

Through the mist you saw three figures standing in the doorway.

You turned off the shower, the mist dissipating slowly from the room.

It was the boy you had punched in the face and knocked down earlier in the day for teasing you in the mess hall about your funnytalk. He had two friends with him, both as big as you and mean-looking; all three were blocking your way out of the shower, each holding a thick dowel from woodshop.

The boy with the black eye said, "L-l-l-look at the big d-d-dummy's hairless d-d-dick."

All three laughed at the imitation of your funnytalk and your completely hairless appearance, their apparent warm joy contrasting sharply with their cold, dead eyes. Their work shirts were rolled up, all three displaying full sleeves of blue tattoos on their muscular arms— swastikas, SS/L.A., WHITE PRIDE, knives, skulls, crosses, CINDY LOU, and other blurred, incomprehensible words. The homemade, fuzzy tattoos only added to their scary, menacing appearance.

Smack, smack, smack.

They repeatedly slammed the dowels into the palms of their hands as they stood there, the sharp sounds reminding you of a distant memory from your past: The high-pitched *crack* of rifle shots in a boxed canyon, an older person shooting squirrels... the sharp *smacks* associated with the spooky images of limp, gray, bloody, lifeless things.

You shivered involuntarily, your wet body feeling clammy.

Black eye smiled coldly and said, "You didn't think I'd just forget, did you, asshole?"

Despite your fear and nakedness, you suddenly rushed at him with reckless abandon, smashing a solid punch into his surprised face, knocking him to the floor, before turning quickly and trying to defend yourself, as the other two waded in quickly, pounding you with their clubs.

A blow crashed solidly to the side of your head—

You saw exploding pinwheels of colored lights, as you dropped down on hands and knees on the wet deck, each succeeding blow only a dull, jarring thud that smashed painlessly against your jaw, shoulder, and leg... the accumulation of thuds finally driving you down flat on your stomach. And then you seemed to be spinning dizzyingly in the swirling water, sucked down into the drain into a cold, clammy blackness...

You awakened to a world of pain, a man's face looking at you, with a concerned expression.

You blinked, able to see out of only one eye.

He smiled.

The man pulled his chair closer to your bed. He was dressed in a black suit, a high, tight, white collar.

It was the priest, of course.

"Don't try to talk," he said, "your jaw is fractured slightly. One eye is swollen closed but not seriously damaged. A bump or two on your head, bruises on your back. More seriously, you have a compound fracture of both the tibia and fibula in your lower leg." He glances down at the end of the bed where your right leg is in a cast and suspended in traction. Looking back at you, he explains, "I am Father Nathan. You are in the infirmary. You were beaten up in the shower in your dorm earlier this afternoon. I don't suppose you remember any of that or know who did this to you?"

You began to shake your head but the motion caused a sharp stab of pain in your jaw.

Father Nathan smiled, making a dismissive wave with his hand. "Okay, I understand, Samuel," he said in a kind voice. "And I know all about the stuttering, the hair problem, and how much you suffer here because of being different from all the other boys… " He paused for a moment, with a bigger smile, then continued: "I would like to come visit you each day as you heal physically, because I think I can teach you to speak better, reduce the stuttering. At least I would like to try. During the visits I also would like to convince you of something that I learned long ago: The importance of the *word*, that it can reach much farther than the *fist*. In any event, you need a friend. Are you interested?"

You hesitated just a second before making a slight nod. You had nothing to lose. If he could really help you speak better, it was worth a try. You did need a friend. And the odd thought, that a word could possibly reach farther than a fist, at first funny, actually intrigued you, made very good sense.

"O-okay," you murmured.

"Good," Father Nathan said, rising and shaking your hand. "Get some rest, now. I'll see you early tomorrow morning."

He left.

But Father Nathan came back often while you were in the infirmary; then, after your release, you visited him many times at chapel. And over the years he did indeed teach you about the power of the word, and helped you to cope with your problems. He'd been a good friend. For some reason, you had never been able to bring yourself to the point of completely confiding in him, sharing with him the secret about hearing the voices of the two Angels.

And now it is much too late to share anything really important with him, you think, the wobbling whine of the unbalanced extractor drawing you back to the present. You concentrate on rebalancing the load, thoughts of the priest and your present problems forced to the back of your mind.

3

After work, at your apartment you struggle with the letter to Father Nathan. You cannot really write about the dread in your heart—the Dark Angel and the apprehension of walking in His shadow forever, being eternally damned, and despite your fluid reading ability, your self-censored written words come very laboriously, and the sentences appear almost juvenile, stiff, and contrived. Unfortunately they're the best you can manage.

> *Dear Father Nathan,*
> *I am fine. How are you?*
> *I live in a swell apartment here in Sacramento near Sutter's Fort. I go to the park there almost every day. I like it here a lot, except it is really hot.*
> *How is the weather now in San Diego?*
> *I practice the breathing and focusing you taught me all the time. It works well. My speech is getting much better, I think. I try to read almost every day. I have been working on* Heart of Darkness *but find it really hard. Any other suggestions?*
> *My probation officer, Mr. Gabriel Chacon, Visits me every two weeks or so. I get along with him real well. I like Mr. Clark a lot too. He is a good boss. He got me a half dollar an hour raise last month. So I am doing very well money wise. I have made two close friends at the laundry, Danny and Wilbur. We kid around quite a bit. They are a lot of fun. There is even a young woman who I like a lot and she likes me, too...*

You pause and drop your pen, thinking about Gisela.

Tonight is her party.

You glance at the clock: 11:40 p.m. The party is probably going full blast right now. You wish you could have explained everything to her. You sigh, then remember one of Mr. Clark's remarks, a suggestion about you trying to make more female friends.

He's right.

On the spur of the moment, you decide that regardless of the possible repercussions with your P.O., you are going to that party and see your friend. You look around and find Gisela's card with directions how to get to her address way out near McClellan Air Force Base. It will require catching the light rail train and riding out along Interstate 80 past Del Paso Heights almost to North Highlands. And then a pretty good hike on foot to her address by the Air Base.

Nevertheless, you smile leaving your apartment, applying another piece of Mr. Clark's advice.

4

You walk over to the light rail station at 12th and E Streets, but don't arrive until after midnight. The reduced schedule from 12:00 a.m. to 6:00 a.m. indicates another train will not go north for nearly forty-five minutes.

You wait impatiently, conscious of the cloying heat even this late at night.

The train finally comes, but, despite only a handful of passengers, it makes an endless series of station stops.

Start, stop. Start, stop. Start, stop…

Eventually, you get off at the next to last light rail station at Longview; and after another fifteen minutes or so of walking, you finally arrive at Gisela's home address.

5

The downstairs apartment door is opened wide, country music playing softly into the night—it's a song you recognize and like a lot, Merle Haggard singing, "Tulare Dust." A young woman dressed in a gray S.C.C. Panthers T-shirt and black shorts is picking up beer cans outside and putting them in a paper sack. She stops and gazes at you, apparently surprised by your bundled-up appearance on such a warm evening. When she speaks it's obvious that she has consumed her share of the beer.

"Hiya," she says, her face heavily made up. "You come for the party?"

You nod.

"Well, you're a little late, fella," she explains, bending over and picking up another can. "Party's over. Someone in the complex bitched about the noise outside. Cops came a little while ago." She squints, taking another good look at you, then smiling kind of flirtatiously. "Wynne and I are helping clean up before we head home." She gestures in the direction of the apartment next door, sucking in a deep breath and giving you a profile of her full breasts, then glancing back at you for some reaction.

"G-Gisela?" you ask, suppressing your negative feelings about her gaudy makeup, flirting with a stranger, and obviously her drunken condition.

Bad, bad, bad.

"Oh, she isn't feeling too well." The young woman makes a vague gesture toward inside.

You move into the open door a step or two and stop.

Another young woman, probably Wynne, is picking up cans and emptying ashtrays into a bag. The room smells of stale smoke and spilled beer. She smiles and says, "Hi," apparently paying no attention to your rolled-down stocking cap and long-sleeved shirt or anything about you. She too appears to have been drinking, but her face is not quite as heavily painted as her roommate outside.

"I-I'm looking for G-Gisela."

She nods, kind of dancing around as she cleans up, paying more attention to the music, than to you.

You move over to the stereo player and turn down the volume slightly.

She looks up frowning.

"G-G-Gisela?"

"She's *sick*," the young woman says with a frown, stepping over and flipping the sound back up. She gestures down the hall and explains over the amplified sound, "Friend helped her to the bathroom."

You stand there silently for a few moments, looking down the darkened hall into an open but dimly-lit empty bedroom at the far end, debating with yourself, wondering if you should go see how Gisela is feeling. She will probably be embarrassed, especially in front of a friend. It's really late. Maybe you should just go home. But you've come all this way; and you want to at least say hello, see if Gisela is okay. Maybe you can explain why you don't usually go to parties, if she is well enough to listen.

You move midway down the darkened hallway to a door, opened just a crack. You guess it is the bathroom. You stop and listen, but you don't hear anything that suggests someone is sick. No gagging, retching. Nothing like that. Instead, someone is breathing heavily, a series of pant-like, gasping sounds, almost like a weight-lifter doing bench presses, except more joyful... And then you do recognize Gisela's voice, except it sounds much lower in pitch than normal and kind of hoarse, "Oh... oh... oh, yes!" This is followed by a long sigh and a string of words in German.

Curious, you cautiously nudge the door in slightly, allowing a little more light into the hall and affording yourself a better view inside. You discover that you are peeking into a mirror at *two* people sitting together on the commode; and you're stunned by an unexpected sight.

The friend is Wilbur.

Rising up off his lap is Gisela, who turns slightly toward the mirror, her dress still hiked up around her hips, wearing no panties, her secret hair exposed to your view. It is fiery orange just like her head, fine and soft like her underarms, but unruly, damp, and creased, revealing her dark brown, wrinkled lips.

She does not look sick, even though her cheeks are flushed deeply.

Wilbur is sitting down on the john seat, his pants and blue polka dot boxer shorts down around his ankles, his exposed stomach, crotch, and upper thighs covered with coarse, black hair, his maleness thickly erect, darkly veined.

You feel disoriented, in a dreamlike state, like when you walk in the shadow of the Dark Angel, everything appearing unreal, as if you're seeing things through someone else's eyes. And even the sight of Gisela's beautiful secret hair, something you have longed to see, does little to stir you from your detached state. Nor does the musk-like smell hanging heavy in the enclosed room and adjoining hallway do much more than flare your nostrils, make your nose itch.

Wilbur and Gisela...

You are not able to complete the thought, put it all together. You feel like you're staring at one of those colored-dot, embedded pictures, not quite able to separate foreground from background, not sure what you are looking at and unable to figure it out. Yet, despite the confusing nature of the scene, you remain rooted in place, staring into the mirror, unable to tear your gaze away, caught up and fascinated by a palpable tactile sensation, a sweaty, tingling, almost electrical feeling being generated by the two in the tiny room.

Wilbur is smiling broadly now, just sitting there, his genital area still completely exposed to view, absolutely unembarrassed, as if he is sitting at a table in the cafeteria at work, just taking a break, *proud* of something he has just said or done. Nonchalant. Not a care in the world.

But now Gisela is reaching behind her to the counter running under the mirror, picking up her black panties. She turns her back to the commode—kind of a shy gesture—where Wilbur still remains seated, his manhood going soft. She pulls on her panties, drops her dress back in place, smoothes her clothes down, and checks her appearance in the mirror, before looking back and saying to Wilbur, "Where's my bra, Willy? What did you do with it?" She smiles sweetly, and her voice sounds more familiar now, not like the husky, panting sounds you heard earlier through the door.

So natural, sweet, and ladylike.

Wilbur laughs lasciviously, like he's just thought of a dirty joke he wants to tell. Then he glances around behind him on the commode tank and rises slowly, her black bra clutched in his fist. "Come here and get it, you red-headed devil," he says, his voice low and husky, his words slightly slurred.

He, too, has been drinking heavily.

Bad, bad, bad.

The tension in the room seems to increase, prickling the hair along the back of your neck.

Looking at him coyly, Gisela turns and backs away a step, her back to the mirror now, and shakes her head. "Oh, no, Willy, I'm really too exhausted by the party and everything. I could not possibly do that again tonight, no thank you, you, you... naughty boy."

"Bet me," he growls, moving close to her with surprising quickness and jerking her into his arms. He kisses her hungrily, clutching her rump in his big hands.

She struggles for a second or two, trying to push him away, then gives in and kisses him back.

For a moment you almost expect to see electrical sparks flying off the two of them...

Then you blink, your thinking beginning to thaw.

Obviously, neither Gisela or Wilbur are aware of you standing just outside the partially opened door in the darkened hallway, because they continue to embrace, their body heat beginning to steam up the mirror.

Wilbur hikes up Gisela's dress, tugs down her panties...

Your heart is heavy now with the growing acceptance of what has happened, and in fact, *is* going to happen again. It takes all your remaining will to stifle a groan, and you know that you should reach out and ease the door completely shut, so neither of the two young women out front stumble onto this degrading, disgusting, and disappointing scene. But you are unable to even move a finger or tear your gaze from the mirror. You are frozen in place, your sensibilities still stunned by what is happening.

Bad, bad, very bad.

Yes, indeed.

They continue to kiss, both opened-mouthed now, their heavy breathing increasing even as they break apart slightly. Then, Wilbur clumsily pushes up Gisela's blouse, exposing her bare, freckled breasts; and he bends over, gently flicking her erect, dark brown nipple with the very tip of his wet, pink tongue—

This is too much!

You drop your eyes in revulsion.

Then, leaving the door still cracked, you try to tiptoe back down the hall and escape from the apartment, but you're forced to stop in the living room, the knot in your stomach suddenly cramping, making you gasp aloud. Sucking in several deep breaths, you reach inside your shirt and massage your belly, digging your fingers roughly into the clenched muscles, eventually easing the cramp.

"Did you find her?"

The slurred voice startles you.

You turn.

It's the young woman, Wynne. She is in the corner near the stereo, and has just turned off the music, apparently preparing to leave.

Before answering, you clear your throat. "Y-Yes, I d-d-did," you reply, your voice sounding far away, different, almost like it belongs to someone else, except for the funnytalk.

She looks at you directly, frowning. "Are you okay, you seem kinda funny, hurt or something, you know?"

You hold up your hand, and signal you are fine, then head for the door, still suffering from the knot of tension in your stomach.

Outside, the other woman has apparently finished her clean up. In any event she isn't anywhere in sight. You are alone. You pause, bend over to catch your breath, massage your abdominal muscles, and ease the lingering ache, while closing your eyes momentarily. But all you see is the mirror reflecting in your mind's eye: Gisela, with her skirt hiked up around her hips and sliding down onto Wilbur's engorged, slippery manhood—

"Oh, no," you cry out into the night, your eyes snapping open, cutting off the vivid image.

Bad, very bad, indeed.

The knot in your stomach has disappeared, and you remove your hand from your shirt, but there is no way to reach in and massage your battered soul.

It's all been too much for you to deal with, your sensibilities frayed, overloaded, and finally shutting down…

6

You find yourself back in your apartment by Sutter General Hospital, sitting on a chair, staring out the window, with absolutely no recall of how you got home from Del Paso Heights. The sky to the East is beginning to lighten, turn pink; it is almost daylight. With an effort of will you stand, shuffle over, and drop on top of your bed, not even bothering to undress or take off your shoes.

Tired, so tired.

Then, behind you, from the open window, you feel a cool gust of air sweep into the room. You continue to face the wall, remaining uncovered, insulated now by an overwhelming sense of despair that has completely numbed your head and heart.

Remarkably, in a few minutes you are able to escape into sleep.

But as is often the case when you are emotionally and physically exhausted, you do not sleep soundly; instead, you toss and turn, wakening yourself often, unable to shake the dreamlike, but vivid, image of an orange-headed woman, standing partially naked in a bathroom mirror with her beautiful secret hair exposed, and a naked, hairy creature squatting behind her on the commode, his maleness thick, slick, and erect, beckoning her with deep, panting, animal grunts.

Bad, bad, oh, so very bad, you think, your eyes tearing up.

FAMILY SECRETS

"Geri, Geri!" Katy shouts over the people moving through Gate 10B, the Saturday 10:00 a.m. arrival from San Diego. "Over here." Standing on her tiptoes, she manages to wave over the heads of most of the crowd. Geri spots her and waves back, smiling broadly.

Katy thinks that her friend hasn't really changed much over the last thirteen years. She's still a tall, lean, attractive, black woman, who moves smoothly through the crowd with an athletic grace, dressed casually in sun glasses, a short-sleeved, gray, V-necked, cashmere sweater, and faded-blue designer jeans. The poise of a gold-medal, ex-Olympic hurdler, or a successful business woman, or even a college professor—Black Female Literature, or something like that. Not anything like a 55 year-old, ex-PAL basketball coach and uniformed sergeant, who worked in the ghetto and recently retired from the SDPD.

As Geri gets closer, Katy spots the streaks of gray in her friend's hair. She smiles, telling herself, it only makes her friend appear even a little more distinguished.

"Yo, girl, wha' sup," Geri shouts—destroying the built-up sophisticated image in Katy's mind—then pushing her glasses up on her forehead, dropping her carry-on, and sweeping Katy up in a clinging hug. "Look at you, now," she says, leaning away slightly, then giving Katy a big kiss on the cheek.

"Yo, yourself," Katy says back, laughing, then hugging her friend tightly for a moment or two. "It's so good to see you." She picks up Geri's carry-on bag. "Any luggage checked?"

"Nope, you know me," Geri says, grinning, "travel light, travel fast, never look back over your shoulder, because no one is able to get close."

Katy nods, leading her out of the terminal to her car in short-term parking.

On the way south on I-5, then east on I-80, Katy gets caught up with Geri's retirement, Herb's recent marlin fishing escapade down at Cabo San Lucas—something he'd planned for five years before *his* retirement—the recent local elections, and the sad state of local tax funding in San Diego County.

"... Money is getting really tight, Katy, for all the non-essential stuff, you know, kid's recreation, schools, police, fire protection, and things like that. But, thank God, we were able to pass a bond to build the *Padres* a brand new state-of-the-art baseball park."

They both laugh.

Katy takes the Watt Avenue turn-off, headed for her place near the college, thinking it's a pleasure to be around her old friend again. There's a comforting sense that she is definitely in *good* company. The thought reminds Katy of the hokey *Allstate* insurance image with the two hands. She nods to herself.

2

At the townhouse, after they get settled, the first thing Geri asks about is the book. "How's the writing going?" She knows Katy's publishing history—she has every story, dated and inscribed—and all about the importance of the upcoming convention in San Jose, the appointment with a top agent.

Katy frowns.

"Actually, I haven't been too productive the last few days." She explains about working part time on the new homicide case, goes over all the puzzling *why* questions, and admits to blocking out on the novel...

"But I don't want to think about the case or writing, not today. Today is a special fun day with an old friend. Time out from everything. I've been looking forward to it."

Geri nods.

"Okay, I can understand that. I've been really looking forward to this trip, too, seeing you and the Phoenix Mercury. Did I tell you about one of my girls—Sidney Williams—from my last Panthers team, four years ago, got a full ride to UCLA? Anyhow, the Mercury drafted her this year, but she's still recovering from an Achilles tendon injury suffered during training camp in June. Not on the active roster now, although she's traveling with the team. She has really high hopes for next season."

Katy chuckles. Geri has proudly mentioned Sidney a half a dozen times in the past four years. "Yeah, sure, I remember you telling me about her, and I did go see her play against both Stanford and Cal, up here, last year when I had time," she says. "Sidney's terrific, got a great chance to make the Phoenix team, I think, if her injury heals properly."

The door buzzer interrupts them.

"That must be John Cato, my partner. I wanted you to meet him, so I invited him for lunch. Okay?"

"Your work partner?" Geri says, lifting her eyebrows quizzically.

"Well, maybe a *little* more than just a partner," Katy admits, headed for the entry. "I think so, anyhow."

She opens the door.

3

The luncheon goes great.

It's obvious to Katy that Johnny and Geri hit it off right from the start. Geri is a real boxing fan, and can talk intelligently about it. She's also sincerely interested in Johnny's volunteer coaching and the program up at Folsom Prison. And his enthusiasm is contagious.

From boxing, the conversation shifts to San Diego and stories about Katy's time playing for Geri and the Panthers, including their first strained meeting at Metro Recreation...

The three of them thoroughly enjoy each other's company, and time passes quickly.

But, a little after 3:00, Johnny suddenly rises and excuses himself. "You two need some time alone to visit before the game tonight," he says to both of them. "Glad I finally got to meet you, Geri." He gives her a hug. Then he turns to Katy, "I've some work I should do, you know."

She nods, walking him to the door, where she kisses him on the cheek. "Appreciate you coming, pal."

He smiles, saying over her shoulder, "Geri, get Katy to tell you about the TV program we just taped last night." Looking back at Katy, he whispers, "Have a good time at the game tonight, kiddo."

Then he leaves.

"Like just your... ah, partner, Katy," Geri says, with a big, wide-mouthed grin of approval. "What TV program was he talking about?"

Katy describes *Saints or Sinners?* and the recent ordeal with Serra Melendez, promising to tape it for her friend.

4

After helping Katy with the luncheon dishes, Geri wanders around the townhouse, finally stopping and picking up a photograph on the fireplace mantle. "This must be your mom and dad and you when you were little?" she says, poking her head and the photo back into the kitchen.

Katy replies, "Yes, it is," setting two mugs of tea on the breakfast counter. "I guess you've never seen a picture of them before."

Geri shakes her head, sets the photo down, and says, "You know, I never even knew my own father." She takes a stool at the counter and stirs her tea absently.

"Is that right?" Katy says, curiously. "That's funny, in the fourteen or so years we've been friends, I think that's the first time I've ever heard you mention anything about any member of your family."

Geri smiles sadly, her eyes distant. "That's probably right. I guess I never really talk about them to anyone, except Herb. They are *all* gone, now, my dad, mom, sister. Yet, they're still a kind of private and very special part of my life."

She pauses and looks directly at Katy, her eyebrows pulled together in a sad frown.

"Why don't you tell *me* about them," Katy says to her friend, reaching out and touching her hand.

It's quiet for a brief moment.

Then Geri nods and says, "Okay."

She looks away into space, sighing, and gathering her thoughts for a moment before starting.

"Well, like I said, I never knew my father. Only photos. He was a soldier in an all-black unit, died in the last days of World War II. My mother raised me and Kris, my sister, alone in Long Beach. And I don't mean a constant stream of *uncles* in and out of the house either. A single parent. We lived in a federal housing project apartment, not like the solid brick buildings around Metro Rec in San Diego, more flimsy-like plywood barracks, but we never thought, *poor me*. Momma was a good woman, worked at the shipyard, loving and caring to me and Kris… "

There's a kind of hitch in her voice as she pauses for a moment; Katy notices Geri's eyes are growing more than a little moist. She's never seen her friend cry about anything. She gets up, goes to a cabinet, and returns with a box of Kleenex, which she places at the older woman's elbow.

"Thanks," Geri says, blowing her nose loudly and smiling kind of apologetically.

"Well," she continues, her gaze looking off into the distance again, "that part of our life ended at a corner grocery store, when I was eight and Kris was twelve. Mama was shot and killed in a botched robbery, you know the innocent bystander bit. Kris and I went to live with an aunt and uncle—my Dad's sister, who actually lived right there in the same housing project.

"At the time, Kris was really getting involved in a rec center basketball league for girls. She was a natural athlete. By the time she was a freshman in high school she was good—rebounder, shooter, ball handler, just *good*. Star on the freshman team. Starter as a sophomore on the varsity. But something funny was going on about that time. I was twelve by then, and would wake up sometimes and find Kris sitting on the foot of my bed, just staring down at me, a look of concern on her face. She never said what was bothering her. But I knew that she was afraid of something, keeping an eye on me, seeming to worry about how I was doing all the time. The summer between her sophomore and junior years in high school, she came to me, and asked me some funny questions about Uncle Fred. Apparently the answers satisfied her, and she never said any more. But I noticed that she continued to keep an even closer eye on me after that. When school started in the Fall she didn't seem to be doing too well. She had lost a little weight, and there were circles under her eyes. Her grades slipped big time—she'd been a straight A student the year before. And then she decided not to go out for basketball. Of course I should have put it all together, known right then and there that something terrible was going on between her and Uncle Fred, but I didn't. Guess I really didn't want to know. Just like my Aunt Ruth.

"It didn't come out until the end of winter of that year, when I came home early from school, walked in, and surprised Kris.

"She was home alone just sitting at the kitchen table, her head down on her chest, kind of sleepy-like. Not like herself at all. She'd always been a real ball of energy, you know.

"So, I asked her if high school got off early.

"She shook her head. 'Didn't go, today,' she said and sighed. 'Oh, babe, I'm sorry you had to see me like this,' she said apologetically, a look of shame on her face. 'But I guess it's time you and me had a talk, time for you to really grow up. Know what's going on with me.'

"Then, she went on and told me all about it. Uncle Fred had been making sexual advances since she was only thirteen or so. She avoided him, initially. But he kept pressing, pressing, putting on the pressure, and finally threatening to hit on *me* if she didn't give in. She was afraid to go to Aunt Ruth, who had always seemed pretty resentful about taking us both in, anyhow. And things were a lot different in those days about revealing sexual abuse to the authorities. So Kris felt there was no other way than to give in to Fred, but *only* if he promised to leave me completely alone.

"It broke my heart, because I soon realized not only what she'd done for me, but what it cost her. Once a bright, talented athlete with a promising future, she never played another basketball game after that afternoon, never went to college, never even graduated from high school, *nothing*.

"Oh, there was something she was doing, and I should have suspected that, too. She died two months after that afternoon of an overdose of heroin—"

Geri blows her nose again.

After a few moments, she continues, "Fortunately for me, Aunt Ruth threw the bum out not long after Kris died. He never got the opportunity to do to me what he'd done to her. I played basketball, ran track, and graduated from high school, then got a job, and eventually got my own place out of federal housing. When I was twenty-two I moved to San Diego, eventually passed the civil service and physical tests, and hooked up with the SDPD. That's where I met Herb. And I guess you know the rest."

Jesus, Katy swears silently.

For a minute or so it's quiet.

"I guess in some ways we pretty much have the same family background," Katy finally suggests in a low voice.

"You know it," Geri replies sadly, still frowning slightly. "In fact, when I first got that call from Gavin McCloud and he told me about you, it reminded me so much of Kris, it hurt me down deep. That first night at Metro Rec I just prayed you were going to be a real player."

Geri stops and shakes her head, the frown completely gone now. "Damn, if everything didn't work out much better than I hoped. You played college ball, graduated from Sacramento State with full honors. Became a writer. A homicide detective. So, I guess sometimes the good things balance out the bad in the long haul, you know." She nods her head.

After another minute of silence, Katy gets up and takes a tissue from the box and blows her nose. She glances over at the clock, 4:30 p.m., and suggests, "C'mon, we have a little time for a walk before we need to make our dinner reservations on the way to Arco Arena. We'll check out Sac State. It's really grown in the last eight years since you were here for my graduation."

5

They get to Arco Arena about half an hour before the game. Because the Monarchs aren't doing real well, there are plenty of good seats available. They have a spot about five rows from mid-courtside

"Hey, there's Sid," Geri says, pointing at a nicely dressed young woman sitting in the first row behind the Mercury bench. "C'mon, I'll introduce you." They go down and visit for ten or fifteen minutes with Geri's ex-player.

Just before they return to their seats, Sid confidently promises them that the Mercury are going to *cream* the Monarchs.

But the game is close, the Monarchs hanging in until the last four minutes. The score ends: Mercury 64, Monarchs 59. Adia Barnes plays well, and Katy enjoys seeing her in person despite the Sacramento team's loss. Of course Geri enjoys herself, too.

6

Later that night, at the airport, they hug goodbye, Katy swearing she will come to San Diego for an extended visit just as soon as the book is done.

As Geri starts toward the departure gate, getting into line, she turns back abruptly and shouts to Katy, "Oh, I just had a thought about the case you're working on. One of your *whys*." Then she glances at several late-arriving and impatient-looking passengers in line behind her and says, "I'll call you tomorrow evening about it." She waves, turns back, and disappears through the gate.

Katy waits until the plane takes off, thinking it was a great visit and glad that Geri finally shared about the loss of her family.

azette

SERIAL KILLER
DOROTHEA PUENTE
FOUND GUILTY OF
MULTIPLE MURDERS

STEWS, SOUPS, AND PUDDINGS

Weekends are the worst.

Usually, on Saturday you wander around aimlessly, maybe spending the morning at the old folks' park watching the different card games, then catching a movie downtown in the afternoon, and reading or watching TV at night. Then repeating this on Sunday. But it's all so strange, feeling unnatural with no schedule, nothing really to do. No one around you. Beginning with your earliest memories, you've always conformed to some kind of a daily routine governed by someone else—foster homes, school, jail, CYA. And since coming to

Sacramento, each working day has a structured routine, with people around. Familiar, comfortable. But during the weekends you are lost, at loose ends.

Except for this particular Saturday.

You sleep until 5:00 p.m., when you finally force yourself to get up, shower, dress, and go down to the 7-Eleven near the freeway and get a burrito and coffee. The burrito is tasteless and the coffee bitter and stale. You return to your apartment, but are unable to read or even watch TV. Too jumpy. Your thoughts keep returning to last night and the bathroom mirror at the apartment in Del Paso Heights. The memory is actually like some kind of weird pornographic movie, involving two people you don't know but recognize, two actors. Everything detached and unreal. Even finally glimpsing Gisela's fiery and beautiful secret hair does little to redeem the depraved nature of the shocking scene—two animals copulating. You are left cold, numb, bummed out every time you replay it in your head.

Even though you have slept most of the day, at 9:00 you crawl back into bed, and escape the recurring pornographic movie by quickly falling asleep.

2

It is almost noontime when you finally rise on Sunday morning, not really feeling well rested, even though you've slept over twenty-five hours in the last two days. You dress, trying to keep your thoughts as distant from Del Paso Heights as possible, and go outside.

It is hot already.

You wander around the block and stop, not feeling like going over to the senior citizen's park today. No. Instead you cut across several streets until you reach F, then, as if drawn by a compelling force, you turn and head downtown.

After twelve blocks you slow, reaching a residential neighborhood of aging Victorians, many in need of a painter and carpenter. Some have signs in the lower windows: ROOMS FOR RENT. Others announce: BOARDINGHOUSE. You walk another half a block, and stop in front of one of the Victorians that has been recently fixed-up and painted a steel gray with maroon and gold trim, with a newly-lettered Gothic sign announcing: ROOM & BOARD. You just stand there staring for a few minutes, wondering why you feel drawn to this particular location today. You take a step or two up the entry walk, actually onto the property and into the shade, but stop suddenly, because the temperature has dropped, plunging at least twenty degrees, and you feel chilled, rubbing your arms vigorously through your long shirt sleeves. For a moment you glance upward, half expecting to see the fuzzy darkness of the Dark Angel hovering somewhere above the trees.

But no. You're not in his shadow.

Then you look at the address and repeat it to yourself silently...

You know this place.

You read about it only last week in an article in the *Sacramento Bee*.

It was once a boardinghouse for male senior citizens, run by an old woman... her name, Dorothea Montalvo Puente. She was arrested in November of 1988 after seven bodies of old men were dug up in her back yard, apparently all once boarders at her house. She'd been cashing their Social Security checks for some time, even though they were dead. Puente was eventually tied to two more dead bodies and convicted of murdering three of the nine in 1993. She was sentenced to life without parole and was presently serving her sentence in Central California Women's Facility near Chowchilla. The funny part of it was the authorities never actually determined the cause of any of the nine deaths, but obviously suspected poison. Puente never admitted to any of the murders, so naturally she didn't reveal anything about an exotic poison. All very mysterious. As a perhaps ironic afterthought, the *Bee* stated in the last line of the article that Dorothea Puente was considered an excellent cook by her boarders, known for her stews, soups, and puddings.

You stand there for a few more minutes, then move closer to the old house, feeling a strong desire to look into the backyard where the bodies had been discovered. But it's fenced and too high to see anything, and you are freezing. Besides you don't want anyone to call the police and report a prowler. So you back off the property, retreating into the sticky heat of the day, and remain on the sidewalk staring at the spooky old place.

Despite all the fresh paint and repairs, you have an overwhelming sense that here at this specific place you are encountering real evil, almost like your first meeting with the Dark Angel. You shudder, wondering if Dorothea Montalvo Puente had ever walked in His shadow. It's possible, you decide. The article mentioned she had been in prison for a long time when she was younger. She'd been a hustler in bars, apparently doping the drinks of her customers before robbing them.

After awhile you step back off the sidewalk to allow a kid to pass on his bike. Only then do you realize that you've been standing transfixed in front of this old Victorian, staring bemused into space for a long, long time. From the angle of the sun, you guess at least an hour, if not more.

Why? you ask yourself.

Why do you care about this Victorian boardinghouse or the woman who once owned it?

Why do you feel a strong, unsettling attraction to this place?

Does it really have anything to do with you?

Maybe, but you aren't sure.

Perhaps you have been drawn here to simply confirm that a place like this actually did exist. That ten years ago, a woman lived here who was truly evil. A bad person, who did terrible things for really a very small amount of money. Her deeds more horrific than anything you could possibly imagine or do.

Bad, bad, bad.

Yes, indeed.

You turn and begin to walk away toward your apartment, rubbing the back of your neck, which is still clammy cold, feeling like you've just emerged from the chilling darkness of a graveyard vault into the light and warmth of day. You stop and look again at the old Victorian, unable to suppress another shudder.

But as you retreat you realize that your spirits have been lifted, your sensibilities sharpened. The streets, the cars, the people, the sounds around you, all seem real. And you sigh deeply, enjoying even the smell of the hot, humid day.

3

When you get home, you are relaxed, able to concentrate. You take up *Heart of Darkness*, which you now find very engaging. You finish it easily by dinnertime, then sit quietly and think about what the story means. Of course it centers on the character of Kurtz. And a transformation? Not really, more like the opposite. A regression to a more primitive, atavistic state. Leading a group of African natives, who worship him like a god, into murder, plunder, and who knows what other evil deeds. Something Kurtz could apparently not resist, despite his best intentions. The absolute power had corrupted him absolutely. But the important question that you think Joseph Conrad poses is: Did Kurtz die with a sense of remorse for his terrible behavior? His dying words, "The horror, the horror," suggest perhaps a death bed redemption, or at the very least an awareness of the evil of it all.

But you are not really sure.

The story is deep—including the odd narrative framing—compelling, Conrad's exact meaning anything but obvious.

You warm some tomato soup, make some cheese toast, and eat lost in thought, still mulling over the meaning of *Heart of Darkness* and Kurtz's possible redemption. And you wonder about Dorothea Puente, who must be 75 years old by now, sitting in a cell in a women's prison in Central California.

Is she sorry?

Is there any possibility of redemption for her?

4

As the day wanes, you begin to grow tense, anticipating another visit. Sure enough, just as night falls, His shadow darkens your room.

It is the Dark Angel, hovering in the night outside your window again. Curious, you squint and peer intently, for once taking a little more time to try and make out the details of his features. See him clearly. But it's no use. His essence is buried in a black hole that sucks in all the surrounding light, the darkness completely obscuring his features, making him an indistinct figure standing in the distance on an overcast, moonless night.

"You expected me?"

"Y-Yes," you answer.

"Then you are prepared for our trip to Del Paso Heights?"

"No, I-I—"

"No?" the Dark Angel repeats, his wing beats seeming to increase in speed and force, stirring and really chilling the air in your tiny apartment. "What do you mean, no? It is time for vindication, again. Time to take vengeance against another of your enemies."

"B-But she was my f-friend."

"Friend?"

There is a long period of silence.

Then, the Angel speaks in his characteristic low growl, but his tone this time is heavy with righteous anger. "She is an adulterous Jezebel, who has enticed your true friend, seduced him into an act of vicious betrayal of his wife and family. Doomed him. And why? Because she is lonely, misses her husband. She has betrayed your faith in her. She is a bad person, an evil person. The most vile of strumpets. She does not deserve your friendship or respect. She deserves only to taste your instrument of vengeance. Get it, *now*."

He is right.

You stumble across the room, clumsy now with your increasing sense of outrage. Gisela betrayed her husband, betrayed Wilbur, and betrayed you. She is indeed an evil Jezebel.

Bad, bad, bad.

Returning across the room, you stop in the middle of His shadow, hold the instrument of vengeance up after flipping it open, but see nothing reflected in the mirror, not even the faintest metallic glint, only the slightest shimmering disturbance in the darkness right where you stand. You and the instrument of vengeance are indeed invisible while in His shadow.

You close and put the razor in your pocket, then rub your arms briskly. It is cold, so very cold in the Dark Angel's shadow. But despite the numbing chill, you feel very confident, and, more importantly, you feel absolutely safe.

You obediently follow Him off into the night, drawn irresistibly into the recurring nightmare.

5

You are in the apartment in Del Paso Heights, quietly looking around, the Dark Angel hovering in the air outside the opened window. But Gisela is not here, the apartment unoccupied.

You wait patiently in the front room, after having glanced absently into the bathroom mirror, feeling that this is all happening to someone else. Not you. You are just watching a dark movie, a spectator with a sense of complete detachment.

At about 8:00 in the evening Gisela walks in wearing a loose fitting, blue sweatsuit, and stops abruptly when she sees you in her living room, a mixed expression on her heavily painted face—startled confusion.

"What are you doing here, Sam?" she asks, recovering her poise quickly. "How did you get in?"

"I-I've come to see you," you say almost perfectly, ignoring the second question.

"Why?" she snaps, her face flushing with anger. "I do not care to see you. You are not welcome here—"

"Oh, I-I've been here b-before," you interrupt, "l-last F-Friday n-night."

"The party?" she says, shaking her head. "You were not at the party. In fact, I am still very hurt about your refusal to come."

"Yes, I was here late that n-night," you insist, the ember of dark outrage beginning to flare up and heat your cool sense of detachment. "You didn't see me, because y-you w-were too b-b-b—" You stomp your foot and break the stammer, "—busy in the bathroom." You nod your head at the look of guilty surprise on her face. "T-That's *right*, with W-Wilbur."

She just stares at you, the guilty look gone now, replaced by an expression of shame.

"No," she whispers with absolutely no conviction in her tone. "You couldn't have… "

"I was in the hall, looking into the mirror through the c-cracked d-door. I-I saw i-it a-a-a—" Again the stammer interrupts you, but you don't even try to break it this time. Instead, you take out the ebony-handled straight razor and casually flip it open, the light glinting off its blade. "Y-Y-You betrayed me."

"*Mein Gott,*" she cries out, a look of terror settling on her features as her gaze locks on the instrument of vengeance.

"What are you going to do?" she asks in English in a subdued tone.

"Take off all your c-clothes," you order, ignoring her question.

She does nothing, obviously frightened witless.

"Now!" you shout, moving a step closer, flashing the razor in front of her eyes, jarring her from her trance.

She responds, clumsily removing her sweatshirt and bra.

"The pants and p-panties, too."

She obeys, tears welling up in her eyes and trickling down her cheeks. "You are not going to hurt me, are you, Sam?" she murmurs meekly. "We are friends."

You are able to only smile cruelly, your pulse racing, the black rage smothering any possible response.

She is standing there now, completely undressed, but covering her lower nakedness with her joined hands, her pose reminding you a little of the naked Dragon Lady at *T & A* downtown, trying to tease the audience of bad people. The disappointing image only further infuriates you.

"Take your hands away," you order hoarsely. "I want to s-see all of you."

She sobs almost uncontrollably now, but her hands drop to her sides in complete surrender.

Beautiful, orange, secret hair.

Soft, dry, silky, not unruly and wet like the other night.

Oh, no.

No, indeed.

You are almost transfixed by the glorious sight, stirred by a strong compulsion to reach out, touch her in her private place. You begin to do it; but suddenly, in your mind, you visualize a distracting image of a hairy creature with an erect, purple-veined, throbbing penis, grunting on the commode, beckoning—

You jerk your hand back, as if it had actually touched the vile appearing appendage.

"Sam?" she says in a strained, timid voice. "Please, do not hurt me."

Strike, now, the Dark Angel orders in your head, activating you from your bemused state.

"Jezebel," you shout perfectly with icy righteous indignation, quickly stepping in close, and smashing her in the jaw with your left fist.

The orange-headed strumpet crumples at your feet, a startled expression frozen on her painted face.

6

Later, in the mirror, you arrange the fiery patch on the front of your baldhead. Then you glance down at your crotch at the beautiful, fine, soft, orange, pubic hair above your partially stiffened manhood.

You sigh and smile—

Then you suddenly frown, after spotting a bloody handprint on the counter just left of the sink, a disturbing sight. You turn, snatch the lone washrag off the bathtub rack and wipe back and forth across the counter, smearing the print. Then you carefully remove and wrap both sticky patches in the washcloth, glance with disdain at the empty commode seat, and hurry out from the small bathroom.

After dressing, you check carefully around the apartment, again aware of the strange, detached feeling of walking in someone else's dream, seeing things through someone else's eyes. Everything appears to be the same as when you arrived, natural and peaceful, except for the naked woman lying quite still on the living room rug, her blood-soaked, sweatshirt laying across her chest.

"It is time to go," the Dark Angel advises, entering through the opened window.

"Yes."

You step back into His shadow, and follow Him out the front door, feeling the now-familiar jittery rush of moral vindication, after having introduced another enemy to the instrument of vengeance.

A bad person, very bad.

Yes, indeed.

7

You are back home, sitting on the edge of your bed, after cleaning and hiding the ebony razor and washcloth-wrapped prizes under the mattress. You still feel exhilarated, knowing that despite the lateness of hour it will be much later before you'll be able to go to sleep, if at all tonight. You will be tired tomorrow at work.

The thought of the laundry reminds you that you have probably unconsciously drawn the authorities closer to yourself by punishing the adulterer. They will more than likely come visiting the laundry soon. Poking around, asking questions. You frown, the thought destroying some of your euphoria. It will be a long day, perhaps stressful. Maybe you shouldn't go.

Call in sick!

No. That would indeed cause suspicion to focus on you. Regardless of how you feel, tomorrow morning you will have to go to work.

For some reason, you suddenly think of the two young women cleaning up at the party Friday night, and the memory of them makes you groan, "Oh, no." They will be able to give the police your bundled-up description, if interviewed. The authorities may now be able to link you to the punished Jezebel, perhaps the others.

You shudder, thinking about being caught and sent to some place even more terrible than CYA for a long, long time—a dark, scary thought.

So, after some consideration, you decide that tomorrow you will not wear your blue, roll-down, stocking cap.

No, indeed.

You search through your closet and finally find a black Giants baseball cap with an orange SF logo on the front. It's wrinkled and dusty, the bill broken down. Despite its scruffy condition, you will wear it to the laundry tomorrow. It is not much of a disguise really, but it will have to do.

Then you lie down on the bed, still dressed, your thoughts drifting, finally settling on Father Nathan. He seems like a figure from the extremely distant past now. Too far away to help. Not quite a complete stranger, more like someone you have read about in a book, like the focal character from *Heart of Darkness*, the man, Kurtz.

A SIGNIFICANT ENTRY IN THE DESCRIPTION COLUMN

K aty awakens relaxed Sunday morning after the terrific visit with Geri, finding she can now fully concentrate on her novel, *The Indigo Man*. She works diligently all day on a critical scene near the end of the book.

The indigo man believes his dyed color is beginning to fade, and, somehow, develops a corollary theory that this actually indicates he is cured of the fatal defect in his character that resulted in a judgment of color thirty-three years ago.

In the scene, the indigo man has stumbled upon a young Freeman boy, playing untended by a stream, tossing bread crumbs to fish. The boy does not notice the indigo man as he creeps closer, entranced by the boy's beautiful features and curly, golden hair. He almost gets close enough to reach out and touch the boy, who despite the angle of sunlight, suddenly senses a foreign presence. He scoots back out of the blinding sunlight and, frightened by the appearance of the indigo man, the boy cries out and scrambles up the slope to his mother, who has suddenly appeared after hearing the boy shouting with fear. Angry, the mother and boy stone the indigo man, who remains standing in place, accepting the abuse. He remains frozen for a long time after the two depart, examining his inner feelings, trying to determine if, despite the fact that he did not trigger aversive conditioning, his attraction to the boy may have still been sexual in nature. He is not sure, but his confidence is badly shaken...

Katy works into the evening on the scene, skillfully leaving both the reader and the indigo man in the dark as to the true nature of his attraction to the boy. Is the indigo man *cured* or *not?*

The scene that Katy will partially recreate later in the indigo man's journal from his perspective will demonstrate his deteriorating confidence in everything, including the belief that his color is fading. He will suspect he's just been fooling himself and fears he will never rid himself of color, that he is going to die with it. This makes him very despondent, for he feels doomed, his indigo color an eternal evil burden.

Katy is finally forced to stop for dinner by a protesting stomach, growling with hunger, so loud it disturbs her thinking. Reluctantly she gets up and throws a frozen dinner of macaroni and cheese into the microwave.

Wow! The clock next to the timer indicates it is after 9:00 at night.

She glances out the window. It's been dark for some time.

Katy smiles to herself, as she waits for her dinner to heat, realizing that she feels really upbeat about the book again. She pours herself a glass of milk. Maybe I *will* finish a complete draft before BayCon, she thinks hopefully.

Half way through her meal the phone rings.

It's Johnny.

"Katy, I'm sorry to disturb your writing," he says, "but the perp has just hit another victim. In Del Paso Heights, near McClellan Air Force Base. A young woman only recently moved here from Germany, married to an Airman. But—get this, partner—she has a job in the laundry over at Sutter General Hospital, which is very close to Mary Ann's apartment. Just a coincidence—who knows? Anyhow, Long John is here ranting and raving, you know, directing traffic, and he wants you in on this full time, *now*. The press is all over the place and knows about our boy taking hair patches from the heads of his previous victims, but not about the pubic hair, yet, thank God. The shit is starting to hit the fan big time, partner."

"I'll be right over, Johnny," Katy says, consciously trying to hold intact the enthusiasm of a moment ago, about finishing the book on time.

No such luck.

The upbeat feeling slips from her mental grasp, like water through cupped fingers, and she sighs deeply with regret.

"Give me the address," she says, unable to keep the edge from her tone.

2

Katy ignores the Channel Ten and Channel Three cameras, the extended microphones and questions, as she tries to shoulder her way through the noisy media picket line outside the apartment in Del Paso Heights—

Then, from her right, a reporter shouts out in a clear voice over the crowd noise, "Hey, Green Hornet, when you gonna catch this current nut case... Red Chief?"

Red Chief?

Puzzled, she slows momentarily, then smiles in spite of herself, recognizing the allusion to the famous O. Henry short story, "The Ransom of Red Chief." She rolls her eyes, making a mock face of disgust at the grinning reporter and continues past the four uniformed police holding the crowd back, hearing Long John's high-pitched nasal voice as she reaches the apartment's open door.

The front room is abuzz with people talking and milling around—

more uniformed police, the forensic specialists, the coroner and his people, and the other three homicide detectives assigned the case.

"Hey, partner, that was fast," Johnny says, coming up and hugging her. "Do you want to look around the other rooms until it thins out in here?"

"Okay," Katy answers, but pauses momentarily to pull on a pair of latex gloves and glance at the victim. At that moment, McHugh and Bundy slip away from the group surrounding the corpse, greet her with brief nods, and head toward the front door.

"They're going to start interviewing some of the immediate neighbors," Johnny explains over his shoulder, leading her in the opposite direction down the hallway.

"Only one bedroom," he announces, as they reach the room at the end of the hall. "The forensic team has been over everything in here already."

Katy wanders around the small bedroom, trying to get a feel for the woman who lived here, noticing the unmade queen-sized bed, and the shoes, underwear, and other dirty clothing scattered about on the foot of the bed, on a pair of unmatched chairs, even the floor.

"What was her name?"

"Gisela Huntington," Johnny answers, trailing behind Katy.

She stops and nods to herself. "Gisela, you were one messy person," she murmurs under her breath, after kneeling and glancing under the bed at several magazines covered with dust bunnies.

"Yeah, sure looks like it," Johnny agrees, obviously overhearing her observation. "She's been living alone for a little while now, maybe that explains it. Her husband was recently sent back to Germany on TAD. Captain Silver is going to try to get in touch with him a little later tonight. It's still pretty early tomorrow morning there."

Katy takes one more look around the bedroom, not noticing anything important, then wanders back down the hall to the bathroom.

The first thing she spots is the smeared blood next to the sink. She peers at the smudge closely. "Forensics seen this already?"

Johnny replies, "Yeah. They think it's a handprint and the blood is more than likely hers. They've taken a sample and a couple of pictures."

She glances again at the smeared handprint then down at the floor, which is spotless, then over at the empty towel rack. He must've put his bloody hand down on the counter… then noticed it, grabbed a towel or washcloth from over there, and partially wiped it up. The print indicates he was facing the mirror, like he probably did at Mary Ann's.

Why? she asks herself, peering at her own image in the mirror.

What did he expect to see?

Himself.

But doing what?

Why was he so curious to see himself just after cutting a woman's throat?

Did he see the same thing at Mary Ann's?

Would he have been just as curious to see himself if there'd been a mirror in the alley off the K Street Mall?

She reads no answers in the mirror, only a slightly frustrated expression on the face peering back at her.

Katy turns and looks over the rest of the tiny bathroom.

Nothing else obvious here.

No other blood drops.

Wait a sec—

Where's the bloody towel or washcloth or whatever he used to smudge the handprint?

"What are you looking for?," Johnny asks, as Katy checks in back of the commode then into the bathtub.

"Well, what about the washcloth he used to smear it? Forensics pick it up?"

Johnny rubs his nose. "I'll check, but I don't remember them picking anything up in here except a blood sample. Maybe our boy took it with him? He'd need something to wrap up his trophies."

They move up the hall, back toward the front room, Katy glancing at the bare walls and down at the frayed, dirty rug, spotting no blood drops, nothing of interest. She stops as the worn hall carpet ends at the front room's stained rug, the two unmatched in color and design—the sight and general feel of the apartment depressing her.

After a moment Katy turns and asks Johnny, "Who found the body?"

"Wynne Stennet, a young woman from the apartment next door. She's a friend of the victim, along with her roommate, Debbie Chudulsky. Both Sacramento City College students. Patrick and Harlan are taking their statements, probably right *now*. Anyhow, Wynne comes over to visit around 8:30 p.m. The front door is wide open and she sees Gisela lying there naked, her throat cut, her bloody sweatshirt covering her breasts. Of course she freaks out, but fortunately doesn't go in and touch anything. She returns next door to her place, and her roommate, Debbie, calls 911."

Katy nods thoughtfully.

Most everyone has cleared out of the front room by now, except for Long John and two of the coroner's men, waiting to bag the body and take it to the morgue.

"I'll see you later at headquarters," Captain Silver says to them, as he backs toward the open front door. "I'm going out to face the media, then I have to make that call to Germany."

"Yeah, we're going to meet with Patrick and Harlan downtown in the command center at 11:00," Johnny says, walking the Captain out. "See you after that."

Katy stays and looks over the body.

Gisela is really young—twenty at the most. Lovely hair, pretty girl. Shapely. The ghastly crimson slash across her throat is shocking.

Sad.

A patch of hair about the size of a silver dollar is missing from both the young woman's forehead and her pudendum.

Katy kneels down and carefully checks the victim's arms, hands, and fingernails.

No defensive marks again.

Probably nothing microscopic under the fingernails either, she thinks.

No struggle. Same as before.

Johnny kneels beside her.

"Of course the forensic people think it's the same guy cut Pearl and Mary Ann. He hit Gisela in the jaw first, like the others—see the tell-tale bruise? Then he cut her throat, using her sweatshirt as a shield to prevent blood spraying him and the room. No signs of any sex again. No semen on the floor. Nothing. He didn't take anything except the two hair swatches. And maybe a towel or washcloth from the bathroom. They have no idea what he was doing at the mirror in the bathroom after he cut her throat… "

Johnny pauses, rubbing his nose, then adds, "Long John is really pissed about the hair patch leak to the press, thinks it probably came late yesterday or earlier today from someone in forensics."

"I bet he's angry," Katy says, standing back up and sighing deeply, still staring down at the victim.

What does this pretty young German woman have in common with the others, women who have been around the park a time or two?

What attracted him to each of them?

There must be something.

She has a sudden flash of insight.

Both Mary Ann and Gisela had red hair, but Pearl was Afro-American, with dark hair, except she did *dye* her pubic hair pink. *I wonder—?*

"Johnny, let's check with Pearl's boyfriend, what's his name?"

"Ah... Charles White."

"Ask Charles if Pearl recently wore her hair dyed red or reddish blonde?"

Johnny jots a note in his C.S. notebook, then snaps his fingers, obviously catching on to her thought process. "All redheads."

Katy nods, walking around the front room. "Did they get any good latent prints this time?"

"A few partials, but probably nothing good enough for a computer match. It would've been nice if he hadn't smeared that friggin' handprint in the bathroom. This dude just doesn't leave much behind."

She walks around the body once more, then says, "Okay," to the coroner's men.

Johnny follows her out of the apartment, stripping off his latex gloves, back out into the night, where Katy takes a deep breath of fresh but muggy air, before taking off her gloves.

The media crowd has broken up by now, after recording Captain Silver's apparently brief statement, and there's no one around to pester either of them with questions.

"Well, of course it's the *same* guy," Katy says, staring off into the clouded night sky. "But we still have all the *same* damn questions. We can assume he left through the front door if it was open. So, did anyone see him leaving? Or coming? What is he looking at in the mirrors? What do these three women have in common, with the exception of maybe red hair? Does he actually know all of them? Is that why there's never any struggle? Why is he taking the head and pubic hair swatches? And maybe a washcloth or towel, this time? Did he wrap the patches in the cloth?"

She shakes her head, annoyed and frustrated by the questions.

"Let's get a cup of coffee before we meet with Patrick and Harlan," Johnny suggests, rubbing his nose, and watching the coroner's men leave the apartment, lock the door, and seal it with yellow C.S. tape.

3

At 11:00 p.m. all four detectives meet in the command center, McHugh and Bundy looking a little smug about something.

Even before they all get comfortably seated, Patrick begins. "We talked briefly to the two girls next door, the one who found Gisela and her roommate. They didn't actually see our perp tonight, but he may have been here for a party *Friday* night. They both talked a little about a guy from her work who she was pretty cozy with... "

He pauses, checking his C.S. notebook. "Wilbur Cox, big guy, but not a stutterer, and married," he reads from the book, then looks up, his voice rising slightly in pitch. "And our bundled up, stuttering giant did make an appearance much later Friday night, and asked specifically for Gisela. So he *knew* her. Most everyone was gone by then, but these two girls got a good look at him, when they were cleaning up, and their description jibes with what we had before. Husky—about 6-foot-5-inch, stutterer, wearing a stocking cap and long-sleeved tan shirt buttoned at the neck, the whole bit. Except he's a little younger than we figured—only twenty-one, at most. Anyhow, we hope to get both girls downtown with a composite artist some time tomorrow morning."

"Good work," Johnny says. "Can we place him or this Wilbur guy at the scene, tonight?"

"I don't know," Patrick replies. "Like I said, the girls didn't see anyone. But we haven't had time to check all the surrounding apartments... Oh, and Harlan has something else kinda interesting."

"Yeah, Dr. Wright called me at home earlier today," Bundy says. "Said it sounds like our boy has a hair fetish. Which has always been clinically common, but is kind of a minor trend right now, really catered to in porno. Extremely hairy beaver shots flashed in some of the magazines—*sorry*, Katy. And a few videos available focusing on unshaven, hairy women. So, our boy may have a collection of these kinda mags and vids, maybe goes to hairy porno flicks. We'll check these places out when we get the composite to show... Oh, another thing. Dr. Wright thinks the guy takes the hair patches, maybe even carries them around with him, because they probably stimulate his hair fantasies, or maybe he just simply likes the feel of them. You know, kinda like a kid liking the feel and nuzzling his favorite blanket or teddy bear?"

"Yuk," Katy says, making a face of disgust at Harlan. "Gross."

He shrugs back, tosses up his hands, and responds defensively, "Hey, Katy, nothing, and I mean nothing, surprises me about a perp anymore."

At that point she shifts the discussion, asking, "Anyone figured out yet or even have an idea what he's doing in front of the mirrors?"

Johnny rubs his nose. The other two just shake their heads.

"C'mon, any guesses?"

After a long silence, Johnny gets up, fills in a couple of entries in the description and question columns on his chalkboard.

Then he turns, and says, "Well, tomorrow, Patrick and Harlan, you guys keep checking with the neighbors, see if anyone actually saw him coming or going *tonight*, and make sure we get a copy of that composite drawing when you get it, okay? Harlan, your idea about checking around the porno movie places and magazine stands with the drawing is a good one. First thing in the morning, I'm going to check on the forensic report on Pearl and then our computer description. And if he's that young, I'm going to clear a special request to CYA, too. Probably have another early afternoon press conference with the Chief and Captain Silver. Later, Katy and I are going to Sutter General Hospital, where Gisela worked a 3:00 to 11:00 p.m. shift Monday through Friday. Talk to her boss and this Wilbur Cox guy, maybe some of the other laundry employees, show them the composite. Look around there. Play it by ear, you know. Anyone got anything else to talk about?"

"Yes," Katy says. "Let's keep the description and composite of the perp *out* of the press as long as possible, so we don't alert him. Like we did until the very end on the Double Jack case. We already let out his description on the street with your C.I.s, and you guys are going to show it around at porno places. That's okay. I don't think the media will talk to any of those people, at least right away. But, Johnny, let's *not* show it around the hospital laundry, yet, and for sure nothing at the press conferences. Maybe you guys can ask the two girlfriend neighbors not to mention anything about the composite to the press."

"Okay, probably a good idea," Johnny agrees, nodding thoughtfully. Then he says, "I'm going in to meet with Captain Silver, now. Let's all touch base here late tomorrow morning... Say about 11:30, okay?"

4

Katy is pooped when she finally gets home, but notices her message-waiting light flashing on the phone. She punches the button.

It's Geri in San Diego:

"Had a wonderful time. Don't you forget about that visit down here real soon either, you hear. Also I had a thought about your case, one of your questions. The one about why the perp is taking the swatches of hair? Now, I don't know much about the psychology of sociopaths or psychos, that's your department. But I do know from experience on the street that people take what they don't have and need or at least *think* they need. Just an observation. Hope it helps. Love you, girl."

Katy hangs up the phone, goes into the bathroom before getting ready for bed, and stares thoughtfully at herself in the mirror, rewinding the investigation tape in her head and letting some of the visual images and thoughts replay again:

Mirrors
Blood drops
Bloody handprint
Bundled up in this hot weather, including a roll-down stocking cap
Mouse's pale description, patting his chest and *the top of his head*
Patches of hair taken from heads and pubic areas
Fetishes
People take what they don't have...

"Oh, Jesus."

Of course!

No hair. What's it called?

And he must be trying on the damn patches at the mirrors.

Why didn't I fucking think of this before?

She rushes to the phone in the bedroom and speed dials Johnny at home.

The phone rings four times, then an out of breath answer, "Hello?"

"He's *hairless*, partner," she says much too loudly, unable to keep the excitement from her voice. "Bald, no hair any place on his body, including the pubic area. There's a medical term for the condition—can't quite come up with it, right now. And I think he's actually trying on the patches at the scenes, then admiring himself in the mirrors—at least at Mary Ann's and Gisela's apartments. That's why he's always bundled up even during this hot weather spell, hiding his hairless condition. That's why Mouse patted his chest *and* head at Reds. We need to include the hairless condition in the computer requests. If he's done time we've got him, partner." She stops to catch her breath.

"That's really great, Katy!" Johnny says, matching her enthusiasm. "I'll upgrade the computer searches, including the one to CYA first thing in the morning... "

Johnny's voice fades out, a thought competing for Katy's attention: *No hair on his body or head.* The image triggers something at the back of her mind.

Something.

She can't quite retrieve it though.

"... Katy, you okay?"

"Yes, I'm fine," she says to Johnny. "Just tired and drifting. But kind of excited."

"Well, try to settle down and get a good night's rest," he says. "Things are going to be popping tomorrow. I feel that special tingle now, you know, just before a case breaks wide open."

"Yeah, me too," she says. But with her it's actually more than a sudden tingling. More like a gradual buildup and spread of an electrical charge, as they close in at the end of the hunt—sort of like in junior high school science, the class holding hands in a closed circuit, hooked up to a magneto, as the teacher gradually winds up the magneto. She feels it in her hands now, slowly working up her arms, her neck, down her back, her groin.

Yeah, they were getting close.

But she senses they would be even closer if she could just pull that *something* up—but exactly what... ?

"Good night, kiddo."

"Good night, Johnny," she answers in a detached voice.

She hangs up the phone and two minutes later crawls into bed, still feeling unsettled about the image of a giant, completely hairless perp; the image does not quite ring a bell, but she knows it *should*.

Another *why*.

Katy turns over and sighs deeply.

I'll sleep on it tonight.

Maybe it'll come to me in the morning.

RED CHIEF

t 3:05 Monday afternoon, when you arrive at work quite a bit later than usual, you find the machines quiet, everyone still in the hallway in front of the laundry, milling about nervously, chattering about Gisela to each other, most of the women speaking rapidly in Spanish.

A confusing hubbub.

"Say, *esé*, you hear about this Red Chief dude and Gisela?" Danny asks, as you stop near him, Terry, and Wilbur, the three clustered in the hallway in front of the first laundry chute. "They say he scalped her, man."

You nod. "C-Channel three n-news at n-noon."

Wilbur says nothing, but has a strange, kind of preoccupied expression on his face. Terry looks a little more confused than normal and a bit rattled by the break in routine.

"Cops are here already," Danny adds, pointing in the direction of Mr. Clark's office.

Oh, that's great news.

You reach up and tug the bill of the Giants baseball cap. Good thing you wore it today, instead of your stocking cap. Maybe they won't even notice you—

Suddenly Mr. Clark's chat the other day pops into your mind, his concern about the *mental behavior that got you sent to CYA*. You're disturbed by the recollection, because it's possible that his concerns might connect you to Gisela's death. He could be in there right now telling the police all about it. Maybe even telling them about the other girl long ago? And that you had been released from CYA only four months ago? Still on probation? Giving them your P.O.'s telephone number—?

"Okay," Wilbur says to you, Terry, and Danny in an uncharacteristically subdued tone. "Let's get to work."

Shelley herds the women off toward the mangle.

In a few moments the big machines are all started up and making their music, but the sounds are not quite so comforting this afternoon.

No, indeed.

You work at the extractor, trying to balance the first washed load, but you're not paying full attention. You can't help glancing repeatedly at the closed office door. Any moment now you expect them to come out, perhaps with drawn guns, to arrest you. Then they will handcuff and take you away to jail and a trial. Of course you will be convicted and eventually sent off to prison with other bad people. And there you will be locked away where it is cold and dark, more than likely all by yourself... Just like that time long ago in the pantry at Daddy Wigs.

You almost cry out, choking off a sob of agony and glancing over at Wilbur and Danny to make sure they don't notice your anguish.

For a few moments you feel faint, your head light, your legs shaky. Which is actually a good thing, because at the same time you turn weak-kneed, you're overwhelmed with a sense of panic, a strong compulsion to flee, to escape this trap. But because of your rubbery legs and disorientation, you remain in place, hanging on to the overhead control box for support. An anchor.

You won't run, you decide, your thoughts clearing. Not now. No one has talked to you, accused you of anything. In fact, no one has even come out of that office, yet.

So, you get a grip on yourself. You breathe deeply and center, regaining control of your legs, and continue working while listening to the music; but you are unable to completely calm your racing pulse or resist glancing every sixty seconds or so at Mr. Clark's closed office door.

Time passes slowly on the clock near the office, taking an eternity to tick off each minute.

Still, no one comes out.

What could they be talking about in there?

The wait is maddening.

You're just dropping a pair of balanced halves into the extractor, when the office door flies open, and Mr. Clark emerges by himself, hurrying right across in your direction.

"Oh, n-no," you whisper to yourself.

Dread knots your stomach muscles. You feel sick.

Just as he reaches the dryer behind the women feeding the mangle, Mr. Clark veers forty-five degrees to your right in the direction of the two washers, shouting and waving his arm. He stops at the bleach urn, after finally catching Wilbur's attention over the sounds of the big machines.

Surprisingly, Mr. Clark did not so much as even glance your way.

The two of them return to the office together.

What's going on? you ask yourself.

What are they doing in there with Wilbur?

After ten minutes, Wilbur comes out of the office with a funny expression on his face—still preoccupied, but he looks really shaken now, too. He says something to Yolanda, who nods and goes into the office herself.

Maybe everyone in the laundry will have to go in one at a time and talk to the police. You hope not, because you can't do it. Not now. You know you will be too locked up with the funnytalk. Which will be incriminating, because you realize that it's highly probable the two women at the apartment in Del Paso Heights have already told the police about your speech defect. If so, when they talk to you, they will know it was *you* there Friday night, even though you are not now wearing your roll-down, stocking cap. You pull the Giants baseball cap down even more over your sweaty brow, the gradually rising temperature of the laundry appearing to close in around you, gripping you tightly, like a giant invisible hand, slowly squeezing every drop of moisture from your body.

Trapped.

You shudder.

You should not have come to work today.

Yolanda steps out of the office, followed by Mr. Clark and the two detectives, a man and a woman.

They are leaving!

You work your way carefully around to the backside of the extractor, revealing only a partial view of your head and shoulders to the others across the laundry. But the two police officers only glance around casually, paying no more attention to you than anyone else.

You watch Mr. Clark and the detectives disappear into the hallway, only then realizing you've been holding your breath ever since they stepped out of the office. Sighing deeply, you feel a little flare of elation. The detectives don't *know* about you, because they would've come for you if they did. Mr. Clark must not have said anything about you to them.

Why didn't he?

Because of Father Nathan?

Or maybe he just doesn't suspect you. That's most likely.

You pick up two halves with the crane, balance them, then drop the load into the extractor.

You should feel even better, but you realize the investigation is still getting closer, even though they may not know about you quite yet. It's really only a matter of time, now. And there is something else bothering you, something nibbling at the back of your mind. Closing your eyes, you center more fully, trying to relax each limb at a time, just like Father Nathan taught you at CYA. Still, you are unable to completely relax, wipe out the last hour of tension. Instead, in your mind's eye you see the female detective again, glancing briefly in your direction. She is tall, graceful, with beautiful golden-red hair worn in a short ponytail. A curious but pleasant expression on her handsome face.

You think… yes! You *know* her.

Someplace, somewhere, you have met before.

"... Sam, Sam?"

It is Wilbur trying to catch your attention.

You nod at him.

"Take a break, man," he says, lifting the extractor control box out of your hand.

2

For the rest of the shift you are unsettled, primarily concerned about the police officers coming back to arrest you, but also trying to place the female detective. You have never been arrested or in trouble here in Sacramento, so it's really unlikely you've met her here before. And yet, you feel you know her from somewhere.

Perhaps in the past?

Yes, you decide after another moment's thought. That's it, of course. You must have known her down south.

At CYA?

No, before that.

But where?

When?

Frustrated, you struggle consciously and unsuccessfully with the problem until 10:15 p.m., when Mr. Clark dismisses the shift early, because of the exceptional mugginess hanging heavily in the basement's air—one of the industrial fans is down for repair. There is a rush to escape the oppressive laundry atmosphere, everyone drenched with sweat but happy about getting off work before 11:00— a rare treat—laughing and joking loudly together.

Everyone except you, hanging back by yourself.

Preoccupied with your own tenuous freedom, you sense that it may be very important to place the face of the red-headed detective. You are absolutely certain you know her from sometime in the distant past.

When?

Where?

3

At your studio apartment, you flip on the TV as your canned chili and minute rice cooks on the two-burner stove in the kitchen nook.

The Channel 10 local news is just ending, the summary of the main storyline... They have been talking about Gisela, linking her to the two other women, saying they were all viciously murdered and scalped by the same homicidal maniac, and referring to him flippantly as *Red Chief.*

Stupid name.

Agitated by the inaccurate characterization, you begin to return to the kitchen, but hesitate a moment, as a woman's face comes on the screen, her attractive features, especially her eyes, holding your attention.

"Good evening," she says, seeming to peer directly at you. "This is *Saints or Sinners?*, and I am Serra Melendez. Tonight I have two very special guests, who everyone in the Capitol wants to meet. Miss Katy Green and Mr. John Cato, homicide detectives with the Sacramento Police Department. You all know them better from newspapers and TV as the Green Hornet and Cato."

It's them.

The same two detectives from earlier today at the laundry.

The Green Hornet and Cato—

Of course!

You smile to yourself.

It has really been a long time, but you recognize her, now.

Yes, indeed.

You forget about your dinner on the stove a few steps around the corner in the kitchen, and you stand in place, entranced by the TV program, especially when the camera moves in on the young woman, Katy Green. You hadn't remembered her name. Too long ago.

During the first series of ads, you bring your dinner into the main room and watch the rest of the program, eating absently, particularly intrigued by the last few minutes of conversation.

"... And you had no relatives to take you in?"

"No... Actually my mother's sister, my only other relative was killed in the car wreck that night, too."

"So, you were raised in a series of foster homes in San Diego by *strangers*?"

"That's right. I lived in four different foster homes from the age of ten until I graduated from high school."

"And *that* background, *that* life style is what formed your character... made you want to study Police Science at Sac State, write stories or books about offbeat characters, go into law enforcement, and eventually be a homicide investigator, tracking down *sick* sociopaths like Double Jack?"

"Actually I think you do learn a *lot* of good things being raised in a group home situation—you know, how to share, cooperate, etc. But to your point, I was personally more influenced by a female police officer who was my coach in a summer PAL basketball league in my junior and senior years in high school. She was my role model. Her name is Geri Robinson, and she taught me to respect myself and strive to be all I could be... "

Yes, you think, as the program winds down.

It *is* her, no question.

You smile thinly, remembering Katy Green said she had lived in four foster homes. You must've lived in at least a dozen before CYA.

How ironic seeing her like this again after all these years.

Then, you frown, realizing it is even more ironic that Katy Green is now hunting you. Trying to catch you and send you away. Not a foster home placement, either. And she's real close.

Yes, indeed.

You shiver.

Then, you get up and flip off the TV, and take your dishes into the kitchen sink. You slowly drink a glass of water, your thoughts drifting back...

You must've been only seven or maybe eight.

You close your eyes and you can see her, as she looked fourteen or fifteen years ago, coming home from her job at Burger King. Watching through the cracked door as she combs her shoulder-length, reddish-blonde hair. Then spotting the underarm tufts of golden-red. And finally the magnificent, reddish-golden, secret hair. So long ago, but still so vivid in your memory.

You blink, seeing her current image again.

Of course she's older, a grown woman now. And her hair is no longer shoulder-length and not quite so red, either—she's more a strawberry blonde. Perhaps she tints it, you tell yourself, as your interest naturally shifts and focuses on her secret hair.

Is it still the same?

A tiny, soft patch?

Reddish-golden?

And beautiful?

The glorious intensity of the fantasy makes the blood rush in your veins, the breath catch in your throat.

You choke.

Tears come to your eyes and you suddenly cough, explosively. For a moment or two you fear that you are going to heave up your dinner. But you take another sip of water, swallow carefully, and dry your eyes with a dishtowel. You suck in a deep breath and let it out slowly.

For now you are fine.

4

Later, just after crawling into bed, you unexpectedly hear His hoarse, throaty voice in your head.

We must visit her.

"W-Why?" you cry out, alarmed by the suggestion implicit in the Dark Angel's statement.

For the same reason as the others, He says.

"No!"

Yes.

"B-B-B—"

You throw back the covers and slip from bed, upset by the direction of the conversation.

Yes, it is important that we find and visit her.

"B-But she isn't an e-enemy," you insist.

Oh, but she is, He says emphatically.

You shake your head, stomach muscles beginning to tighten with growing dread.

Yes, the very worst of your enemies. For she is the beginning of all the bad things, the origin of the need for vindication. If not for her, none of this would've happened. Not even CYA.

"B-But she intended n-no harm."

Her intent is not a factor, the Dark Angel insists, a ruthless advocate for His own point of view.

"Y-Y-Yes it i-i-i—" you stammer ineffectively, only able to stamp your bare foot in vain.

She is the ultimate cause of all your problems, He repeats loudly in your head.

You can't believe the stubborn position He is taking.

"No, s-she was a friend back t-then."

Friend? You are joking, the Dark Angel says, in an impatient, derisive tone. *She never cared anything about you back then. What did she do when she finally caught you spying on her?*

You don't even try to answer, your confidence crumbling, shaken now by His relentless argument. The girl had screamed when she first caught you looking at her, even called you a number of filthy names, then made a big fuss to the foster parents—

And then what happened? Do you remember?

Of course you remember. You were quickly sent off to the transient home at Daddy Wigs for a second time, then finally another foster home—the fourth placement in less than a year. And you never saw her again until today at the hospital laundry, and again on TV tonight.

So let us not get confused about friendship, the voice growls deeply. *Her intent now is not very friendly, either. Far from it. She and her partner are exceptionally successful at what they do. You heard what they are called—the Green Hornet and Cato, after a pair of comic book super heroes. But these two are hunters of real men. She intends to hunt you down unmercifully. And you will be taken away again, only to a very dangerous place this time, a dreary place probably even more depressing than the California Youth Authority at Chula Vista. For a long time, perhaps forever.*

It is true.

Impossible to refute.

She intends to do just that. And she is getting very close.

Katy Green is little different than the other three. All real enemies...

The Dark Angel pauses, then adds, *But she will be the last—*

"The l-last?"

Yes, He says in a low and persuasive voice. *After she tastes the instrument of vengeance, it will be finally finished. Over. Forever. You will be completely free of all your enemies, no longer requiring my assistance. I will take back the instrument of vengeance. You will in all likelihood never see me again. You will be free.*

Free?

You will not have to ever walk in His shadow again?

No longer condemned to a life of eternal damnation?

He will let you go?

It is difficult to believe.

Believe it, the Dark Angel says, privy to even your innermost concerns.

A quiet minute passes.

You are convinced.

"But how do w-we find her?"

For another moment there is silence.

Then: *I can find her, if need be. But maybe she will come to us. Yes, that may be easier and much wiser.* He makes a sound almost like a chuckle.

"I-I don't understand."

Call her the Dark Angel suggests, then pauses, obviously working out the details of his idea. *Yes,* he continues, *and then tell her who you are, confess what you have done, say you are sorry. That you saw the TV show, and realized that once long ago the two of you lived in the same foster home in San Diego. Emphasize you are truly remorseful about the vindications. You wish to give yourself up, but only to her, an old friend. No one else, no other detectives or police officers present. That you want to meet her somewhere private, alone.*

"She would n-never meet m-me alone. The other authorities would n-never a-allow i-it. A-At the very least, t-they would be near in h-hiding."

Maybe it would not make any difference, if you can get close enough before they can stop you. You pick the spot carefully, anticipating where they will be positioned to observe the meeting. Take it into account. Then, think like a magician. The art of misdirection. Strike when they are not expecting it, from a position they do not anticipate. Then successfully escape while they are still paralyzed in a state of shocked surprise.

You are tired, confused.

You blink.

Think about it.

Yes, you will think about it.

Plan carefully.

You will need to plan very carefully. You will need to see them without yourself being seen. Maybe you will need a disguise along with an appropriate spot to use that disguise, with an escape route mapped out ahead of time.

You have the glimmer of an idea. Just a hint, but...

Maybe it can be done. You nod to yourself.

You can do it.

Yes, indeed.

Then, silence for a few more minutes.

He is completely gone from your thoughts now. You can relax, a weight off your mind. Think more clearly. Plan.

But not tonight, tomorrow; you will think and develop your idea tomorrow morning.

Exhausted by the stressful day and the intense discussion with the Dark Angel, you crawl back into bed and close your eyes, only one thought lingering now in your head: Freedom.

THE CIRCLE CLOSES

T he four homicide detectives meet Monday morning in the command center at SPD headquarters downtown, shortly before 11:30 a.m.

Johnny brings McHugh and Bundy up to date on Katy's late night revelation about their perp's bald, hairless condition, and explains about him displaying himself in the mirrors wearing the victim's hair patches. Then Johnny makes the appropriate entry in the description column and turns back to face them, a slight frown on his face.

"That's the good news," he says, picking up a folder from his desk. "The forensic report on Pearl LeDoux doesn't really add much. You can all read it and judge for yourselves." He distributes copies.

"Our boy just isn't leaving anything behind... "

He pauses and rubs his nose. "The *Boss* is really jerking Long

John's chain, because of the scalping leak and the media sarcastically calling our boy, Red Chief. He doesn't think it's a bit funny and he's not happy. There's another press conference today scheduled for 1:00 p.m. That one should be a lotta fun. I told Long John I feel we're getting close. He says close isn't good enough—we've got to catch this guy before he hits another victim, period."

Johnny looks at Katy, smiles, and adds, "You were right, you know. Pearl did wear her hair reddish blonde in the recent past. So our boy is definitely partial to redheads. Maybe the Chief can release that tidbit today. Probably be a good bone for the media to chew on." He turns back to the chalkboard and makes another entry.

Katy swivels her chair around to face McHugh and Bundy, both sitting to her left. "You guys get that composite sketch?"

Harlan makes a face. "The girls couldn't come down early, after all. I guess the one who first found Gisela isn't feeling too hot, she didn't sleep very well. Bad dreams about her friend. And the other one had to turn in a summer school paper at 11:00. So, we're going to take the artist out to their place at 1:00 this afternoon, when they're both available. We'll get you guys a copy by tonight. Okay?"

Katy nods.

"Naturally we'll talk to them some more, after the sketch is done," Patrick adds. "And we'll check out the last of the un-interviewed neighbors, too. Who knows? Maybe this time someone will remember seeing our boy coming or going."

Katy smiles inwardly. The press may call him Red Chief, but now that the detectives feel they're getting closer and closing in, they all are calling the perp: *our boy.*

"Sounds good," Johnny says, stepping away from the chalkboard. "I got back my computer searches. No stuttering giants released from prison or a mental hospital in the last three months. But I'm going to ask for another search going back six months, after giving them Katy's bald, hairless description update. And I'll clear a priority request with all that to CYA, too. If we're lucky we may see something by tonight or, at the very latest, tomorrow morning."

"Oh, I called around to the porno magazine and vid outlets," Harlan interjects. "Three of them have some of the hairy stuff. We'll go by with the composite picture of our boy, later. There's also one movie joint that shows this kinda stuff that we'll check out when it opens, tonight after 7:00."

"Yeah, that's all good stuff," Johnny says, a little grin back in his tone. "Let's touch base here after dinner tonight, say about 8:30. Okay?"

2

At 2:55 that afternoon, Katy and Johnny meet the laundry supervisor, Derek Clark, in the lobby of Sutter General Hospital. He walks them through a confusing maze of corridors down to a hallway finally leading into the laundry, which occupies almost the entire basement of the hospital.

The laundry crew is already waiting in the hallway to begin work, standing around, talking excitedly among themselves.

Katy looks over the group carefully. There appears to be only one really big guy, but he's not bald. "Is everyone always here on time for work?" she asks Clark, pointing at the employees.

He glances briefly at the milling crowd and nods. "Yes, normally, *except* for Terry, who's a little slow. His mom usually brings him right at 3:00 or sometimes a bit later."

"Then he's not here, yet?"

Clark shakes his head.

"And what does Terry look like?" she asks. "Does he have a speech defect?"

"Yes, he does talk sort of funny," the supervisor answers thoughtfully, leading them around the quiet mangle down a narrow aisle toward his office.

Katy feels a hint of excitement tighten her stomach muscles.

Clark pauses momentarily with his hand on the office door. "He's a black man, big, heavy-set, mildly retarded, socially backward, but a real hard worker."

Black? Shit, that's *not* our guy, Katy thinks with a sinking feeling of disappointment.

She waits for Johnny to catch up, letting Clark enter the office by himself. "I Didn't see our boy in the laundry crowd. Did you?" she quickly whispers, as the two of them follow the laundry supervisor into his office.

Johnny shakes his head.

"It'll be better to talk in here," Clark explains, pulling up two folding chairs, then sitting down at his desk. "Gets pretty noisy out there when they first start up all the empty equipment."

Katy glances about the tiny, clean cubicle, noticing the neat, orderly appearance of the desk top, the empty IN and OUT baskets, and the obligatory photos of the laundry supervisor's family—a wife, a teenage boy, and a younger girl.

"Well, what can I do for you?" Clark asks, leaning back in his swivel chair and trying not to look too nervous.

"Just a couple of questions," Johnny says in an off-hand way, "then maybe we'll talk to a few of your employees in here in private. How long had Gisela Huntington actually been working in the laundry?"

"Let's see… three weeks, I think, but let me check to be sure," the supervisor replies, taking out some papers from a file in the bottom drawer of his desk. "Yes, that's right, fifteen work days. These are her time sheets."

"What exactly did she do?"

"She worked on the mangle, folding linen. That's what all the women do, fold or feed. The men load the washers, extractor, dryer, except for Terry. He cleans out the laundry drop chutes and sorts dirty linen—"

All the laundry machinery suddenly cranks up at once, filling the air, even in the closed office, with a vibrating, teeth-chattering, jarring dissonance.

"Wow," Johnny says.

Clark shrugs apologetically.

"She got along okay with the other women?" Katy says, speaking loudly over the din.

"Yes, she sure did. She was a pleasant young woman. Good worker, too."

"And the men? She got along with them okay?"

"I don't think she had much contact with them, being so new and all. Of course she was married. You knew that, right?"

Johnny nods. "She didn't flirt with any of them or anything like that?"

"I don't think she did, but I never observed her at breaks. The other women on the mangle would know."

"She have any special friends here?" asks Katy. "Among the other women, who all seem to be Hispanic, right?"

"Yes, mostly Mexican-American," Clark answers. "And I think she was closest to Yolanda, who is our youngest girl, nearest in age to Gisela."

"How about other people in the hospital?" Katy asks. Coming in she had noticed the hospital was a big, multi-storied building. Probably hundreds of employees.

"I don't *think* so," Clark answers thoughtfully. "Three weeks is just about long enough to find your way around down here in the basement, learn your job, where the cafeteria is, the location of the bathrooms, the days we're paid, that sort of stuff. And really we're kind of socially isolated from the rest of the hospital located down here. Terry delivers carts of clean linen to the six hospital floors above us, once a day in the early evening. Sometimes one of the other men does it. But that's not normally part of the women's responsibilities." He shakes his head. "No, it's unlikely she had the opportunity in just three weeks to get to know anyone else on the floors above us."

"So, you wouldn't have any idea who might not like her and want to do something like this to her?" Johnny asks bluntly.

Clark shakes his head, blinks, and sits upright in his chair. "Gosh, no, I wouldn't have *any* idea."

"Okay, Mr. Clark," Johnny says, as if concluding the questions. Then as an apparent afterthought, he asks, "How about Wilbur Cox? He know her very well?"

Clark looks taken aback by the nature of the unexpected question. "Well, no, I don't think so. Wilbur has been here longer than anyone, my second in command. And he's married, too… except—"

The laundry supervisor dismissively waves away his last thought.

"Go ahead, what were you going to add?" Johnny says, encouraging Clark to finish the sentence. "Let us worry about it being significant or not."

"Well, I really shouldn't even mention this, but Wilbur does sort of tease most of the women on the mangle," Clark says in a hesitating manner. "Old, young, it makes no difference. I don't think it means much of anything. Just his way, you know. And, now that I think about it, I don't remember ever seeing him and Gisela even talking, much less flirting. So, it's nothing, I'm sure."

"Well, maybe we should ask *him*, see if he did flirt with her," Katy suggests to the supervisor.

Johnny nods his agreement. "How about asking him to step in here for a minute?"

"Sure," Clark replies after a momentary hesitation, rising from behind his desk, with a slightly sheepish expression on his face now, obviously feeling a little guilty about what he'd said. He steps out of the office into the laundry.

"You still don't want to tip our hand with our boy's actual description?" Johnny asks, when they're alone.

"No," Katy replies. "Let's wait. The press will probably be talking to Clark sometime today. The description would be out by tonight, all over TV. Tip him off, maybe make him bolt. Let's just squeeze this guy, Wilbur. See what he knows. He must've been a lot closer to Gisela than his boss suspects. Maybe he knows of other boyfriends."

Johnny nods. "Gotcha."

The laundry supervisor returns to the office, leading in a big guy with thick, dark, curly hair, dressed in Levis and a light denim work shirt with the sleeves cut off at the shoulders. His arms are heavily muscled and matted with dark hair. Clark unfolds another chair. "This is Wilbur Cox. Detectives Green and Detective Cato."

Katy and Johnny shake hands with Cox.

"Mr. Cox, you know what happened to Mrs. Huntington last night, right?" Johnny begins.

"Yeah, I do. A tough deal."

"It sure was," Johnny agrees. "Did you know her very well?"

"Ah, no," Cox replies back, shaking his head emphatically.

"Then you wouldn't know if she maybe had a boyfriend?"

"No, I wouldn't," Cox answers.

"Or have any idea of anyone who could do something like this to her?"

"No."

"Did you actually hear about this last night?" Johnny asks.

"No, this morning."

"I see… Oh, for the record, where were *you* last night, Mr. Cox?"

"Home," he quickly answers back. "Me and the wife and kids had gone to the zoo during the afternoon, then had a picnic supper at William Land Park, and we got home kinda late. After 8:30. Then me and the wife watched a rented video—*The Hunt for Red October*—after she fed the kids a snack and put them to bed. About 11:30, both of us went to bed."

"You didn't even have to think about all that, Mr. Cox," Johnny says, a tough expression on his boxer's face. "That's funny, you know. Usually we ask someone a question like that, they have to think at least for a few moments, you know. But *not* you. Funny, eh?"

A hard look flashes momentarily into Cox's narrowed eyes, then softens, as he insists, "Yeah, well, I was home last night, you can *bet* on that."

"And you really didn't know Mrs. Huntington very well?" Katy asks, noticing that it's getting very warm down here in the basement, and Wilbur Cox is beginning to sweat heavily, the front of his work shirt soaked a darker navy-blue color already.

He glances across the desk at his supervisor, like a student searching for some tutorial guidance from a teacher, then shakes his head, his forehead heavily creased now—a nervous, guilty look of concern. "No, I didn't."

"Then, you wouldn't have been invited to her party last Friday night?" asks Johnny in a colder voice, scooting his chair a little closer in Cox's direction.

For a moment only the din of the machines intrudes on the awkward silence of the office.

"Ah, actually," Cox eventually answers in an almost contrite tone, "I *did* go to that party."

"Oh, and did anyone else from the hospital go," Katy asks him, "or even get invited?"

Cox looks at her directly, his worried frown deepening, then replies in a voice barely audible over the equipment noise, "No, I don't think anyone else from work went to it." He sucks in a big breath, then his eyes light up a little as he adds, "Wait, I think Yolanda may have been invited."

"Yolanda was her best friend here at work, but didn't go to the party, although she was invited," Johnny says, with a look of puzzlement. "But you, who hardly knew Mrs. Huntington at all, did go. Seems rather odd. I don't really understand, Mr. Cox. Can you enlighten me?"

Wilbur Cox shifts his gaze back to Johnny, sighs loudly like he's giving in, then admits in a deeper, man-to-man tone of voice, "Look, officer, I did go to that party last Friday night, and Geez's old man wasn't there. You probably know he's back in Germany on temporary duty in the Air force. She's been kinda lonely lately. Anyhow, me and Geez had a few beers together, fooled around a little, and... well, you know, one thing led to another... I'd appreciate it if my wife didn't have to know about any of that. Okay?"

"Okay," Johnny says agreeably, but his expression still tough and hard. "We do need to check out your alibi for last night, Mr. Cox. Although we don't need to talk to your wife about anything you did at the party on Friday, if you are telling us the truth about last night. You are, right?"

"Man, I *swear* I wasn't anywhere near Del Paso Heights last night."

Johnny glances over at Katy, who nods and says, "Maybe you could ask Yolanda to step in here on your way out, Mr. Cox."

Cox pops up from the folding chair and is out the door in two seconds flat.

A minute later, Yolanda knocks politely on the office door.

"C'mon in," the laundry supervisor says and introduces the young woman to the two detectives.

"Yolanda," Katy begins, "you didn't go to the party Friday night at Gisela's apartment. Why?"

"Oh, it was too late," she replies with a slight accent, "and my papa, he wouldn't allow it."

"You live at home with your family?" asks Katy.

"Yes," the young woman answers, wringing her hands nervously in her lap.

Katy leans close and pats her gently on the shoulder. "We only have a couple of more questions. Do you know if anyone else from the laundry or the hospital was invited to that party?"

Yolanda replies, "Gisela said she invited Wilbur."

"Why? Had she been going out with him?"

"I don't think so. He's married. But she never really told me."

"Was Gisela seeing anyone else, going out with anyone that you do know about?" Katy asks, smiling encouragingly at the young woman.

Yolanda shakes her head. "I don't think so. She maybe joke a little bit with Wilbur here at work, but that is all. I think she was a *good* girl, Detective Green."

"You have no idea about who could've done something so horrible like this to her?"

"No," the young woman answers, dabbing at her eyes with a handkerchief.

Katy looks at Johnny, who says, "Okay, Yolanda. Thank you for your help."

Then he turns toward the supervisor. "We appreciate your cooperation, Mr. Clark."

They all follow Yolanda out of the office into the busy laundry.

Katy glances first at the mangle and the women working on it, then across the floor at the big washing machines and the two men there, and finally at another large piece of equipment in the far right corner, operated by a guy in a Giants baseball cap.

My God, how do they stand the racket, the wet heat, and the dust in the air? she asks herself, hurrying to catch up with Johnny and escape the noisy, muggy, dirty place.

3

Back at the command center before the 8:30 meeting, Katy examines their chalkboard, glancing thoughtfully over all the columns of entries, but dwelling on the revised description:

Husky, 6'5"
Stutters
21 years old
Wears stocking cap, long-sleeved, tan shirt, buttoned at the neck
Suffers from alopecia

Something about that last entry—the bald and hairless bit—still sticks in her mind, a thorn constantly pricking her unconscious—

"All right!" Johnny shouts from the fax machine. "Got an early response and printout from CYA. Dude fitting our giant, hairless, stutterer description was released about four months ago down in Chula Vista. And get this, partner—his probation was almost immediately transferred from San Diego up here to Sacramento. I wonder why? Got his local P.O.'s number. I'm calling him right now."

"What's his name," Katy asks.

"Ah… Samuel Kubiak," Johnny replies, reading it off the fax, as he picks up the phone—

Katy is stunned!

"Holy shit," she murmurs to herself. *I should have remembered.*

Sammy. Of course.

As Johnny dials the phone, she slips back to when she was fifteen, living in San Diego in her penultimate foster home.

Sammy Kubiak was big back then, too, she remembers, even though he was only about eight years old. One of the youngest boys in the home. A creepy kid actually. Bald, hairless, not even any eyebrows or eye lashes. His speech locked-up in a hopeless stammer. He'd scared the living shit out of her one night, when she caught him spying on her through a slightly cracked door—she'd been naked. An eight-year-old peeping tom, back then.

And a brutal killer, now.

Jesus.

"His P.O. doesn't answer, dammit," Johnny says, slamming down the phone in frustration. "*No*body there. Only a canned recorded message. Won't be able to get our boy's home address, work place, or anything else important we need before 9:00 a.m. tomorrow morning, at the earliest. Friggin' state bureaucrats." He rubs his nose roughly with exasperation, then glances over at Katy.

"Hey, what?" he says in a softer, concerned voice, stepping close. "What's wrong, kiddo? You look like you've seen a ghost—"

"I know *him*," she says in a barely audible whisper, still shocked by the revelation.

"Who?" Johnny asks, looking confused.

"Our boy, the guy the press calls, Red Chief, Samuel Kubiak."

"Personally? You know him personally?"

Katy nods, blinks, then focuses on Johnny's face and sighs deeply, shrugging.

"We lived together years ago for several months in the same foster home in San Diego. I know I should've remembered earlier, as soon as I knew about the giant, bald, hairless bit, but I was focusing on an adult not some young kid in my distant past—"

"Hey, it's okay," Johnny says, patting her hand. "I can't even remember what I ate for breakfast."

4

At 8:45 p.m., all four detectives finally gather in the conference room command center.

Both Harlan Bundy and Patrick McHugh look wrinkled, hot, and exhausted, wrung out by running around all day in the stifling heat, which still lingers outside even at the late hour. They both get a cold drink from the break room Coke machine before plopping down heavily in their seats.

Johnny brings them up to date, letting Katy share her stunning news.

Then, Harlan, in a tired voice, tells Johnny and Katy about drawing blanks with all the rest of the Del Paso Heights neighbors, and nothing at the porno places either, including the sleazy, run-down movie theater that they had just left. No one they talked to remembers *ever* seeing a young, stuttering giant in a roll-down, stocking cap.

"... At least it had some half-ass air-conditioning," he concludes, referring to the manager's seedy office at the movie theater, then taking another drink of his Coke.

"Hey, get a load of this composite," Patrick says, with a little gasp of enthusiasm, giving them each a copy of the artist's sketch from a folder, then pointing at their chalkboard description.

"Yeah, it sure *looks* right," Johnny agrees, glancing back and forth from the drawing to the chalkboard. "I didn't see anyone like that at the Hospital this afternoon. Did you, Katy?"

She stares at the drawing for a few moments, a frontal view of a young man with a dark stocking cap rolled down over his ears, then sighs, and absently shakes her head, still seeing an eight-year-old kid in her mind's eye. "Hard to imagine Sammy so much bigger and all grown up, now... and a ruthless psychotic killer to boot."

After making a couple of additions to their board, Johnny suggests, "Let's knock off for tonight. Everyone's beat. Not much we can do until tomorrow morning, anyhow. We'll all meet over at Adult Probation at 9:00, ready to go from there, okay?"

They agree.

Johnny walks Katy out to the passenger side of his sky-blue Mustang. "You okay, partner?"

"Yeah, I'm fine, thanks," she answers and smiles, giving him a hug, before sliding into the car. "Must be the heat's finally starting to bug me. When's it ever going to end?"

He looks up into the night sky, cloud cover almost blocking out all of the stars, and shrugs.

They head off to her place with all the windows rolled down in the car, neither saying anything on the trip.

5

When they reach her townhouse, they both sit quietly for a moment in the car, looking at each other, Katy aware of the extra tension in the sticky air—like waiting to be kissed on a first date. Finally she leans over and nuzzles Johnny's neck. As usual he's not wearing any aftershave or cologne, but she can smell the fresh scent of his soap—*Irish Spring*? She kisses him softly on the mouth, feeling a faint stir of excitement deep in her loins—almost like when the old magneto from junior high school was beginning to get cranked up real good.

"Hey, pal, did you bring a toothbrush?" she asks in a voice matching the sultry night, lifting and wiggling her eyebrows in a Groucho imitation, trying to cover her own nervousness with a bit of silliness.

Johnny just stares at her for a moment, a serious expression on his rugged features, then asks, "You sure about this, Katy?"

She peers deeply into his blue eyes, just able to make out the tiny triangles of amber bursting from his black pupils in the dimness cast by the parking lot lights. *Yeah, she's sure.* But she doesn't answer out loud. Instead, Katy slips out and goes around the Mustang, opens his door, takes his hand in hers, and leads him home.

Inside the front door, they clench and kiss again in the refreshingly cool darkness, opened-mouth now, their tongues touching and exploring, the contact setting off a stronger tingling in Katy's loins.

Suddenly, she can sense Johnny's growing excitement pressing just above her groin.

They break apart, Katy feeling a giddy kind of rush, almost like when she was a teenager and her first serious boyfriend clumsily slid his hand down inside her panties and his fingers touched unexplored, bare skin.

She laughs aloud at herself. It's been a long time, girl, but not that long...

"C'mon, pal, let's take a shower."

She leads him into the bathroom, but doesn't allow him to turn on the lights. They undress in the dark and enter the cramped shower stall mostly by feel, Johnny laughing out loud, now.

"Hey, what's up with the lights off? You didn't pay your P.G.& E. bill or what?"

She adjusts the temperature of the water, before answering.

"I'm a little self-conscious, okay?"

Johnny gently caresses her shoulders, then allows his hands to slowly slide down her arms and trace the flare of her hips, before reaching behind Katy and firmly clutching her buns in his hands, as if gauging their size and weight. Then he nuzzles her neck, her chest, and gently kisses both breasts, before letting out a sigh and pulling her body loosely against him.

"You feel just *great* to me, Katy," he says huskily.

"You do, too," she replies, hugging him back tightly as the warm water cascades over their heads and joined bodies.

After soaping up and washing each other in the dark, they quickly rinse off and get out.

Katy flips on a night light near the bathroom door, then tosses Johnny a clean towel.

"You got a problem, pal," she says, toweling herself off, then moving a few steps into the darkened bedroom, before letting the towel slide to the floor.

He follows, leaving the bathroom door wide open, the dim light framing his nakedness for a brief moment.

They kiss again, wetly, passionately, their still-damp, nude bodies pressed tightly against each other. Skin against skin, body temperatures quickly rising, even in the chilling coolness of the air-conditioned bedroom—

"C'mon," Katy says in a lower, huskier voice, shivering, then leading Johnny to her bed.

They make love for the first time, not clumsily like two overly-eager, first-time lovers—quick, wet, and frantic; but more like a pair of long-time dance partners, each sensitive and responsive to the other's moves—gentle, kind, considerate, yet breathlessly passionate.

Loving sex.

Afterward they lie quietly in each other's embrace, catching their breath.

I knew he would be like this, Katy thinks, touching his broken nose. She grins, tracing the scar tissue over his eyebrows with her forefinger. "That was great, pal, but I thought you boxer types were all tough guys," she whispers. "You know, hard and rough with your women, and usually not quite so thoughtful."

He pulls her close and kisses her roughly on the mouth. "You know what, kiddo?" he says in a tight-lipped Brando impression.

"No."

"I coulda been a contender… *if* it hadn't been for all the babes. Hunnerds of 'em."

"*On The Waterfront*, pretty good," she says, acknowledging the famous movie line before his pause and dumb macho ad lib, chuckling, and gently slipping out of his arms. "How about a cold drink?"

Katy gets up, and looks at him for a response, her eyes a little better adjusted now to the room's darkness.

He's nodding to himself, staring at her naked body with an almost salacious look on his face.

"What?" she asks, self-consciously tugging on a black-and-white kimono from the foot of the bed.

"You are definitely a *girl*, partner," he replies with a crooked, ironic smile, "just as I suspected when I saw you at the pool the other night. How about that? And one terrific body, too. Kinda like Cher's, you know. Tall, elegant, and very sexy. What have I been missing these past four years?" He hits himself in the forehead with the palm of his hand, before slipping into a Sonny Bono parody. "I shoulda jumped your bones long ago, but I gotcha now, babe."

She picks up a pillow and smacks him with it over the head. "Just for that last crude, chauvinistic remark, I'm not bringing you a drink. You can just get up and get it yourself."

She storms off in a mock huff into the kitchen, stopping at the fridge.

Johnny follows, after pulling on his shorts.

"What do you want?" she asks, holding open the door. "Root Beer, 7-Up, or iced tea?"

"The 7-Up, you raging feminist," he says, grinning and kissing the back of her neck.

6

The phone rings the next morning just before 7:00 a.m.

Katy glances over at Johnny, who blinks and lets out a long, deep groan of protest before he rolls away.

She answers, "Hello?"

She listens for a few seconds, then covers the mouthpiece. With the other hand she shakes Johnny's shoulder. He rolls back over. "It's *him*," Katy whispers excitedly, nodding emphatically.

Johnny looks puzzled for a moment, then mouths the question: *Our boy?*

Katy nods, listening carefully, occasionally answering the unseen speaker, "Yes" or "No."

Then finally she replies, "Okay, I'm sure I can arrange that."

She listens for a few more seconds.

"No, just me… Okay, I understand. 11:45, sharp. I'll be there, alone. Count on it."

She looks at Johnny then hangs up.

"Well, what did he want?" Johnny asks, glancing at her curiously, as he begins to throw on his clothes.

"He wants to turn himself in," she says, shaking her head in amazement. "Yeah, he wants to give up, but just to me. In a special place, a park between 27th and 28th Streets on I Street, not really too far from Sutter General Hospital—"

"When?" Johnny asks, completely alert now.

"Later this morning, 11:45."

She goes on to explain all the instructions to Johnny, who listens carefully until she finishes.

"Well, you are not going there alone, *period*," he says, rubbing his nose. "Let's hustle over to that park right now and check it out. See what we can set up for your safety, before our boy gets there."

Katy dresses slowly, lost in thought.

"You know, it's funny. He saw *Saints or Sinners?* last night on TV and recognized me. After all this time. Can you believe it?"

Obviously annoyed by her dallying, Johnny says, "C'mon, Katy, snap it up, we have a lot of ground to cover before noon today."

7

"Whoa, it's crowded already, even so early," Johnny says incredulously, looking around at all the old people in the park, dressed alike in their faded tans, blues, and grays, as they walk along the main path. "We'll have plenty of cover, *if* we dress right."

They stop on Katy's signal, almost in the center of the senior citizen's park, at a bench with a green trash receptacle next to it.

"You sure this is the right spot?" Johnny asks her.

She nods, glancing around. "Yeah, this is the bench he designated. The green barrel, there. Main path leading right and left to the edges of the park. And this smaller path behind the bench, leading to the restroom building back there near 28th Street."

Johnny says, "Okay, that means he can come at you in how many different directions?" He turns, facing another bench directly across the main path, looking over it at the duck pond that extends like a moat almost to 27th Street. "He won't come from that way. So we cover this main walkway both ends, and that path behind you." He glances up at the tree limbs drooping over the bench. "Damn, I don't like that," he says, indicating the trees lining the walk, making an almost solid canopy over this central section of path. "I don't see how we can get a rifleman zeroed in on this exact spot from high up on a building on either 28th or 27th—"

"We won't need one," Katy says. "You, Harlan, and Patrick can cover each of the paths. We know exactly what he looks like, right. You guys will see him coming long before he gets anywhere near me."

"Yeah," he agrees half-heartedly, rubbing his nose. "And we'll have plenty of back-up units on the adjoining streets." He points at the end of each of the paths. "We'll have you wired so we can stay in close contact, of course. And you'll be well armed, carrying your new Sig Sauer. 45, right?"

"It'll be just fine," Katy says, squeezing his shoulder confidently. "I believe him. He wants to give up to me. That's all."

Johnny's tone lightens up a little. "He better or he's a dead man," he says. "Okay, let's set it all up. We'll have you back here, wired up, and sitting on that bench by… 11:15 at the very latest, with everyone else in place undercover by 11:30. I need to get in touch with Patrick and Harlan, right now. They'll have to meet with Kubiak's P.O. by themselves before coming over here, get a current photo, find out where our boy lives and works, anything else important, just in case we need it later." He looks around again at all the old people out so early and grins wryly. "Guess I've seen enough, for now."

Then, Johnny takes Katy's arm. "C'mon, let's get busy, kiddo."

MAGICAL MOVES

fter the early morning telephone conversation with Katy Green, you wander around your tiny studio apartment, carefully selecting those items to include in your backpack. Sadly, you will have to leave a lot of things, including most of your books and the new TV. But you know this apartment will no longer be a safe haven. The detectives will be coming here very soon, hunting for you, probably as early as this afternoon.

Yes, indeed.

A little later in the morning you go down to a pair of businesses on J Street and purchase the items you require for your disguise.

Then, you return to the apartment for the last time and begin to carefully apply the disguise. Somewhere you've read that altering both body posture and the way you move are the key ingredients in any really effective disguise. You will try to remember that.

Smiling to yourself, you pick up the bulging backpack and glance fondly around the tiny apartment, your eyes resting for a moment on the books stacked under the reading lamp. You frown. It's the first time in your life that you've ever really lived alone. You will miss the privacy, the times you were able to read and study in complete solitude, or pick out a program you wanted to see on TV without any argument, or turn on the radio anytime of night or day as pleased you.

After dropping your apartment key on the kitchen table, you reluctantly walk out the front door without glancing back. This was a good place, you think sadly.

A very good place, indeed.

Just before 11:00 in the morning, you arrive in the park, at your scouted spot, almost an hour early for the scheduled meeting. You glance around at the hundreds of old people, taking up most of the benches and tables or just milling around, providing plenty of cover, for *now*. You grin to yourself, then slip the backpack off, and set it down next to you. Closing your eyes, you breathe slowly, and center for a few moments. Now, for a little experimental posture adjustment, you think, eyes still closed. You bend forward, roll your shoulders together, letting out a long, slow breath and relaxing your chest. For the next few moments you visualize your great bulk shrinking inward, hoping your new posture and the way you move will make you *appear* smaller, even to a more than casual observer.

Think like a magician.

After a few moments, you blink.

After another look about, you take the three props from inside the backpack, and you place one on the ground at your feet, keeping the other two in hand.

You are ready.

Again you smile.

It won't be long now.

Freedom!

Just the thought of the word makes your pulse race.

Again, you force yourself to breathe slowly… calm down.

Under control mow, you whisper, "I'm in place and ready."

The Dark Angel, hovering out of sight, somewhere above the trees, replies in your head, *Yes, I can see that you are. And they will never spot you. You are almost invisible even in broad daylight, blended so perfectly into the background. A real magic act.*

You do not respond, content to sit quietly, still bent over, shrunken, occasionally peeping surreptitiously out at your immediate surroundings, waiting patiently, like a spider in its hidden lair, ready to pounce on unsuspecting prey.

Things are going well, just as planned.

Yes, indeed.

2

Just after 11:20, Katy sits down on the bench next to the green trash barrel. She is comfortable but wound tight and a little nervous. "Okay, I'm seated in place," she whispers from the corner of her mouth into the dark button pinned under her windbreaker's collar.

"Yeah, we all have you in direct view," Johnny says reassuringly through the earplug. "I'm about seventy-five yards to your right in the little crowd around the card game. Harlan is a little closer, just off the path to your left, standing in the middle of that bunch kibitzing the chess players. Patrick is fifty yards or so directly behind you, hidden in back of the restrooms. All our back-ups are in place on the three surrounding streets. So, rest assured, if our boy comes anywhere near this park and you today, we've got the bastard."

She takes a deep breath, feeling a little better but still not completely relaxed, glancing over at the pair of old guys sharing the bench directly across the path from her—one whittling long shavings into a pile, the other reading the *Bee*—before glancing again at her watch.

Time creeps by too slowly:

11:34 a.m.

11:38 a.m.

11:40 a.m.

11:42 a.m.

11:43 a.m.

11:44 a.m.

Katy tenses as it draws closer to the 11:45 a.m. meeting time, peering both left and right up the path, then turning and glancing over her shoulder along the trail leading to the restrooms. She doesn't actually see any of the other detectives… but that's probably good. Sammy won't spot them either.

The meeting time comes and goes. No Sammy.

At 11:50, Johnny whispers in her ear, "Our boy is a little late."

"No one's seen him yet?" she asks, covering her mouth with her hand before speaking, already knowing the answer, but wanting to keep Johnny talking, not feeling quite so alone when she can actually hear his voice.

"No, nothing yet, kiddo. I'll check the back-up on the street."

Katy reaches inside her jacket around her right hip and adjusts her back holster, pausing, sliding the .45 almost clear of the holster but not quite into view, drawing comfort from the solid feel of the hidden weapon. Then, momentarily alarmed by her potentially revealing lapse in judgment, she jerks her hand back into her lap and checks the nearby bench occupants to see if either of them noticed her fondling the automatic weapon.

Apparently not.

Thank God.

She sees that the one old guy has dropped his newspaper into his lap and is busy now squinting at *his* watch. After figuring out the time, he sighs, carefully folds up the *Bee*, gets up, and strolls away to her left in Bundy's direction. The other old fellow remains seated, intent on his whittling.

"Nope," Johnny says, his voice slightly tighter than normal, "no one has spotted anyone even close to the composite description, yet. How are you holding up, Katy?"

"Fine," she says, covering her mouth and checking her watch again: 11:55 a.m.

"Well, hang in there, kiddo."

"Okay."

Katy drops her hand away from her face, trying to make the movement appear completely casual. She cannot quite shake the creepy feeling that she's being watched by someone other than her colleagues. Someone…

She sucks in a long, deep breath.

In a few minutes, Johnny comes back on, in a surprised voice. "Hey, *hey*, what's happening around here? Where's everyone going?"

Katy glances right, then left.

The crowded park is rapidly thinning out, the majority of the seniors all appearing to get up and leave at almost the same moment, as if on some kind of cue like: *Abandon ship.*

For a moment, she's puzzled, then she realizes it's noontime.

"They're probably hungry, just going home for lunch," she whispers into her collar mike.

"Yeah, okay, I guess that figures," Johnny whispers back and sighs audibly.

In another minute, there are only a dozen or so people remaining in the entire park, everyone else having left.

Johnny and Harlan look way too young for their faded clothes, each standing alone now that everyone is gone, looking about suspiciously, heads cocked, talking to the collars on their jackets, sticking out like a pair of stubborn cowlicks. She twists around, but can't spot Patrick, who must still be hidden somewhere behind the restrooms. Good. Turning back she notices the old guy across from her hasn't left yet for lunch. He's still bent over his stick, whittling away, the long shavings curling and dropping down into a thick pile on the newspaper spread between his feet. He must be paid piece work, Katy jokes to herself, trying to ease the tension she still feels.

3

Maintaining your position, you glance from the corner of your eyes to the left. It's noon, the old people are all beginning to leave the park for home.

Just as planned.

You grin inwardly to yourself.

There's an obvious police officer, about fifty yards away, a young fellow dressed in brown, but standing out awkwardly all by himself now, talking into a hidden mike.

You carefully shift your gaze right.

Uh-huh.

There's another one, standing out all alone, too, even though he's wearing clothes like the seniors. You chuckle quietly, having validated your belief that the authorities wouldn't be aware of the daily noontime exodus from the park that would leave them completely exposed.

There is another hiding behind those restrooms, dressed in gray clothes, the Dark Angel says in your head. *But they are all too far away from the woman to be of any assistance. And there are no snipers in the buildings nearby. Too difficult to aim and get a shot through the tree cover.*

Again, just as planned.

You smile to yourself.

It is time to execute your surprise magician's move.

Yes, indeed.

You pull your backpack to you, put one prop away, slip out the instrument of vengeance, and leave the pack where it rests. Then you wrap up what remains of the other prop, keeping the instrument of vengeance hidden in your right hand. You rise noisily with a loud sighing effort, like a old man fighting gravity and his protesting, creaky, arthritic limbs...

But you've slipped up, forgetting to consciously maintain your doubled-over, shrunken appearance as you stand.

Slowly, you limp toward the woman, seated on the nearby park bench.

4

"Still hasn't shown up, Katy," Johnny says in her earplug, almost with a sense of relief. "It's 12:30. Maybe he got spooked by something, isn't coming at all. What do you think? Want to call it a day?"

"You may be right," Katy answers into the button behind her cupped mouth, disappointed but a little elated at the same time. "Let's wait just a few more minutes, okay?"

"You're the boss, kiddo."

Even the senior citizen whittling across from her is now giving up, apparently going home for lunch. He shuffles slowly toward her with all his shavings neatly wrapped in a newspaper, obviously headed first for the green trash can next to her bench—

Something about his appearance sets off an alarm in Katy's head.

She examines the old man more carefully.

It's the creases. *Yes.*

They just aren't right, she decides—they look almost drawn on his face, like a young actor playing an old person in an amateur play. And he seems to be changing shape as he slowly moves closer, rising up and growing larger right before her eyes.

Katy springs to her feet.

It's him!

Jesus.

The disguised giant moves quickly now, apparently realizing he's been spotted, closing the distance between himself and Katy, lunging, and striking out at her with his left fist.

But, with a boxer's fine-tuned reactions, Katy quickly dips her knees, easily ducking the punch that sails harmlessly over her head.

At the same time she hears Johnny barking in her right ear, "It's our boy! It's Kubiak! He's slipped by our surveillance and is attacking Katy."

Just a nanosecond too slow, Kubiak tries to slash at her throat with a straight razor he's held concealed in his right hand. But Katy athletically twists slightly to her left, and simultaneously hunches her neck down behind her right shoulder, the razor's blade slicing harmlessly through the upper sleeve of her windbreaker.

After missing his target, Kubiak stumbles clumsily and almost falls flat on his chest, bracing himself on the walkway with his free left hand, but giving Katy the moment she needs to recover and to pull herself together.

Fumbling, she reaches around and yanks out her .45 from the back holster above her right hip, just as her giant attacker pushes up from the path, turns, and flees, grabbing his backpack as he hurtles the bench across the main path.

"He's trying to escape—" Katy shouts into her mike, dropping into a Weaver Stance, her voice catching in her throat as she feels a sharp, stinging pain in her right shoulder. She glances with slightly blurred vision at her arm. A bright red stain is spreading out, soaking her upper sleeve where Kubiak slashed open the windbreaker.

Blood.

Jesus, he must've nicked me!

She blinks away the tears and focuses, trying to aim the automatic, but her grip is weak now and she jerks off a round too quickly, as

Kubiak splashes across the shallow duck pond, headed for 27th Street.

Katy's shot isn't even close, hitting ten feet behind the fleeing giant in the water. She shifts the weapon to her left hand, and sights down the barrel, but she's shaking too badly even to attempt another shot.

"Shit," Katy cries out in frustration. He's getting away. He must've planned to escape that way across the shallow pond, accurately anticipating a lack of back-up cover in that direction—

A pair of loud gunshots erupt almost at the same time from just behind her and to the far right.

But Kubiak keeps moving, shifting this way and that unpredictably, like a football fullback juking invisible tacklers.

Patrick thunders up beside Katy, handgun out, swearing into his button mike, "Now, God Damn it!" Then: "Jesus, Katy, you're hurt, bleeding."

She replies in a tight-lipped, small voice, "I think he may have nicked my shoulder with his straight razor. It's not bad."

Johnny comes running up, shouting something into his mike.

Harlan has taken off across the pond in pursuit of the disguised giant with his handgun out, but he's trailing at least fifty yards behind Kubiak.

"Okay, we have an ambulance back over here on I Street," Johnny shouts loudly, sweeping Katy into his arms. "You're gonna be okay!"

She closes her eyes, feeling drifty but safe now, not really paying any more attention to the hectic activity transpiring around her.

5

As you reach 27th Street, you snatch the folded shopping bag from the crook of the tree branch where you had planted it earlier, and continue running until you hit the corner, then turn right on J Street.

A half block up is the alley.

Hurry.

Breathing heavily, you dart in there and take a towel from your backpack. Quickly, you wipe off the make-up, all the heavy lines. Then you strip off the gray toupee, mustache, and the wrinkled, tan work shirt. You pull on a raggedy, old, blue sweatshirt and the Giants wrinkled baseball cap, turning the bill around so the *SF* logo faces backward. Catching your breath now, you carefully shove everything back into the shopping bag including your backpack.

In less than a minute you're back out on J Street mingling with the crowd of shoppers, a young punk casually swinging your own shopping bag, making your way downtown, trying to walk at an unhurried pace and control your racing pulse.

You risk one backward glance.

Apparently you have evaded the detective chasing you on foot across the pond, because no one seems to be following you at the moment.

Around the corner back near the park, you hear sirens screaming, and in less than a minute a pair of patrol cars cruise slowly along both sides of J Street, which is one-way headed downtown, the officers searching the shopping crowd for you. Obviously checking for what you looked like a few minutes ago when you dashed across the pond. They don't stop, not spotting their prey in the throng around you.

A minute later another patrol car speeds by without stopping either.

You take a deep sigh of relief and grin to yourself, hurrying along, finally turning right on 12th Street.

Only when you eventually reach Ahern Street do you slow down. You glance around to insure no one is watching, then you dump the shopping bag and everything else except for your backpack into a trash barrel on the corner.

After that you turn around the scruffy Giants cap, which matches the unwashed, seedy appearance of your sweatshirt, and you walk up the block to *Fishes and Loaves*.

You sit down and rest in the middle of a group of mostly homeless people sitting across the street on the sidewalk, chatting, smoking, and waiting for dinner to be served at 5:30. No one pays any attention to you.

You are safe, the Dark Angel explains in your head.

You nod and smile to yourself, not answering Him back aloud.

But slowly your smile fades to a frown.

You may be safe, but so is Katy Green.

The instrument of vengeance did not bite deeply.

You are not free, not yet.

No, indeed.

THE LIGHT ANGEL

A cross from *Fishes and Loaves* you wait alone, until twilight finally deepens. Then, you leave the area where some homeless have camped out in the protective shadow of the Dark Angel.

2

Katy is resting on the front room couch at her townhouse when Johnny arrives about 8:00 p.m. with a concerned frown on his face.

"How do you feel?" he asks, setting down a pizza box and some clothes he's carrying on the coffee table.

"Okay," she says. "Only took eight stitches. Just a little more than a superficial scratch really. They gave me some antibiotics and pain pills, but I haven't taken any of the pain medication yet. Didn't want to go to sleep. Just been lying here thinking about Sammy and me raised by the same foster care system down in San Diego County. Funny how we turned out so differently. Me a cop, now, and him a psycho killer. What made the difference in his case? Is it all really just genes, biochemistry? Or maybe it's environment, like the negative ridicule Sammy was subjected to because of the stuttering and the different way he looked? You can just imagine what it must've been like in CYA for him. Maybe it's a combination of those and other more subtle factors, too. But who the hell knows the answer, right now?"

After a thoughtful moment of silence, she manages a self-conscious grin and dismissive shrug, then changes the subject. "What is it with my shooting arm, partner? All the crooks trying to put me out of the hoops business or what?"

Johnny laughs.

"Hey, that's right, it's Tuesday. Guess you didn't go over to the ARC gym tonight?"

She shakes her head and asks, "How did the chase go?"

"Well, he got away despite all the back-up and planning," Johnny replies, a disappointed expression in his eyes. "Didn't show up at his apartment near Sutter's Fort or his job, either. Hey, you'll never guess where he works?"

"Where?"

"Sutter General Hospital laundry."

"No shit!" she says, sitting up with a grunt of pain. "How'd we miss him yesterday afternoon?"

Johnny shrugs. "I don't know, because Derek Clark, the supervisor, says he worked the whole shift. He was the guy on the extractor, that big piece of equipment right off the washers in the far corner... "

Aha, the guy with the Giants cap, she thinks, remembering and nodding to herself.

"And he's probably still running even now," Johnny adds, opening the lid of the pizza box. "We have people standing by at the Greyhound Bus Depot, the Amtrak station, and the airport with a blowup of a photo we got from his P.O. But no one's spotted him at any of the transportation centers yet. For all we know, he's hitched a ride out of town already, or even stolen a car, and is halfway to Mexico or Canada. In any event, we've got an APB out… "

Johnny pauses, then asks, "You hungry, kiddo?" He points at the pizza.

Katy shakes her head, her shoulder beginning to throb. "Not yet." She glances at his pile of clothes and stuff. "You staying here tonight?"

He makes a silly attempt at a sexy grin. "Figured it'd be a good idea, for a couple of reasons, you know. Okay?"

She says, "Sure, but I'm not feeling too romantic, pal, right now, anyhow. Think I'll take some of that pain medication after all."

He nods, taking a big bite from a wedge of pepperoni pizza.

3

Katy wakes up, feeling parched.

She gets up quietly, glancing over to make sure she isn't disturbing Johnny, then slips her kimono around her shoulders. The room is chilly. She must've forgotten to turn off the air-conditioning before they went to bed earlier. The red numbers on the clock beside the bed read: 1:30 a.m.

Swallowing dryly, Katy moves down the hallway, thinking her thirst must be caused by the antibiotics or maybe the pain medication. She hadn't wanted any of the pizza, although Johnny had made her take a couple of bites. She still isn't hungry—only dying of thirst.

At the open fridge, Katy selects a 7-Up and drinks it from the can greedily, finishing it in four long gulps. She puts the empty aluminum container in the recycling bag and sighs to herself, stretching. I'm not the least bit sleepy right now, she thinks. Maybe I can get a little writing done. She feels a twinge of guilt. It's the first time she's even thought of the novel in the last twenty-four hours. Oh, well…

She moves into the entryway to the front room, heading for her computer located in the guest bedroom.

Katy stops suddenly, as if colliding with an unseen wall, detecting an out-of-place sound from the darkness across the room near the fireplace. The angle of the streetlight through the front window vertical blinds casts a deep shadow all along that side of the room.

She cocks her head.

What is that sound—

Breathing?

Yes.

It sounds exactly like someone is catching their breath... Standing right there hidden in the darkness next to the fireplace, not even twenty feet away... and probably staring back at me.

Jesus. The hair along the back of her neck is standing on end, her arms goose-pimpled.

"Who's there?" she asks, her voice a squeaky whisper, thinking: *How'd he get in here?*

She squints, but makes out nothing... except hearing more of the noisy breathing.

4

The Dark Angel is above you, lost in the darkness of the vaulted, almost cathedral-like high ceiling of this expensive townhouse—

Oh, oh!

Katy Green is up, coming down the hallway from her bedroom, wearing something over her shoulders... But nothing else.

You shrink back into the wall just left of the fireplace, gathering the darkness around yourself, like a magical cloak, holding your breath and freezing in place, hoping she doesn't notice you quite yet.

She doesn't.

She turns and goes into the kitchen and pulls open the refrigerator door.

At that moment her nakedness is exposed despite the garment over her shoulders, framed by the light from inside the fridge...

Her firm breasts.

Her flat stomach.

And her golden-red triangle...

Almost groaning aloud with delight, you clasp your empty left hand to your mouth. It's almost like that time so long ago, when as a young boy, you lay at the foot of your bunk bed, holding your breath and spying through the crack of the foster sisters' door.

She is drinking a can of something.

The light blinks out suddenly when she closes the door of the refrigerator and tosses the can in a bag.

Then she stretches, the robe still concealing nothing in the dim light. Neither her breasts, nor her magnificent secret hair!

Your heart thumps wildly in your chest.

Beautiful.

You gape and blink, no longer able to hold your breath, almost gasping.

At that moment, she takes one step into the front room across from you—

And stops suddenly, peering in your direction, cocking her head slightly.

You must be breathing too loudly.

You remain frozen in place, not moving a muscle. But you can't possibly hold your breath a moment longer.

It is time to strike, the Dark Angel commands in your head.

You ignore him.

Now, wake up you fool.

You sigh.

"Who's there?"

You do not answer her.

You are discovered, and you are not a boy, anymore, the Dark Angel growls in your head. *That time was long ago. She called you vile names, gave you up. Now is the time to pay her back.*

You are forced to admit that this time it is much different than that other time so long ago. So many bad things have happened to you.

Including beating that young girl.

CYA.

And now, you are compelled to walk in the shadow of the Dark Angel, rendering justice to all your enemies.

Much different, now.

Yes, indeed.

Still, you hesitate.

Have you forgotten so soon. She is the origin of all your past troubles. And now she is the hunter, a very real threat, dedicated to sending you to a dark, dreary place. But you can change all that, now. You have the opportunity to finally be free.

Freedom.

Yes, you think, your underarms clammy with sweat despite the chilling air.

Cut down your enemy.

Your vision tunnels…

You are gazing at the woman through someone else's eyes, moving like a marionette dancing to silent music in a dark dream.

Now.

You feel a rush of indignant anger.

Followed by an almost blinding rage.

You step aggressively forward from the shadows, flipping open the instrument of vengeance.

5

A huge figure suddenly appears out of the darkness across the room like an apparition, making Katy's pulse race wildly, a lump caught in her throat. She can't even cry out for help.

Oh, my God, it's him!

And he's been spying on her since she walked out of the bedroom, just like that other time so long ago. Still a peeping tom. But much more dangerous, now.

She shudders in the cool darkness, as he moves forward, pulling her kimono around herself protectively, as if it were an effective shield, covering up her vulnerable nakedness.

"No, leave i-it," he snaps, the light glinting off the blade of the straight razor he holds in his right hand: A very real threat that he knows how to use.

Entranced, Katy peers at the bare glistening blade.

Cold, hard steel.

A lethal weapon.

And, yes, he has used it effectively before…

Three times.

The alarms in her head are all ringing, rousing her from her lethargic state, making her blink, flooding her with adrenaline.

She does not plan on letting him cut *her* throat, not without a fight.

No way.

Katy goes on offense, attacks.

6

The woman surprises you, suddenly charging, clawing at your face with her sharp fingertips, and trying to knee you in the crotch.

You drop the razor, too busy defending yourself.

Then, catching her arm, you jerk her close, attempting to kick her feet from under her. But she is like a cat, agile and wiry strong, athletically twisting from your grasp and picking up something from near the fireplace—

7

Fighting for her life now, Katy snatches up the poker from the rack near the fireplace and swings it viciously at Kubiak's head.

He manages to partially deflect the blow with his huge hand, the poker only glancing off his head, but bloodying his ear.

Howling with pain, he moves close and jerks her off balance.

Katy drops the poker, which is useless in close, and tries to follow up with a slapping punch to his face.

But he doesn't even blink.

Then, the giant smashes a fist, the size of a softball, into the side of her jaw.

She's stunned. But feels no pain.

Only a weakness in her legs, then a sagging, sinking sensation… down, down, down into a chilling blackness that closes in around her.

Katy struggles, fighting to hold onto her consciousness, knowing it is all over if she completely passes out.

8

You grab up the instrument of vengeance from the rug and kneel over the prostrate woman.

But you hesitate.

Now, the Dark Angel says, *end it, now. Your last enemy. Freedom.*

But His voice seems so far away. You glance up into the vaulted darkness, and, though you feel the cool air around you being stirred by his wing beats, you see nothing moving.

The woman groans.

You look around for something to use as a screen for the spurting blood.

Ah, one of the newspapers stacked next to the fireplace logs. You pick one and turn back to the woman, who is beginning to move now, trying to get up. She is almost fully awake. You must be quick before she completely recovers her senses. You screen yourself with the newspaper and lean close to slash her throat with the razor—

Sam Boy, wait!

It is the other one, the Light Angel, and His voice is strong, so close… Overhead.

You glance up again, the cool air beginning to swirl about now with hurricane force, as if a great battle is raging in the darkness above you.

But you see neither of the Angels—

A sound explodes in your ears, and at the same time a sledge hammer smashes against your chest. You exhale loudly, the air slammed from your body as you rocket backward.

2

Katy looks up into a blurry face, blinks, clears her vision.

Johnny?

"Are you okay?"

"Yes, I think so," she answers weakly. "What, what happened?"

"It's Kubiak," he replies, sliding a cushion from the couch under her head. "He got in here somehow and—"

"He's here?"

"It's *okay*," Johnny says, gently brushing her hair from her eyes. "I took care of him," he adds, glancing up from her in the direction of the fireplace. "He's down, big time."

Katy sees the gun and pushes herself up to look at Kubiak.

Sammy is lying on his back, his hands folded innocently across his bleeding chest, gasping for breath, peering up into the ceiling… And he appears to be seeing some—

Yes, he's smiling.

10

The brightness is blinding.

But, squinting tightly through narrowed eyelids, you can just make out His presence hovering above you, completely illuminating the darkness.

Glittering metallically.

Great white wings, flecked with gold.

A shining golden robe.

His face radiating kindness.

At last you have seen Him—The Light Angel!

But the blinding light is beginning to dim, and you feel so chilled and very, very tired—

But the Light Angel is bending down toward you now, beckoning for you come to him.

Time to go, Sam Boy, He whispers softly in your head, as you close your eyes.

Yes, indeed.

11

"He's gone, Katy," Johnny says, gently forcing her back down. "You don't have to be concerned with him ever again."

Katy closes her eyes.

Yes, it's finally over.

EPILOGUE

K aty recovers from her superficial wounds in a few days, but she isn't able to finish her novel in time to attend BayCon. She doesn't even go to the science fiction convention.

Eventually, though, another agent agrees to represent her and sells the novel. But the editor insists on changing the title to *The Burden of Indigo* and publishing it under her male pseudonym, Gene O'Neill, arguing that they'll be able to tap into her short story audience.

The novel sells surprisingly well for a psychological study, and a year and a half after the Red Chief affair, Katy Green becomes a full-time writer.

John Cato retires from the Sacramento Police Department shortly thereafter and becomes a partner in a San Francisco private detective agency, with an old colleague, Hap Sullivan, a retired San Francisco police detective.

They move to an apartment in the Marina area of San Francisco, where Katy continues to write full time, play 3-on-3 basketball, occasionally visiting her old friend, Geri Robinson in San Diego, and also doing a little consulting work for *Sullivan, Cato, and Associates*.

The End

… and stay tuned for the next book in the series:
The Crime Files of Katy Green #3: Deathflash

ALSO FROM DARK MOON BOOKS:

A WORLD OF HORROR

Every nation of the globe has unique tales to tell, whispers that settle in through the land, creatures or superstitions that enliven the night, but rarely do readers get to experience such a diversity of these voices in one place as in *A WORLD OF HORROR*, the latest anthology book created by award-winning editor Eric J. Guignard, and beautifully illustrated by artist Steve Lines.

Enclosed within its pages are twenty-two all-new dark and speculative fiction stories written by authors from around the world that explore the myths and monsters, fables and fears of their homelands.

Encounter the haunting things that stalk those radioactive forests outside Chernobyl in Ukraine; sample the curious dishes one may eat in Canada; beware the veldt monster that mirrors yourself in Uganda; or simply battle mountain trolls alongside Alfred Nobel in Sweden. These stories and more are found within *A World of Horror*. Enter and discover, truly, there's no place on the planet devoid of frights, thrills, and wondrous imagination.

"This is the book we need right now! Fresh voices from all over the world, bringing American audiences new ways to feel the fear. Horror is a universal genre and for too long we have only experienced one western version of it. No more. Get ready to experience a whole new world of terror."

—*Becky Spratford; librarian, reviewer,* RA for All: Horror

Order your copy at www.darkmoonbooks.com or www.amazon.com
ISBN-13: 978-0-9989383-1-8

ALSO FROM DARK MOON BOOKS:

Death. Who has not considered their own mortality and wondered at what awaits, once our frail human shell expires? What occurs after the heart stops beating, after the last breath is drawn, after life as we know it terminates?

Does our spirit remain on Earth while the body rots? Do the remnants of our soul transcend to a celestial Heaven or sink to Hell's torment? Can we choose our own afterlife? Can we die again in the hereafter? Are we given the opportunity to reincarnate and do it all over? Is life merely a cosmic joke or is it an experiment for something greater? Enclosed in this Bram Stoker-award winning anthology are thirty-four all-new dark and speculative fiction stories exploring the possibilities *AFTER DEATH . . .*

Illustrated by Audra Phillips and including stories by: **Steve Rasnic Tem, Bentley Little, John Langan, Simon Clark, Lisa Morton, Joe McKinney, Ray Cluley, David Tallerman**, and exceptional others.

"Though the majority of the pieces come from the darker side of the genre, a solid minority are playful, clever, or full of wonder. This strong anthology is sure to make readers contemplative even while it creates nightmares."
—Publishers Weekly

"In Eric J. Guignard's latest anthology he gathers some of the biggest and most talented authors on the planet to give us their take on this entertaining and perplexing subject matter . . . highly recommended."
—Famous Monsters of Filmland

"An excellent collection of imaginative tales of what waits beyond the veil."
—Amazing Stories Magazine

Order your copy at www.darkmoonbooks.com or www.amazon.com
ISBN-13: 978-0-9885569-2-8

ALSO FROM DARK MOON BOOKS:

Darkness exists everywhere, and in no place greater than those where spirits and curses still reside. Tread not lightly on ancient lands that have been discovered by this collection of intrepid authors.

In **DARK TALES OF LOST CIVILIZATIONS**, you will unearth an anthology of twenty-five previously unpublished horror and speculative fiction stories, relating to aspects of civilizations that are crumbling, forgotten, rediscovered, or perhaps merely spoken about in great and fearful whispers.

What is it that lures explorers to distant lands where none have returned? Where is Genghis Khan buried? What happened to Atlantis? Who will displace mankind on Earth? What laments have the Witches of Oz? Answers to these mysteries and other tales are presented within this critically acclaimed anthology.

Including stories by: **Joe R. Lansdale, David Tallerman, Jonathan Vos Post, Jamie Lackey, Aaron J. French**, and twenty exceptional others.

"The stories range from mildly disturbing to downright terrifying . . . Most are written in a conservative, suggestive style, relying on the reader's own imagination to take the plunge from speculation to horror."
—*Monster Librarian Reviews*

"Several of these stories made it on to my best of the year shortlist, and the book itself is now on the best anthologies of the year shortlist."
—*British Fantasy Society*

"Almost any story in this anthology is worth the price of purchase. The entire collection is a delight."
—*Black Gate Magazine*

ALSO FROM DARK MOON BOOKS:

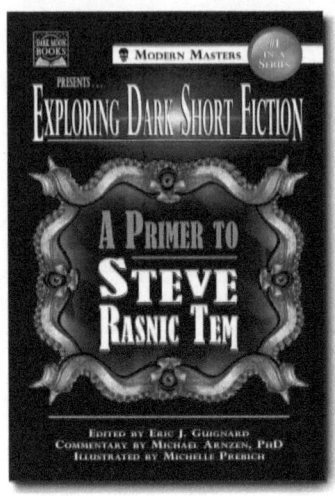

Exploring Dark Short Fiction #1:
A Primer to Steve Rasnic Tem

For over four decades, Steve Rasnic Tem has been an acclaimed author of horror, weird, and sentimental fiction. Hailed by *Publishers Weekly* as "A perfect balance between the bizarre and the straight-forward" and *Library Journal* as "One of the most distinctive voices in imaginative literature," Steve Rasnic Tem has been read and cherished the world over for his affecting, genre-crossing tales.

Dark Moon Books and editor Eric J. Guignard bring you this introduction to his work, the first in a series of primers exploring modern masters of literary dark short fiction. Herein is a chance to discover—or learn more of—the rich voice of Steve Rasnic Tem, as beautifully illustrated by artist Michelle Prebich.

Included within these pages are:

- Six short stories, one written exclusively for this book
- Author interview
- Complete bibliography
- Academic commentary by Michael Arnzen, PhD (former humanities chair and professor of the year, Seton Hill University)
- . . . and more!

Enter this doorway to the vast and fantastic: Get to know Steve Rasnic Tem.

Order your copy at www.darkmoonbooks.com or www.amazon.com
ISBN-13: 978-0-9988275-2-0

ALSO FROM DARK MOON BOOKS:

Exploring Dark Short Fiction #2:
A Primer to Kaaron Warren

Australian author Kaaron Warren is widely recognized as one of the leading writers today of speculative and dark short fiction. She's published four novels, multiple novellas, and well over one hundred heart-rending tales of horror, science fiction, and beautiful fantasy, and is the first author ever to simultaneously win all three of Australia's top speculative fiction writing awards (Ditmar, Shadows, and Aurealis awards for *The Grief Hole*).

Dark Moon Books and editor Eric J. Guignard bring you this introduction to her work, the second in a series of primers exploring modern masters of literary dark short fiction. Herein is a chance to discover—or learn more of—the distinct voice of Kaaron Warren, as beautifully illustrated by artist Michelle Prebich.

Included within these pages are:
- Six short stories, one written exclusively for this book
- Author interview
- Complete bibliography
- Academic commentary by Michael Arnzen, PhD (former humanities chair and professor of the year, Seton Hill University)
- . . . and more!

Enter this doorway to the vast and fantastic: Get to know Kaaron Warren.

Order your copy at www.darkmoonbooks.com or www.amazon.com
ISBN-13: 978-0-9989383-0-1

COMING SOON FROM DARK MOON BOOKS:

Exploring Dark Short Fiction #3:
A Primer to Nisi Shawl

Praised by both literary journals and leading fiction magazines, Nisi Shawl is celebrated as an author whose works are lyrical and philosophical, speculative and far-ranging; "...broad in ambition and deep in accomplishment" (*The Seattle Times*). Besides nearly three decades of creating fantasy and science fiction, fairy tales, and indigenous stories, Nisi has also been lauded as editor, journalist, and proponent of feminism, African-American fiction, and other pedagogical issues of diversity.

Dark Moon Books and editor Eric J. Guignard bring you this introduction to her work, the third in a series of primers exploring modern masters of literary dark short fiction. Herein is a chance to discover—or learn more of—the vibrant voice of Nisi Shawl, as beautifully illustrated by artist Michelle Prebich.

Included within these pages are:
- Six short stories, one written exclusively for this book
- Author interview
- Complete bibliography
- Academic commentary by Michael Arnzen, PhD (former humanities chair and professor of the year, Seton Hill University)
- ...and more!

Enter this doorway to the vast and fantastic: Get to know Nisi Shawl.

**Order your copy at www.darkmoonbooks.com or www.amazon.com
ISBN-13: 978-0-9989383-4-9**

ALSO FROM DARK MOON BOOKS:

Hearing, sight, touch, smell, and taste: Our impressions of the world are formed by our five senses, and so too are our fears, our imaginations, and our captivation in reading fiction stories that embrace these senses.

Whether hearing the song of infernal caverns, tasting the erotic kiss of treachery, or smelling the lush fragrance of a fiend, enclosed within this anthology are fifteen horror and dark fantasy tales that will quicken the beat of fear, sweeten the flavor of wonder, sharpen the spike of thrills, and otherwise brighten the marvel of storytelling that is found resonant!

Editor Eric J. Guignard and psychologist Jessica Bayliss, PhD also include companion discourse throughout, offering academic and literary insight as well as psychological commentary examining the physiology of our senses, why each of our senses are engaged by dark fiction stories, and how it all inspires writers to continually churn out ideas in uncommon and invigorating ways.

Featuring stunning interior illustrations by Nils Bross, and including fiction short stories by such world-renowned authors as John Farris, Ramsey Campbell, Poppy Z. Brite, Darrell Schweitzer, and Richard Christian Matheson, amongst others.

Intended for readers, writers, and students alike, explore *THE FIVE SENSES OF HORROR*!

Order your copy at www.darkmoonbooks.com or www.amazon.com
ISBN-13: 978-0-9988275-0-6

ALSO FROM GENE O'NEILL AND DARK MOON BOOKS:

DOUBLE JACK

—Book #1 in the series, *THE CRIME FILES OF KATY GREEN*

The novella that started it all!

It's night, Sacramento, and single female drivers who break down on the side of Interstate-5 are relieved to see the highway safety CalTrans truck arrive to give assistance… until they realize that's not what the 400-pound ex-boxer who gets out has in mind…

Such is the M.O. of serial killer, Jack Malenko, who preys on women in distress in full sight of passing traffic. Assigned to the notorious case are homicide detectives Katy Green and Johnny Cato, dubbed by the press as Sacramento's "Green Hornet and Cato." However, from the beginning of this case, the two detectives seem to continually be one step behind their huge killer… and each day that passes brings worse news and fresh victims.

How fast can they track down the predatory monster to save further lives, and if they do find him, can they save their own lives in the violent encounter?

Discover why readers have been applauding this stark, fast-paced noir series by multiple-award-winning author, Gene O'Neill! Read *DOUBLE JACK* and then continue the shocking case files of Sacramento's "Green Hornet and Cato":

- *THE CRIME FILES OF KATY GREEN #2: SHADOW OF THE DARK ANGEL*

- *THE CRIME FILES OF KATY GREEN #3: DEATHFLASH*

Order your copy at www.darkmoonbooks.com or www.amazon.com
ISBN-13: 978-0-9988275-8-2

ALSO FROM GENE O'NEILL AND DARK MOON BOOKS:

DEATHFLASH

—Book #3 in the series, *THE CRIME FILES OF KATY GREEN*

Young Billy Williams has been elevated to status of Shepherd of the Flock—leader of a zealous religious cult—and granted gift of the Deathflash, the ability to see the soul as it departs its mortal form at demise.

Billy is also given an ancient knife-like talon and "commanded to do the Lord's work," which he does fanatically, slaying drug addicts in San Francisco who are poisoning their bodies with heroin...

Retired police detectives Katy Green and Johnny Cato find themselves drawn into the grim case of the murdered underclass, whom no one seems to care about until the brother of a victim comes forward with his incredible suspicions...

So begins a journey of addiction, tracking a killer through the dope dens and seedy rehab houses of the Tenderloin district. But as more time passes, junkies begin to die faster and faster, for Billy Williams has given himself entirely to his own addiction: the rush of viewing the *Deathflash*.

Discover why readers have been applauding this stark, fast-paced noir series by multiple-award-winning author, Gene O'Neill! Read *DEATHFLASH* and then continue the shocking case files of Sacramento's "Green Hornet and Cato":

- *THE CRIME FILES OF KATY GREEN #1: DOUBLE JACK* (a novella)

- *THE CRIME FILES OF KATY GREEN #2: SHADOW OF THE DARK ANGEL*

Order your copy at www.darkmoonbooks.com or www.amazon.com
ISBN-13: 978-0-9988275-9-9

ABOUT THE AUTHOR

G ene O'Neill has seen over 175 of his stories and novellas published, several also reprinted in France, Spain, and Russia. Some of these stories have been collected in *Ghost Spirits, Computers & World Machines; The Grand Struggle; In Dark Corners; Dance of the Blue Lady; The Hitchhiking Effect;* and *Lethal Birds.* In addition, he's published six novels.

Gene has been a Bram Stoker Award® finalist twelve times. In 2010 *Taste of Tenderloin* won the haunted house for collection, and in 2012 *The Blue Heron* won for Long Fiction. Upcoming in 2017 are the four trade paperback versions of the *Cal Wild Chronicles* from Written Backwards Press, a number of short stories, and a novelette. A long novel, *The White Plague Chronicles,* is a work in progress, parts to an interested publisher.

Photograph by Jason V Brock

Gene lives in the Napa Valley with his wife, Kay. He has two grown children, Gavin, who lives in Oakland, and Kaydee who lives in Carlsbad and rides herd on his two grandchildren, Fiona and TJ.

When he isn't writing or visiting grandchildren, Gene likes to read good fiction or watch sports—all of them, especially boxing.

www.ingramcontent.com/pod-product-compliance
Lightning Source LLC
Chambersburg PA
CBHW021010120726
47905CB00009B/2936